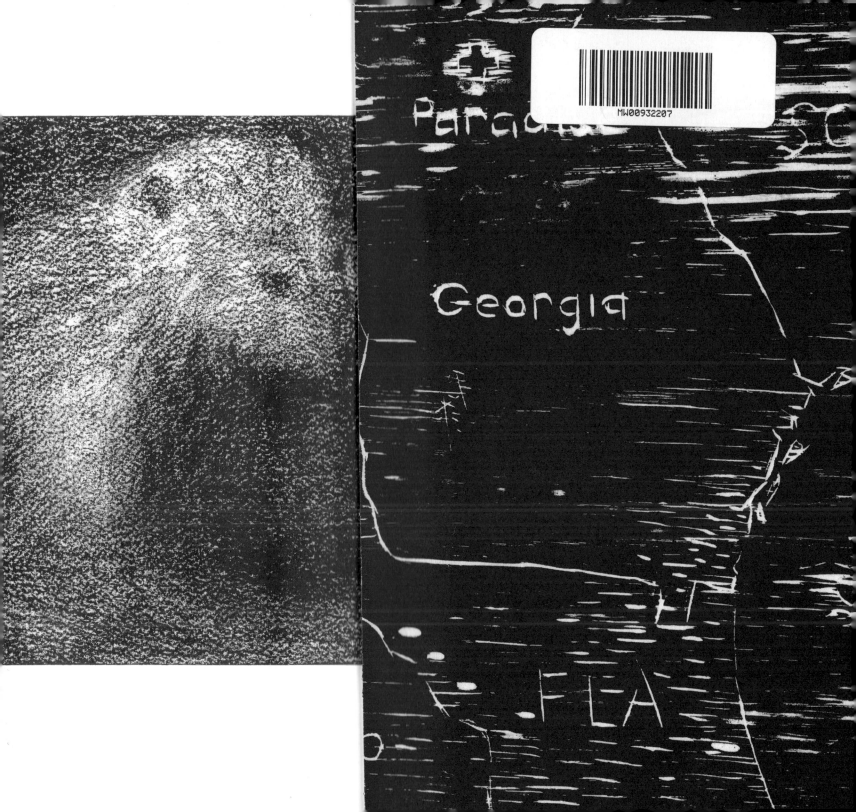

Paradise SC

Georgia

FLA

A Pla

I

A Place for

Delta

Written by Melissa Walker

Illustrated by Richard Walker

WHALE TALE PRESS

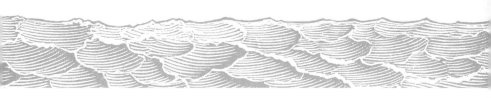

WHALE TALE PRESS
343 Hertford Circle
Decatur, GA 30030

Book design and production by
Shock Design & Associates, Inc.
shockdesign@mindspring.com
www.shockdesign.com

Library of Congress number: 2009929691

ISBN:978-0-9824784-0-0

Manufactured in the United States of America

First Edition

10 9 8 7 6 5 4 3 2 1

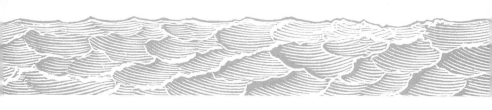

This book is dedicated to those

who love adventure and mystery—

in other words, to kids everywhere.

PART I

Prologue

IT WAS A HOT SUMMER DAY IN GEORGIA. Eleven-year-old Joseph Morse was sitting at the computer reading an email from his aunt Kate, who was working for a wildlife biologist in Alaska. Joseph's mother, Rachel, was looking over his shoulder. Neither said a word until they came to the end of the letter that would lead to an adventure unlike any they could have imagined.

Dear Joseph,

The most amazing thing has happened. Shortly after I arrived at the field station, Dr. Yu spotted a small polar bear cub stranded on an ice floe. There was no sign of the mother. I think I told you about Chipic, the Eskimo man who works for Dr. Yu. Chipic and his brother Avik rescued the cub in their umiak. Dr. Yu asked me if I would take care of the cub until we could decide what to do with her. When he can, Chipic comes to help.

The cub is female and her name is Delta. Dr. Yu thinks she's much smaller than she should be.

She weighs about twenty-five pounds, but normal weight at her age is about fifty pounds. Delta may be small, but she has a loud voice!

The best part of taking care of her is giving her a bottle. Then she makes sounds unlike any I've heard before—it's kind of like a cat purring, but louder. Sometimes she sounds like a helicopter. Delta can sleep for as long as three hours at a time, but when she's awake, she either wants to take her bottle, play with toys, hide in boxes, or climb up my legs. Somebody has to be with her all the time, even when she's sleeping. The truth is, I've got more to do than I can handle.

You asked about how long the days are here. This time of year the sun never sets, and it's as bright at midnight as at noon. We won't see the sunset until early August.

Now that you know something about what it's like to take care of a polar bear cub, I have a proposal for you. Soon after Chipic rescued the cub, we realized that we needed someone else to help with her care. I suggested you would be the perfect person. Dr. Yu has approved your coming. If you decide to do this, you'll fly from Atlanta to Anchorage. Chipic will meet you there and fly with you to

Barrow, the most northern town in the United States. I promise this summer will be one you'll never forget. Please say yes!

Love,
Kate

"So what do you think?" asked his mother Rachel, who was reading along with Joseph.

"I think I better pack my stuff," he said. "I have to do this. It's a chance in a million—or maybe a billion!"

Joseph was so excited that he hardly knew what he was saying. All he could think about was that he was going to the Arctic to take care of a polar bear cub. What he hadn't thought about—or didn't know—was how the experiences of his family had shaped his life and created this mind-boggling opportunity.

CHAPTER 1

Looking Back

This story begins in the summer of 1982, at an old homestead in the mountains of north Georgia some twenty years before Joseph received the email inviting him to come to the Arctic.

"Wake up, kids, and see your new home," Lisi said as she turned into the dirt lane that led to an old sprawling farmhouse. It was around midnight and a full moon illuminated the peeling white paint on the large dilapidated house. First eight-year-old Kate and then her ten-year-old brother, Ben, sat up and rubbed their eyes.

"So what do you think?" Lisi asked.

Kate looked at her mother with her bright blue eyes wide open. "It looks like a haunted house to me," she said quietly, as if she didn't want to wake any ghosts.

"Oh, Kate, there's no such thing as a haunted house," Ben said. He rolled down the window of his mother's old Volkswagen van and stuck his head out into the cool, moist summer night. "Wow," he said in a whisper. "It does look like a haunted house."

The moon bathed the clearing with soft light, creating shadows that swayed in the light breeze. The old white house seemed to glow.

"Be quiet for a minute and tell me what you hear," Lisi said.

For a few minutes, nobody said anything. Kate, Ben, and their mother Lisi sat listening in silence. At first all they could hear was the rhythmic chorus of night creatures.

"Crickets?" Ben asked.

"I think so," Lisi said, "but maybe tree frogs, too. Whatever creatures are making such a racket, they're singing in unison, each making the same exact sound at the same time as all the others." Lisi said. "Do you hear anything else?"

Kate and Ben strained to hear something above the night noise. No one moved or said a word. Finally Kate broke the silence.

"I think I hear running water," she said.

"Look," Ben said, "the moon is shining on a pond of water over there."

"And there's a stream running into the pond," Kate said.

As their eyes adjusted to the dark, they were able to make out features of the landscape—a pond, a stream flowing down the hill and spilling over an outcropping of rock, and beyond that a forest of large trees.

"Okay," Lisi said, "let's go in the house." Neither Kate nor Ben wanted to leave the car.

"How about we wait 'til morning?" Kate suggested.

"Yeah," Ben said. "We can sleep in the van."

"I don't think so," Lisi said, pointing to the back of the van filled with bags, brooms, mops, and tools. "But you two can stay here while I check out the house."

Ben and Kate groaned as Lisi opened the door and stepped outside into the moonlight. They watched her cross the yard, climb the steps, walk across the porch, and disappear into the dark house. Then all they could see was the light of the flashlight, first at one window and then another.

After waiting what seemed a long time, Kate called out, "Mom, come back." No response, no sudden surge of light, no sound except the steady, shrill chorus of crickets. Then the pale, moving glow of the flashlight went out. Alert and wide-eyed, the kids peered into the moonlit summer night waiting for their mother to return.

"What's happening, Ben?" Kate whispered.

"Don't worry. Mom's just making sure everything is all right. She's probably trying to find a light switch," Ben said in a strong voice, not wanting to sound frightened.

Finally, they once again saw light flickering inside the house. The door opened with a creak, and Lisi walked across the porch and down the steps toward the van.

"Why didn't you turn on the lights?" Kate asked, on the verge of tears,

"I didn't turn on the lights because there's no electricity. We have running water, but no hot water, and no refrigerator. Good thing I bought a bag of ice."

"So, what's inside?" Ben asked.

"As far as I can tell, nothing except some old furniture that came with the house and boxes that the movers left," Lisi said.

"I'm hungry," Kate said.

"I'm hungry, too. We'll have peanut butter sandwiches, a cup of milk, and a banana," her mother said, pulling out a small box of groceries and opening the ice chest.

"That's all we've had today," Kate said.

"And that's all we'll have tonight. Tomorrow I'll make blueberry pancakes."

Once inside the house, the children found themselves in a long hall. To the right was a room that would have been called the parlor when the house was built in the early 1800s. This is where the children and Lisi would soon find themselves getting together with friends, having tea, reading, telling stories, and playing games. Along the walls, the movers had stacked boxes full of their belongings. Kate and Ben looked around and then wandered into the dining room to the left of the hall. Moonlight streamed through the windows illuminating a ten-foot-long table that had been in the house since before the Civil War. In the middle of the table was a sign in Lisi's handwriting telling the movers that no objects, no moving boxes, nothing should be placed on this beautiful, antique heart-pine table. In years to come, this table would be the center of their family life—the place where the children did their homework, where special meals took place, and where the family gathered alone or with others to discuss serious matters. Behind the dining room was the kitchen, and behind the parlor was a large room that would become Lisi's bedroom.

Back in the parlor, Lisi had spread quilts and pillows for sleeping on the floor. The children collapsed on these makeshift beds, half asleep before Lisi could cover them with light blankets. Still Kate felt a little afraid in this huge almost empty house. Fourteen hours had passed since the Morse family piled into the van and drove from New Orleans to this old farmhouse in the mountains of north Georgia. Lisi, who had just finished graduate school, would soon start teaching biology at a nearby college.

They had left the sweltering heat of New Orleans and woke to cool mountain air the next day—July 6, 1982.

By the time Ben and Kate woke, the sun was above the trees on the eastern side of the property. Lisi had been up for almost an hour, just long enough to pick blueberries, set up the camp stove on the porch, and cook the first stack of pancakes. Smelling the food cooking, Ben woke first and then called to his sister. Kate opened her eyes.

"Where are we?" she asked.

"Our new haunted house, remember?"

Kate looked around at the box-filled room with its peeling paint and cobwebbed corners. "Actually, this is not a new house. Mom told us it's almost 150 years old. But I agree with the 'haunted' part."

"Ben! Kate! Come out to the porch for breakfast," Lisi

called. She had made a table by placing boards across two of the packing boxes. The three of them sat on the porch floor and ate blueberry pancakes—their first meal together in their new home. After breakfast Ben and Kate looked around both inside and outside the house. First they checked out the porch. On one side was a swing, which Ben and Kate tried out. On the other side, they found three old rocking chairs that were in need of repair and paint. Before they began cleaning up the house, Lisi took Ben and Kate exploring, first behind the house, then around the pond, and finally up the hill on a trail by the side of the stream.

Lisi had first come to this part of Georgia the summer before to do field work for her research on salamanders while Ben and Kate had stayed with their grandmother down in the Mississippi River Delta. Before she returned to New Orleans, Lisi learned of a job opening in the biology department of a nearby college, and she had applied for the position.

Later, when Lisi came to interview for the job, she went house hunting, and found the old farmhouse, which came complete with forty acres. The house was solidly built and had been in one family since before the Civil War. Until Lisi bought it, the house had been empty for more than a year after the last member of the family had died. Lisi knew right away that she had found a good place to raise her children. After living in a cramped apartment, this rambling old house and the land and trees around it seemed like paradise. And that's exactly what she called the place.

Rumor had it that the man who built the house had been lucky mining for gold back in the 1830s. Some said that he was so rich that he never had to work again, and that the orchard, the vegetable garden, and the chickens and other animals were for his own family. By the time Lisi bought the property, the vegetable garden was overrun with weeds. But the plum and fig trees were still bearing fruit, and Lisi thought there would be a good crop of apples in the fall.

The chicken house in the back was falling down, but nearby there was a small springhouse in good shape with the door nailed shut. Ben and Kate were curious about the springhouse and wanted to look inside, but Lisi warned them that snakes might live there. Young trees were taking over what had once been a small pasture. The entire cleared area was less than five acres. The rest of the property was wild. There was no sign that the woods had been cut in the last hundred or more years.

Eight days passed before the electricity was turned on. Lisi cooked on a camp stove set up outside, and they used kerosene lanterns inside to see at night. When the power was finally turned on, they had become accustomed to doing without. The biggest difference was that now they could turn on the ceiling fans and take hot baths.

Kate never knew her father who died in a helicopter crash just before her birth. Ben, who was just two at the time, didn't remember him at all. His name was Sam Morse, just like the man who invented the telegraph. After his death, Lisi was very sad, but fortunately there was enough money from Sam's life insurance for her to be able to stay home with Kate and Ben until they were four and six years old. Then she went to graduate school to study biology so that she could teach in college. And with what was left of the insurance money, she made a down payment on forty acres and this old farmhouse.

As a single mom, Lisi had to work hard to support the family, but as a college teacher, she would have time to be with her children. She would not have to work in the summer or during school holidays, and she would be able to pick up her children from school in the afternoon. Her job began the same day that Kate was to start the third grade; Ben would be in the fifth. They didn't know anybody in Georgia, and Lisi was worried that it would be hard for the children to make friends, especially since they now lived in the country. Time would tell.

For the next few weeks, Lisi—with Ben and Kate's help—made the house their home. For several days they slept on the floor while Lisi cleaned and repaired what was broken. Ben washed windows while Kate cleaned up mouse droppings and spider webs. Lisi sanded the floor in the living room, and they helped her varnish it. Then they painted the walls in the rooms they would use. The outside painting would have to wait until Lisi had saved enough money to pay someone to help.

Upstairs were four more rooms; one would be Kate's room, and another would be Ben's. The other two rooms were empty and shut off from the rest of the house. Each of the children's rooms had a bed and an old piece of furniture called a wardrobe, or armoire, that served as a closet. Their few clothes and shoes fit inside with room to spare.

Each child brought a prized possession from New Orleans. Ben's special object was a soccer ball—the one his father had bought when he was born. Lisi had given it to him on his sixth birthday, and whenever he could, Ben practiced kicking it. Ben built a small platform with a wooden box and a piece of plywood

11

that he found in the attic. There the ball stayed as a reminder that someday he would join a soccer team. As it turned out, that someday would be soon.

Kate's favorite possession was a stuffed animal, a polar bear that her grandmother had given her. She named the bear Delta for the Mississippi Delta where her mother was born and where her grandparents still lived. As soon as her bed was set up, she propped Delta on her pillows. Only then did she feel that the room was hers.

Lisi's special possession was a photograph of Sam Morse, the father of her children. He had been a medic in the Vietnam War. When he came back to New Orleans to go to medical school, he volunteered one weekend a month as part of an emergency team that rescued people from fires, sinking boats, and other catastrophes. On a mission to bring back an injured man from an oil rig in the Gulf of Mexico, he was killed when his helicopter crashed in a storm.

One afternoon Lisi and Kate went exploring together. Ben didn't want to go, and he spent the time kicking his soccer ball around the pasture. As they walked up the creek, a light rain began to fall, and Lisi pulled their matching yellow slickers from her pack. As they walked along, Kate asked her mother what her favorite animal was.

"Well, I'm not sure I have a favorite, but since I'm a herpetologist, I'm especially interested in reptiles and amphibians."

"You mean like snakes, turtles, and alligators?" Kate asked.

"Yes, all of those, and salamanders, and many more."

"What's interesting about salamanders?" Kate asked.

"Follow me, and I'll show you," Lisi said. About two feet from the rapidly running stream was a decaying log. When Lisi lifted the log, Kate saw something she had never seen before. First she saw flashes of bright red, but as she looked more closely, she understood that she was seeing dozens of little creatures squirming and wriggling in the wet, exposed soil.

"Salamanders," she heard her mother say in a whisper. "Red salamanders."

"Are they reptiles?" Kate asked.

"No. They're amphibians. These are young ones."

"Do you want me to be a herpetologist when I grow up?"

"I want you to do work that you love. I'm lucky. I get to study and teach about interesting creatures. I want you to find work that you like as much as I like mine."

After a few moments of silence Kate said, "I'd like to see a wild bear."

"Well, you just might see one in these woods, but we don't want bears close by. That's why we won't have chickens or rabbits, or other small animals. Bears, like foxes, will rob a chicken house, and even take seeds from a bird feeder."

"Will they eat vegetables from the garden?" Kate asked.

"They might. That's why I only want a small garden that we can easily fence in. Before we plant next spring, we'll build a fence to keep out bears and deer, too."

A few days later, Lisi took Ben and Kate along the stream bank all the way to the property line at the edge of her land and explained that they were not to go on the other side. "When you roam the woods by yourselves, don't go beyond this spot. Notice this outcropping of rock and the even bigger one over there?"

she said, pointing to a six-foot-tall, flat-topped slab of granite. "Beyond these rocks is wilderness. Hunting season starts in October. Hunters with bows and arrows and rifles will soon be roaming the forest looking for deer. We don't want them on our property, and we definitely don't want to go into the woods with shooting going on."

"So who owns the wilderness?" Ben asked.

"The wilderness is federal land. It belongs to all of us," Lisi said.

"So why do hunters get to go in the wilderness, and we can't?"

"Ben, we can go in there. If I had a hunting license, I could go in and kill a deer. But I don't want to hunt." The next day Lisi took them back to walk the property line, and together they marked it with "No Trespassing" signs.

CHAPTER 2

Friends

Before school started, Ben joined a soccer team and got up early to go to practice. He had never played on a team, but the coach said that he was a natural and told Lisi that Ben would be a really good soccer player.

Kate was nervous on the first day of school. She didn't know anybody, and so she took a seat in the back of the room and pretended to read. Then she looked around at the other kids. They all seemed to know each other. Just as she was thinking that she would never make new friends, the girl sitting next to her turned to her and smiled.

"You're the new girl. My name's Rachel Carson. I was named for a famous writer."

"My name is Kate Morse."

"Kate is a good name," Rachel said, "but Morse is a funny name. It rhymes with horse."

"My dad was Sam Morse. He died in a helicopter accident."

About that time the bell rang, and the first day of third grade began. That first week of school the girls sat next to each other at lunch, but they really didn't have a chance to talk until school was out on Friday. On the other days, Rachel went straight to her mother's office without talking to anybody, but on Friday she took her time.

So at the end of the first week of school, Kate and Rachel sat on the school steps and got to know each other better. Kate explained that she lived in the country in an old farmhouse with her mom and her brother, Ben. Rachel said that she wished she had a brother but that her parents were divorced. Her father, she said, had left the family to live in Alaska.

"My dad has trouble settling down. Mom says that Georgia was too tame for him. She's a veterinarian and wanted to live in a small town, but my dad is an adventurer."

Not wanting to pry—her Mom had told her not to ask personal questions—Kate didn't ask what she meant by an adventurer. But she wanted to know more about Rachel's dad.

When Lisi drove up to the carpool lane after school, Kate ran out, pulling her new friend by the hand. "Mom, this is my new friend Rachel. Her mom is a veterinarian, and her dad is an adventurer."

"I'm glad to meet you, Rachel. Maybe you can come out to the country to play with Kate sometime."

"My mom lets me visit friends on Friday, but nobody has invited me. Could I come today?" Rachel asked politely.

"Please, please," Kate begged.

"We'll have to ask Rachel's mother," Lisi said.

"That's easy. Her office is just two blocks away. After school I walk over there and do my homework while she finishes working. I'll meet you there. It's the brick building on the corner."

A few minutes later, the two single moms were getting to know each other. Amy had to work another two hours, and she said it would be great if Rachel could go home with Kate rather than sitting around the office on a Friday afternoon. Fifteen minutes later, Lisi turned off the county road into the lane leading home. "Welcome to Paradise," she said.

"Wow!" Rachel said. "I know about this house. I've heard it's haunted."

"I thought it looked haunted when I first saw it, but I don't believe in ghosts. Do you?" Kate asked.

"Not really," Rachel said, "but some people do. I've also heard that there's gold hidden around here somewhere. Maybe in the house."

"Okay, girls, let's go get a snack," Lisi said, interrupting the discussion of ghosts and gold.

As the girls burst through the front door, Rachel was still wondering what might be in the house. "This is a really big house," she said.

"We only use five rooms," Kate said.

"That's a lot of rooms," Rachel said, thinking of the small cottage she shared with her mom.

"Actually some of the empty rooms have been used by animals. We found that raccoons and squirrels had nests in the attic, but Mom closed up the holes so they couldn't get in," Kate said. "Now we only have mice."

"My mom takes care of farm animals and pets," Rachel said. "But sometimes people bring her wild animals that have been lost or hurt. We raised a fawn whose mother was hit by a car. My mom will try to save anything."

"What does your mom do with wild animals after she saves them?" Kate asked.

"She takes them to a wildlife rehabilitation center,"

Rachel said. "My dad also knows a lot about animals. He writes me about animals in Alaska."

"Does your dad work with animals there?" Kate asked.

"Actually, I'm not sure what he does. He writes to me from different places," Rachel said.

"I'd love to go to Alaska," Kate said.

"Maybe we could go there to visit my dad and see some really big animals. He said he would take me to Kodiak Island where there are huge grizzly bears," Rachel said.

"I'd like to see a polar bear," Kate said.

"My dad has been to Barrow, Alaska, close to the North Pole, and he's seen polar bears," Rachel said. She talked a lot about her dad, as if to remind herself that she had one. "My dad's not like other dads. He likes to go places and do things that other people don't get to do."

"My dad was different, too. He liked to help people, even if he had to risk his own life. That's how he died," Kate said. For a moment both girls were silent. Finally Kate spoke.

"We have bears here in Paradise, but I haven't seen one yet."

About that time, Lisi called the girls to the kitchen for a snack—hot chocolate and cookies. Later that afternoon, Ben's soccer coach brought him home. He ran in the house shouting, "We won! We won! And I made a goal!"

Kate looked at her brother and said, "Well, I have a new friend, and she loves nature as much as I do."

"I love nature, too," Ben said, "but I love soccer more."

For that first year, Rachel was Kate's only close friend. Kate liked to play with her brother, but as they got older, he was busy with his own activities—soccer, soccer, and more soccer. More than a game for Ben, it was his connection to his father, who had played soccer in college.

He also liked to go camping with kids on the soccer team. The year Kate and Rachel became friends, Ben was in the fifth grade. When he came home, he ate supper and went to his room to do his homework. Kate missed the days when they explored the woods together, and she was jealous when he went on a camping trip without her.

CHAPTER 3

Tracks in the Snow

On Fridays, Lisi picked up Kate and Rachel after school. Rachel's mom worked until late afternoon, and after work she would drive out to Paradise to get Rachel. Sometimes she would bring Ben home from soccer practice, and often she would stay and visit with Lisi.

One cold Friday afternoon in December, Lisi and Amy settled down in front of the fireplace with a pot of tea. The girls were playing a board game on the floor, and Ben was in his room. A light rain was falling, and the temperature was dropping. Nobody noticed the whistling wind. When Lisi suggested they stay for supper, Amy was glad. She didn't want to go home and cook alone. Lisi brought out fresh baked bread, a pot of chili, and a blackberry pie. As she was scooping ice cream to put on the warm pie, the lights went out. Except for the light from the fireplace, the house was completely dark.

"I think I know what the problem is," Ben said, looking out the window at the ice collecting on trees and power lines.

Lisi got up and found candles, matches, and kerosene lanterns. Soon the kitchen was glowing with light. No one said anything until they had finished the pie and ice cream.

Then Lisi broke the silence. "Well, one thing's for sure: no one is going out tonight in this weather. Looks like we're going to have a spend-the-night party."

Soon Lisi brought out sleeping bags and blankets so they could sleep near the fire. There was enough wood to last the night and maybe another day or two. Amy would sleep on the sofa, and Lisi dragged out a single bed mattress for herself.

"This is like camping out," Kate said.

"Not really, Kate," Ben said. "We have a roof over our heads."

"Well, let's just say we're camping inside," Lisi said, trying to make peace.

For the next hour or so, they gathered around the fire and roasted marshmallows. Droopy-eyed and tired, the girls finally crawled into their sleeping bags. Ben pulled his bag to the other side of the room. Lisi and Amy sat on either side of the fireplace and spoke in soft voices into the night. Ben listened to the murmuring talk and was able to hear most of what they said.

"So, what do you know about this house?" Amy asked.

"I know it's always been in the Paxton family, that people talk about the house being haunted, and that Old Man Paxton, who died last year, was the last member of the family. He had no children, and he lived here all his life. Did you know him?" Lisi asked.

"I once came out to examine a wounded doe that had wandered up to the garden here," Amy said. "We were able to remove a bullet from her leg and treat the wound. Old Man Paxton provided her with food until she was able to go back to the wild. So how did you find this house?"

"Paxton left the house and forty acres around it to the college. When I accepted the job, I explained to the head of the biology department that I wanted to buy a house in the country with land around it. The college had just decided to sell the house, and I bought it before anyone else could look at it. It's perfect for us," Lisi said.

"How old is it?" Amy asked.

"It was built around 1840 by Otis Paxton who struck it rich in the north Georgia gold rush of the 1830s. The story goes that he took bags of gold to the new U.S. mint in Dahlonega and had it made into coins. He was rich enough to build this place with the best material he could find."

"Have you heard that there may be gold hidden in the house or on the property?" Amy asked.

"Yeah, I have, but I don't believe it." Lisi said. "Someone must think so, though. When I first came to see the house, I found holes in the yard, some old and some recent. There were even openings in the plaster and ripped up floor boards upstairs. I had all of it fixed before we moved in so Ben and Kate wouldn't know anything about it."

"I'd be awfully tempted to look for the gold," Amy said.

"Well, if gold turns up, it'll be mine. I have a clear title to the house, everything in it, the land around it, and everything under it."

"Have you thought of having a real treasure hunt?"

"Not really. I don't want Ben and Kate to think about striking it rich. And I certainly don't want outsiders to think they might find gold in Paradise," Lisi said.

Ben was getting sleepy, and when Amy and Lisi started

talking about their own lives, he lost interest and burrowed down into his bag. Before long he was dreaming about looking for gold coins.

"Mom, wake up," Ben shouted as he looked out the window at a world covered with a blanket of snow. Large white flakes were falling, but the wind had died down. A thermometer outside the window read twenty-five degrees. Inside it was forty degrees except in front of the fire where everyone gathered wrapped in blankets.

Usually Ben ignored Rachel and Kate when they were playing together, but this morning he tried to convince them to join him for an outside adventure. First Lisi insisted they eat a big bowl of oatmeal.

"Oatmeal takes too long to make. Besides, we don't have any electricity. We can't cook," Kate said, pleased with herself.

"You guys are forgetting the camp stove on the porch," Lisi said. Then she winked at Amy and said, "Since the kids don't want oatmeal, I'll make our coffee first. But I have to say, no one is going out on a day like this without first having a hot breakfast."

"Mom, that's not fair," Kate said.

Rachel looked at her mom, shrugged her shoulders, and said, "Not a problem for me. I eat oatmeal every morning. It's yummy."

That settled it. Lisi had been trying for months to convince Ben and Kate to have oatmeal for breakfast, but they always wanted something else. Ben, wanting to impress Rachel, acted as if he didn't mind at all what he ate.

With that, Lisi went out on the porch, lit the camp stove, made coffee, and then boiled a pot of water and added oatmeal, raisins, cinnamon and sliced apples. In a few minutes she filled five bowls with the steaming concoction. On top she sprinkled brown sugar, nuts, and chocolate chips.

Soon, the kids were scraping the bottom of their bowls and putting on coats, gloves, hats, and boots. Rachel borrowed a pair of boots that Ben had outgrown. "Before you take off, I want to take a photo of you three," Lisi said as she followed them outside. Once she went back into the house, Ben announced that he would be the leader. Kate and Rachel agreed to let him take charge. "Kate, you and Rachel check out the pond, and I'll walk upstream to see what's going on." Water at the edges of the pond was frozen, and that morning there was no sign of life.

"It's amazing how much can happen in a week," Kate said. "Last Saturday I sat on this log and watched a snapping turtle sunning on that rock. Now the rock is covered with snow and the pond is icing over," Kate said.

"Where do you think that turtle is now?" Rachel asked.

"Probably at the bottom of the pond. It's warmer down there."

"Not much to look at here. Let's find Ben," Rachel said.

"Ben," they shouted, expecting him to answer. Together they called out as loud as they could, but there was no answer. Rachel let out a shrill whistle. Still the woods were quiet.

"Maybe he's trying to scare us," Rachel said, "All we have to do is follow his tracks. Let's be quiet and surprise him."

As they set off upstream, Ben's tracks were easy to see. But after a few minutes, Kate stopped suddenly and said, "Look, animal tracks, big ones."

Rachel dropped to her knees and carefully studied the tracks. "It's a bear, all right. Look, it crossed the creek right here." Then she asked Kate if she could tell whether Ben or the bear came first. Rachel's dad had taught her to "read" animal tracks, and she was eager to teach Kate. "Look carefully and you can tell which were made first."

"I got it," Kate said. "There's more snow in the bear tracks, so the bear was here first. If it keeps on snowing like this, all the tracks will be covered in a few minutes. We better find Ben soon."

In the excitement of tracking a bear the girls didn't even think about what they would do if they found one. Still wanting to surprise Ben, they spoke softly and stopped calling out for him. There was so much snow falling that they couldn't see more than a few feet ahead.

Then Kate stopped and said, "I can still see Ben's tracks, but the bear tracks have almost filled in with snow."

Kate was beginning to worry. Ben's tracks were getting closer to the "No Trespassing" signs. The tracks were going that way, and the girls kept following them. Rachel and Kate stood near the edge of the wilderness and saw tracks leading beyond the property line. Kate turned to Rachel and said, "I think we have to keep going. Ben may be in trouble."

Tramping uphill through the woods was more difficult than hiking by the side of the stream. Rachel stumbled over a rock covered with snow and knocked Kate down. At first they rolled in the snow laughing. Then they were quiet.

"This isn't fun anymore. I can't see Ben's tracks at all. I

think we should yell and scream. Maybe he would answer us." Kate said.

"I don't think so," Rachel said. "If we make noise, the bear may run. It might run toward Ben or toward us."

"OK, but it's hard to keep quiet," Kate said.

"Don't worry, I know how to track, and I can still see faint signs of footsteps," Rachel said.

But Kate wasn't sure she believed that. As far as she could see, there was nothing but white. To her eyes, snow covered the trees and hid all evidence of Ben's progress. Kate felt two ways at once—excited to be in the wilderness tracking a bear, but worried that something bad had happened to her brother.

Rachel watched the ground and continued to follow what was left of Ben's tracks. Suddenly Rachel shouted, "Look, we're on the right trail."

About twenty feet in front of them was Ben's red hat. Rachel looked back and saw that her friend was upset. When Kate said she thought a bear might have gotten her brother, Rachel stopped and asked, "Look around. Do you see signs of a scuffle?"

"Well, no, but the snow could have covered it," Kate said, and then she noticed that the hat was only lightly dusted with snow. Since there was still a lot of snow falling, not much time could have passed since Ben lost his hat.

"Here's what I think happened. What do you notice about this flat rock?" Rachel asked.

"There's not much snow on it."

"Right. I think Ben stopped here to rest, wiped off the rock, sat down, and took off his hat. He probably left it lying on the ground. He's got to be close by. Let's go a little farther," Rachel said, as she picked up the hat and tossed it to Kate.

Ben's tracks were fresher now, and there hadn't been time for the snow to fill them. While Rachel studied the tracks, Kate looked around. She was the first to see the den—an opening in a rock outcropping barely large enough for a bear to enter. Kate pointed to the den, but Rachel motioned for her to follow the human tracks that led up a steep hill. There at the top of the hill was Ben with his finger to his lips, warning them to be quiet. Pointing toward the den, he mouthed the word *bear*. Shivering with cold and excitement, Kate and Rachel settled down and waited.

Then it happened. First the backside of what turned out to be an adult black bear emerged from the cave, and then came the back feet. With its head still in the den, the bear seemed to be cleaning house with its front paws. Leaves and dirt came out of the opening and piled up in a mound. Then the bear came out briefly, looked around, and sniffed the air.

Rachel, Kate, and Ben sat as quietly as possible, waiting for what would happen next. The bear raked more leaves into the pile, climbed back into the den, and used the leaf pile to close the opening. Still the children sat quietly. They wanted to give the bear time to settle down and go to sleep.

Finally Ben took a deep breath and motioned for the girls to climb down the side of the hill away from the den. Soon they were following the tracks Rachel and Kate had made, and when they crossed between the two rocks, they left the wilderness and the bear behind.

Ben was the first to break the silence. "Mom's not going to be happy. If we tell her about the bear, we'll have to tell her we went into the wilderness."

"Ben, you know we have to tell her," Kate said. "She trusts us to tell the truth."

"Yeah, I know," Ben said. "How about you tell her?"

"Well, if I tell her, I'll have to say that you were the one to cross over the property line, and that Rachel and I had to follow you because we were afraid you were in trouble."

"Never mind. I'll tell her." When they finally reached the house Ben announced, "Mom, we're back!" at the top of his lungs.

They barged into the living room where Amy and Lisi were sitting by the fire. "Hi, kids," Lisi said, "What's all the noise about?"

Suddenly they became very quiet. Then Kate blurted out, "You're going to be very angry. We did a bad thing."

"Actually, we just broke a rule," Ben said, interrupting his sister. "But it was the right thing to do."

By then Amy and Lisi were sitting up straight. "Tell us what happened," they both said.

"First, we saw the tracks," Kate said.

"No, first, I saw the tracks," Ben countered.

"Well, actually Kate and I saw Ben's tracks first." Rachel said.

"And then we saw the bear tracks," Kate said.

They went on like this for a while, until finally Amy and Lisi thought they could piece together part of the story.

"Let's see," Lisi said. "Ben went up the creek first, saw bear tracks, and followed them into the woods. Then Kate and Rachel followed the tracks of Ben and the bear until they found Ben sitting on a rock. Then all of you came running back to tell us about it. Is that it?"

"Well, almost. Ben was sitting on the rock because he was watching the bear building a den," Kate said.

"Yeah, and we watched her go in and cover up the hole with leaves," Ben said.

Lisi took a deep breath and didn't say anything for a minute. She finally said, "Well, following a bear through the snow is never a good idea, and you could have been hurt."

"Well, she didn't have a cub," Ben said. "There was only one set of tracks."

"That's right, mom. You told us that a mother bear with a cub might attack people but this bear was alone," Kate said.

"Okay, okay," Lisi said, "What's the bad thing you did?"

"We followed the bear past our property line and into the wilderness," Ben said.

Then Kate interrupted, "Well, really Ben followed the bear, and Rachel and I followed Ben."

"And the bear," Rachel said, finally getting a word in.

Amy and Lisi looked at each other, and finally Lisi said, "Maybe we should have gone out with them."

"Then they wouldn't have had such an adventure," Amy said.

For a moment everyone was quiet. Then Lisi got up to warm milk for hot chocolate. Ben let out a sigh of relief.

As time went by, the Morses and the Carsons became like one family. Amy and Lisi began to think of themselves as best friends, sometimes even sisters. Since neither of them had siblings, they were happy to have each other.

CHAPTER 4

Spring in the Wilderness

That spring, Ben began to spend more time alone exploring the woods. Lisi sometimes worried about him in the forest, but he reassured her that he would stay on their property. She knew that Ben needed to be on his own. After all, he was eleven years old. One Friday night in early April, Rachel spent the night with Kate, and when they got up on Saturday morning, Ben proposed a hike. The day was warm and sunny, and there was no need for a jacket. They headed out right after breakfast, leaving Lisi reading and drinking coffee outside in the sun. The girls were once again following Ben, but this time he stayed nearby. Since he was leading the way, he was the first to spot tadpoles in the stream, bright orange mushrooms pushing out of the ground, and a bird nest almost hidden in the fork of a red maple.

Further into the woods, Ben noticed a large oak tree with a cavity at the bottom. Thinking some creature might be living in the hole, Ben quietly crept toward the tree and peered inside. The light was dim, and at first he was not sure what he was looking at. Then he made out the diamond pattern on the backs of what seemed like six, eight, maybe ten rattlesnakes all tangled together. Ben jumped back so fast that he tripped and fell. Scrambling to his feet, he turned and ran as fast as he could toward Kate and Rachel.

Out of breath, he shouted hoarsely, "Snakes! Diamond-backs! A whole bunch!"

Resisting the urge to run back to the house and tell Lisi what Ben had seen, the children resumed the hike, walking slowly and looking out for snakes with every step. Then Rachel told Ben she wanted to lead the way. She picked up the pace but stopped from time to time to look around. When she reached the spot where they had first seen the bear tracks, she turned away from the creek. It seemed to Ben that she was going the same way they had gone that snowy day. Ben and Kate silently followed until they realized they could see the "No Trespassing" signs. Just at that moment, Rachel stopped in front of a decaying log. When the others joined her, she pointed down at the log. "What do you think happened here?" she asked.

Ben squatted down to examine the log. He ran his fingers along the rough narrow grooves that seemed to have been scratched into the log with something sharp, and he noticed squirming larvae all along the log. He looked at the ground where he saw beetle-like insects scurrying around.

Then he stood up. "Do bears eat bugs?" he asked.

"You got it," Rachel said. "Bugs and larvae, too. In fact, they'll eat almost anything when they come out of hibernation. I think the bear has been here recently. These are fresh scratches. Let's look for more evidence."

As they spread out looking down at the ground, Kate stopped suddenly. "Scat!" she shouted, bending over and poking something dark and wet with a stick. This time Rachel was the first at the scene.

"It's scat alright. Fresh scat," she said. "If we want to see what made it, we'd better be quiet."

Not wanting to let the girls know that he had never heard of scat, Ben came up without speaking. There was no doubt what he was looking at. "It's scat alright," he said, wondering why his sister didn't just say "a pile of poop."

"Where do you think the bear is?" Kate whispered and waited for Rachel to answer. But Rachel was still and didn't say a word. She brought her finger to her lips, shushing the others. They stood still and silent.

"Listen," Rachel whispered, pointing up toward the wilderness. Sure enough, they all were able to hear the sound of something passing through dry leaves. Looking the way that Rachel was pointing, Kate was the first to make out a dark shape moving just inside the wilderness. As she blinked her eyes, the shape came into focus. Just as she whispered the word *bear*, they heard a scuffling sound made by two small cubs running toward their mother.

Then the mother bear turned and looked in the direction of the kids. She sniffed. She stood up on her hind legs. Then she made a woofing sound—a low-pitched, threatening woof command. Before anybody could register what was happening, the cubs were scurrying up the closest tree. Finally the mother lowered her front legs, paced around the tree, and looked up at her cubs, woofing one more time. Ben, Kate, and Rachel were frozen in their tracks. No one moved or made a sound. Lisi had told them what to do if they encountered a bear: stay calm, do not run, back slowly away.

Without saying a word, first Ben and then the girls began

to step backward. Somehow they all managed to stay upright. When the bears were out of sight, they turned around and walked silently toward home. This time they could tell Lisi about their adventure without thinking they had done a bad thing.

Ben was the first to speak when they came back to Lisi, who was still reading in the sun. "Mom" he said, trying hard to keep his voice steady and normal, "our bear has cubs, and we saw them climb up a tree."

"Just before that, she made a sound like a dog's woof. I think she was warning them of danger," Kate said.

"And she stood up and looked at us," Rachel said.

"And what did you do?" Lisi asked, trying to seem calm but thinking about what could have happened.

"We did what you told us to do. We kept still and quiet and after a while, we backed slowly away. We didn't turn around until the bears were out of sight. Even then we didn't run," Ben said.

By now the kids were smiling and seemed very pleased with themselves. Ben gave Kate and Rachel a stern look. The girls both understood that they would not tell Lisi about the snakes. Not now.

CHAPTER 5

Growing Up

Although they didn't see the bears again that summer, Kate thought about them all the time. She wished that she could see the cubs nursing, learning to forage for food, and growing bigger and stronger. But she knew better than to go looking for them. She'd promised her mom that she would stay on their property; in return Lisi had promised Kate that she would take her into the wilderness when the time was right.

What with soccer practice and games on Saturdays, Ben was hardly ever at home. Only on Sundays did he have time to go into the woods, and even then he was busy collecting leaves and rocks and arrowheads. Usually he went alone. Always he looked out for snakes.

The next winter, one cold Friday afternoon, Lisi picked up Kate at school. Rachel and Amy were going to Atlanta, and Ben was spending the night in town with a teammate. When they got home, Lisi built a fire and made hot chocolate with marshmallows. When the fire was blazing, they snuggled up together on the old green sofa to read. A while later Lisi suggested that they have some vegetable soup.

"Well," Kate said, "can we have something special?"

"And what would that be?" Lisi asked.

"How about French toast and maple syrup?"

"Suits me," Lisi said.

"Let me cook tonight. You stay here and read the paper. I'll call you when it's ready." This was the first time that Kate prepared a meal for her mother. They both remembered that night as a special time together. After helping her mom clean up, Kate went to the window and looked out. "Do you think it will snow?" she asked.

"It's been more than cold enough for snow, and probably cold enough to send the bears into hibernation," Lisi said. "Remember this time last year we had our first snow."

"Mom," Kate said, "turn on the outdoor light." She looked up at her mother and smiled. "Snow. It's starting to snow."

By the time they crawled into bed, the now heavy snowfall had covered the ground. It snowed all night. When Kate woke up, Lisi had prepared a breakfast of oatmeal and hot apple cider.

"How about we go into the wilderness today?" she asked.

"Mom, really?" Kate blurted out. "You mean it? Why today?"

"Well, there's about three inches of snow on the ground. We'll be able to see the tracks of animals and follow our own tracks back out."

In less than fifteen minutes, they were dressed for the cold. Lisi packed a thermos of hot cider. "You lead the way," Lisi said as Kate set out on the same route they had taken on the last adventure.

This time they noticed small tracks—birds and squirrels. Near the creek there were lots of deer tracks. At the back of the property near the boundary, Kate spotted tracks she didn't recognize. "What do you think, Mom?" Kate asked.

"It could be a dog, but I don't think so. I say coyote."

"Could it be a wolf?" Kate asked.

"Not a wolf," Lisi said. "You tell me why not."

"Because the wolves have all been killed around here. I wish they would come back."

"Some people are talking about bringing the wolves back. Maybe some day you'll hear them howl again in our woods," Lisi said.

Without saying a word, Kate walked past the "No Trespassing" signs into the wilderness. Lisi followed, knowing that Kate was heading for the spot where she, Rachel, and Ben watched the bear close herself in her den the year before.

Kate turned to her mother, put a finger to her lips, and whispered, "We don't want to wake the bear." She was hoping that the bear had gone back to the den with her cubs.

After walking about a half mile into the wilderness, Kate pointed to an outcropping of rock. She led her mother to the same flat spot where she and Rachel had found Ben watching the bear the same time the year before. After they had settled down, Kate pointed to the den. Sure enough it was once again closed up with twigs, leaves and small limbs.

"She's in there with the cubs," Kate said.

"Could be," Lisi said. "A mother bear sometimes comes back to the same den where she gave birth— especially if no one has disturbed it."

For the next half hour, they quietly sat sipping hot cider and watching the den. The forest was silent. If there were animals nearby, the snow muffled their movements. As they followed their own tracks back to the house, Lisi was pleased that Kate understood without having to be told that all living things are important. She expected that Kate would grow up to do something unusual, something out of the ordinary. More than likely Kate would choose to work with animals, but probably not as a veterinarian like Amy. She had never had a pet—no dog, no cat. She was much more interested in wildlife and wild places.

CHAPTER 6

Ten Years Later:
Summer 1992

"Welcome to Paradise," Ben said as he pulled into the lane leading to the old homestead where he grew up.

"Wow," his friend Mike said. "You do live in the country."

"Yep, and right up against the wilderness."

"It's so dark here. If it weren't for the full moon, we couldn't see anything," Mike said as he looked around at the pond, the garden, and the trees beyond.

"It was a night just like this when my sister and I saw this place for the first time. We thought the house seemed haunted. That was ten years ago, but I can remember it like it was yesterday. I'd never been anywhere except New Orleans and the Mississippi Delta. And I'd never seen a mountain. Coming here was a big deal for me," Ben said.

"So why are there no lights in the house?" Mike asked.

"Probably they've gone to bed. I had hoped we could surprise them, so I didn't tell them exactly when we were coming," Ben said, looking at his watch and noticing that it was almost midnight.

"Let's just go to sleep and surprise them in the morning. I'm exhausted," Mike said.

And so they sneaked into the house and crept into Ben's

room. "You take the upper," Ben said as he took off his shoes and crawled into the lower bunk. In no time they were sleeping, and it was broad daylight before they woke up.

Ben and Mike were roommates at the University of Virginia. They both had soccer scholarships and were teammates as well as good friends. They had just finished their sophomore year in college, and they had driven from Charlottesville in Mike's old Toyota pickup truck. Mike was from Montana and had never been to Georgia, or for that matter south of Virginia. He and Ben planned to hike as much of the Appalachian Trail as they could that summer.

It was almost noon when they woke to the smell of bacon cooking. Lisi must have known he was home, Ben thought. She only cooked bacon on special occasions. As Ben walked into the dining room, Lisi was putting the last items of a huge breakfast on the long heart pine table—scrambled eggs, biscuits, grits, blueberry pancakes, jam, maple syrup, and yes, bacon.

"Mom, you've outdone yourself," he said, giving Lisi a hug.

"And you've grown another two inches," his mother said, standing back to get a good look at her tall, handsome son. "You don't look like a boy anymore."

"Mom, I'm not a boy. And neither is my friend Mike," he said as he glanced at his friend who was standing awkwardly in the doorway.

"Mike, I'm so glad to finally meet you," Lisi said, holding out her hand.

Just as he was about to take her hand, Lisi changed her mind and reached up to give Mike a hug, too. "You're even taller than Ben," she said as she stepped away to look at him.

"Actually, less than an inch—I'm about 6'2"."

"Well, Ben didn't get the height from me," Lisi said. "His father was a tall man."

"Enough of this talk," Ben said, just as Kate burst through the door carrying flowers from the garden. Everyone was talking at once—Kate asking for a vase, Ben introducing Mike to Kate, and Lisi trying to get everyone to the table.

When they finally settled down, Lisi explained that they were about to have a genuine southern breakfast. "Help yourself, Mike. Here's something you may not have had," she said passing him a bowl of grits.

Mike spooned out a serving of grits and sampled it politely. "Very good," he said, not mentioning that cheese grits were always on the menu in the dining hall of the university.

Breakfast went on for more than an hour, and when they finally pushed away from the table, Ben and Mike had put away a huge amount of food. Ben excused himself, saying that he was going to lie down for a few minutes. Mike helped with the cleanup, and when the kitchen was finally put back together, Kate offered to take him around the property.

"You don't want to go back to bed," Kate said. "There's too much to see around here."

Mike put on hiking boots and met Kate down by the pond, where she was watching a snake swim away from her toward the other side.

"Water snake. Not poisonous," Kate said.

"How do you know it's not a water moccasin?" Mike asked.

"Easy. This is a long, thin snake. Its head is low in the water, and it swims with its body under the water. When I first came out, it was sunning itself on that rock, but when I walked up, it slid down into the water. This snake will probably climb a low lying tree and stretch out on a limb," Kate explained. "Water moccasins don't do that."

Mike and Kate settled down on the same rock where the snake had been sunning itself, and just as Kate had predicted, it slithered out of the pond, across the muddy bank, and up a sycamore tree, disappearing as it glided out onto a limb some six feet above the ground.

"I would never know there was a snake in that tree if I hadn't watched it go there," Mike said.

"Lots of creatures live in trees—not just snakes and birds, but frogs, squirrels, insects, and even raccoons. And mother bears will chase their cubs up trees if they sense danger."

Kate paused, looked at Mike, and smiled. "I'm talking too much," she said. "And besides, you probably know all that already."

"Well, not really. Since I grew up in Montana, I don't know much about the woods around here."

"I didn't know you were from there. I'll be starting at the University of Montana in Missoula in September."

"Yeah, Ben told me that. Maybe when I come home, I can show you around my neck of the woods."

"So you like to hike?" Kate asked.

"I sure do. Ben and I have been talking all spring about backpacking on the Appalachian Trail. Our plan is to hike from Springer Mountain in Georgia to Damascus, Virginia. Ben thinks we can make it in easily in forty days if we don't leave the trail, or forty-five days if we take layovers."

"What's the rush? Wouldn't it be better to take your time?" Kate asked.

"We have to get back for soccer practice in August, and I want to go home to visit my family," Mike said.

Standing up, Kate showed him her favorite spots—the garden, the orchard, and the springhouse. She told him what she knew of the history of the house: that it was more than 150 years old, that people whose families had lived in the area for generations thought there was gold hidden inside or maybe around the house, and that some still say it's haunted.

Before they went back to the house, Kate and Mike walked the trail to the back of the property and into the wilderness. Along the way, she pointed out wildflowers, a salamander nest, and the tree where Ben had seen a snarl of rattlesnakes. She showed him the cavelike cavity where a mother bear had made a den and given birth to twins. When they emerged from the woods, Lisi was sitting in the swing reading a book and didn't look up. Ben had finally gotten out of bed, showered, and dressed in clean clothes; he was walking down the lane, supposedly picking blueberries, but actually looking out for Amy and Rachel, who were coming for supper. Kate looked up at Mike and once again apologized for talking so much.

"That's okay. I'm interested in all of this—and you're interesting, too," he added with a smile.

For supper, Lisi prepared all of Ben's favorite foods—mountain trout, squash casserole with cheese, spring garden salad, yeast rolls, and for dessert strawberry shortcake.

"I never see you girls in dresses," Ben said as he looked around the table. Kate and Rachel both had on sundresses—Kate a blue-and-white one, Rachel a yellow daisy print.

"Actually, we went shopping yesterday, just for this occasion," Kate said.

"Well, you two look very nice," Ben said.

"Thanks, Ben. That was the idea," Rachel said flashing him a flirtatious smile.

Mike, who fit easily into the family conversation, asked just the right questions to learn more about the four women. "Dr. Morse, tell me about your salamander research," he said, looking respectfully at Lisi, who was not accustomed to being addressed as "Dr. Morse" by anyone other than her students. At home, she was "Lisi" or "Mom," but she didn't correct Mike or ask him to call her by her first name. After all, she had worked hard to earn a Ph.D., and it was courteous of Mike to use her professional title.

After listening attentively to Lisi, Mike turned to Amy and asked about her work. "Well, of course there's the routine cat and dog practice, but I end up caring for all kinds of animals, both domestic and wild. Most of the wild animals I rescue go to a rehabilitation center. Those that can go back to the wild," Amy said.

For the rest of the evening, the talk went back and forth, sometimes in response to Mike's questions but often as Rachel, Kate, or Ben interrupted with stories of their own. By the time the strawberry shortcake was served, Mike knew that Rachel was coming to the University of Virginia. Ben hadn't mentioned

Rachel at all, but watching the two of them together, Mike knew they liked each other a lot.

"Mike, you haven't talked about yourself at all," Rachel said.

"He won't brag about himself, but I'll tell you he's a star soccer player. Without Mike, we wouldn't have won the championship," Ben said.

"So, are you going to play professional soccer?" Kate asked.

"I don't know yet. I'm also interested in medicine. I'm taking pre-med courses—chemistry, biology, physics—the usual. But that's enough about me. Dr. Morse, you and Dr. Carson go out to the porch. I'll clean up the kitchen," Mike said.

"You don't get to do that by yourself. I'll help," Ben said as he jumped up and started clearing the table.

"And you're not leaving us out either," said Rachel.

Each in her own rocking chair, Amy and Lisi shared a pot of tea. They were quiet for a while as they listened to the sounds of laughter and music coming from the kitchen. Lisi was the first to speak.

"Just ten years and our children have become adults. Seems like yesterday when we first sat in this swing and talked about whether they should go into the woods without us. Now Ben is taking off on the Appalachian Trail, and Kate is going to Montana where she'll be in the woods with grizzly bears."

"And Rachel is going off to the University of Virginia where she doesn't know anyone except Ben," Amy said. "You know we really haven't talked about what's going on between those two.

Has Ben mentioned anything to you?"

"Not really. But it's real clear they're attracted to each other. What does Rachel say?" Lisi asked.

"Nothing about Ben other than that they've talked on the phone. Then the other day, she asked if I would be upset if she married before she graduated," Amy said.

"Whoa! That's scary. So what did you say?" Lisi asked.

"Well, I went on about her needing to get her education before even thinking about marriage, and she promised me that married or not, she wouldn't leave college without her degree. She never mentioned Ben, but I think they're in love."

Lisi took a deep breath and was quiet for a while.

Finally Amy broke the silence. "I wouldn't be surprised if they get married—and sooner rather than later," she said in a whisper. And in fact that's what happened. They were married in summer just before Rachel's sophomore year. Their son Joseph was born in May 1994.

PART II

CHAPTER 7

Kate in the Arctic

MORE THAN TWENTY YEARS HAD PASSED since that snowy day in north Georgia when Kate, Ben, and Rachel followed a bear to her den. Kate, now a wildlife biologist and graduate student, was in a helicopter traveling to a research station east of Barrow, Alaska. There she would spend the summer assisting Dr. Yu, her professor at the University of Montana, studying where female polar bears build their dens and have their cubs.

Looking down from the helicopter, she saw lakes and ponds, some no larger than a backyard swimming pool and others miles across. Nothing could be more different from the north Georgia mountains or the forests of Montana, she thought.

The pilot, Max, flew over the observation tower where Dr. Yu watched for polar bears and other wildlife. Dr. Yu gave a signal that he was busy and wouldn't be coming in that night. "Looks like you'll be alone tonight, but Chipic is there now to show you around," Max shouted over the noise of the helicopter.

"Who's Chipic?" Kate shouted back.

"I can't hear you," Max said.

46

With that, Max came in over the landing pad, hovered for a minute, brought the helicopter down, and shut off the engine.

"What were you saying about Chipic?" Kate asked.

"Chipic is the man who makes everything work around here. His job is to help the scientists. Most of his family has never left the Arctic, and Barrow is the only town they know. Chipic started working for the scientists here when he was a teenager. About ten years ago, he got a scholarship to go to college in Fairbanks. Ask him about that. I've got to get back to the airport."

Max flew helicopters and small planes, carrying people throughout the Arctic—tourists, oil company employees, and scientists. Usually when he went to Fairbanks, he did errands for Dr. Yu and brought supplies back to the station. He wasted no time gathering up Kate's duffle bag and carrying it across the wooden walkway that connected the landing pad to the research station, with Kate following behind. "You travel light," he said.

"Dr. Yu warned me not to bring more than I absolutely need," Kate said.

"Looks like you did a good job," Max said as they approached the rectangular boxlike building that would be Kate's home for almost three months. Standing just outside the door was a handsome, tall, Eskimo man.

"You must be Kate," he said.

"And you must be Chipic," she said, looking up into his dark, twinkling eyes.

"That's me," the young man said with a smile as he took Kate's duffle bag from Max.

"See you guys later. I've gotta take some oilmen out to a prospecting site," Max said as he turned and waved good-bye.

"Where is that?" Kate said.

"I can't talk about my oil clients. But Chipic can tell you anything he knows," Max said.

"Is that right, Chipic?" Kate asked.

"Max likes to tease people. In fact I can't talk about everything I know. Many people up here have secrets. I'm lucky. I don't have to work for the oil industry," he answered.

Inside, Kate took a deep breath. "I'm so glad to be here," Kate said as she sat down on one of the two chairs in the room.

"Did you have a rough day?" Chipic asked.

"The truth is I'm terrified of helicopters. My father died in a helicopter crash," Kate said.

"No wonder you're nervous," Chipic said.

"Flying in commercial planes is fine, but I really don't like small planes and helicopters," Kate said.

"You know you can't accomplish much in Alaska without flying. Most places you can't get to except in a plane or chopper. Stay where you are, and I'll fix a pot of coffee," Chipic offered.

In a few minutes, he poured two cups of coffee, gave one to Kate, and sat down. "So, let me introduce you to your accommodations. Everything you do happens in this one room. Behind that screen in the corner is a composting toilet. We have problems making these toilets work in the Arctic," Chipic explained. "We have to add heat to help the composting process. We do that with a gadget that Dr. Yu invented using electricity from small solar panels."

"So, what else do I need to know?" Kate asked.

"Okay. Behind that curtain is the mat you'll use for a bed, three shelves for your stuff, two pillows and a blanket. I brought you the extra pillow. In the opposite corner is Dr. Yu's private space. Most of the time he's in his tower, but if the weather turns bad, he'll stay here," Chipic said.

"And the shower?" Kate asked.

"Max brings in all the water you have in five gallon jugs. To shower, you fill this bag attached to a small hose with a spray nozzle and hang it on this hook. On the floor is a small grate for water to drain into a barrel below. You'll also pour dishwater into the grate."

"Oh, I've got it. Showers are short and cold," Kate said, laughing. "And what else?"

"Let's see. Over there's the two-burner propane stove for cooking and heating water, and a plastic dishpan for washing dishes. Leftover kitchen waste, like coffee grounds, can go in the composting toilet. In that corner is the propane heating stove, but you won't need to use it much. The solar panels on the roof charge the batteries for our computers."

"So the solar panels turn light from the sun into electricity?" Kate asked.

"Yeah, that's right," Chipic said. "Let's get back to the basics."

"Like food? I don't see any," Kate said.

"What's left is in some boxes under the cooking counter. We're kind of low right now," Chipic said. Kate looked in the boxes and saw powdered milk, canned salmon, instant oatmeal, dried fruit, and one bag of chocolate chip cookies.

"Max will be flying to Fairbanks early in the morning, and while he's there he'll buy supplies. He always brings back fresh fruit that lasts a few days," Chipic explained.

"How about sweets?" Kate asked.

"Oh, yeah. Max always brings cookies and candy."

"I brought a loaf of bread, a jar of peanut butter, and some chocolate bars. That should be enough for me until Max gets back, as long as we don't run out of coffee," Kate said.

"Don't worry; I'd never let that happen. Anything else you need to know?" he asked.

"Where do I work?"

"That piece of plywood supported by wooden crates is your work space," Chipic said.

"When do you think Dr. Yu will come back?" Kate asked.

"Probably tomorrow, but you never know. He'll radio me and let me know when he's coming back, but not until he's ready. He doesn't want anyone else picking up his signals. Oh, yeah, one more thing: Dr. Yu asked me to remind you not to mention any of the details of what we're doing in email. You can talk about daily life but don't mention the tower or the data you enter into the computer. If your family should ask, just say that you are working hard and that you like what you do but don't get too specific." Chipic explained.

"Why is that?" Kate asked.

"Well, one worry is that there are people up here who might harm a polar bear, even a mother with a cub, if they knew where to look," Chipic explained as he opened the door to head out into the tundra.

After he left, Kate stood outside the door looking at what seemed to her more like a desert than anything else. What color she saw was a dull yellowish brown—no red, no green, no blue. There were no trees and no bushes, only clumps of grass that she later learned were called tussocks. The only other plants she saw were tiny, dwarf-sized, and strange to her. Beyond the field station, there was nothing to cast a shadow on the landscape. She was aware only of light and silence.

Back inside, she sighed and looked around at the simple room. Before she took this job, Dr. Yu explained that the field research station where they would live and work for the summer was made mostly of plywood and was built on top of posts set into the frozen ground. Had the building been constructed directly on top of the ground, heat from inside would have melted the permafrost under it and caused the station to tilt and maybe even collapse.

She had thought she knew what to expect but was surprised that Dr. Yu's field station was so small. There were four windows in the station, large ones facing north and south and small ones in each of the two sleeping areas. Outside, horizontal bars of steel protected each window from bears that might try to break in. Inside, over each window, a roll of black canvas could be pulled down to block the light.

It would be difficult for her to be confined to this small space, but there were too many hazards in the tundra for her to go out alone. Only Chipic and Dr. Yu came to the field station on foot, and they knew how to step on top of the tussocks to avoid sinking into bogs, how to get past standing water, and how to find their way through sudden storms and whiteouts.

Kate was accustomed to doing research in places under difficult conditions where she slept on the ground and bathed in cold mountain streams. She had tracked wolves in Wyoming and monitored black bears and grizzlies in Glacier National Park, but she had never been confined to one small room.

"Okay," she said, talking to herself, "you better get busy."

In her sleeping space she arranged books, writing supplies, and her journal on one shelf and her clothes and boots on the other two shelves. In a small bag next to her sleeping mat, she kept all her other belongings—her toothbrush, soap, sunscreen, and so forth. She placed Delta, her small stuffed polar bear, on a pillow. Next she set up her laptop computer on her makeshift desk and sent off a short message to Lisi. "Arrived safely. More later," suggesting that she was busy. Kate assumed she would mainly use the computer for writing and keeping records for Dr. Yu. Next she put out two photographs. One she had taken the past Christmas when she was at home in north Georgia. In it were her mother; her mother's best friend, Amy, Ben; Rachel— now Ben's wife—and their son, Joseph. The second photo was of Kate, Rachel, and Ben; the three of them stood in the snow in this photo taken by her mother on that day, so long ago, when they tracked a bear.

Looking back at the family picture, Kate's eyes settled on

her nephew Joseph. Eleven years old, he was tall for his age and had thick, dark brown hair, blue eyes like hers, and a winning smile. He loved to roam the woods, the same ones Kate, Rachel, and Ben had explored. He knew their favorite places—where Lisi's salamanders lived, the hollow tree where they found a tangle of rattlesnakes, and the den where they watched a bear settle in for the winter.

Kate always looked forward to seeing Joseph when she went home for holidays, and she hoped that someday when he was old enough, she could take him on one of her adventures. Although she lived mostly out west and now in Alaska, she always stayed in touch with Joseph. She had promised to write to him while she was in the Arctic. She sat down at the computer.

Dear Joseph,
Remember you said you wanted to come to Alaska with me? Well, I wish that were possible. Right now I'm alone in the research station, which is a small rectangular structure about sixteen feet by twenty-four feet. That may sound like a lot, but this one room has to be a kitchen, a storage space, two sleeping areas, an office, and a bathroom—if you can call it that.

The plane that I took from Fairbanks to Barrow was full of Eskimos who laughed and talked the whole trip as if they were at a party. Luckily I had a window seat, and I couldn't take my eyes off the scene below. Mostly the tundra seemed empty, but we also flew over the Yukon River and the mountains of the Brooks

53

Range. The pilot pointed out a herd of caribou, which looked like a dark mass moving across the tundra. As we were approaching Barrow, we flew out over the Arctic Ocean. The ocean is not smooth at all, but a jumble of chunks of ice, small icebergs, and what look like frozen waves. I saw a whale swimming in one of the openings in the ice. These openings are called "leads."

A pilot named Max met me at the airport and brought me straight here in a helicopter. He left me with an Eskimo named Chipic, who showed me around the research station. It's about midnight here, and the sun is shining as brightly as it does at noon. A cold north wind is blowing and the temperature outside is near freezing, but it's comfortable inside because the sun shines in one window or another nonstop.

Joseph, I've got so much to learn about the Arctic. It's as different from north Georgia as a place could be. I'm a little homesick shut up in what feels like a large box. Don't worry. I'll get over it as soon as I have work to do.

Write and tell me what you're doing this summer.
Love,
Kate

For supper Kate ate a peanut butter sandwich and a small bar of dark chocolate. Thinking that she would read for a while, she crawled into her sleeping bag. But she soon dropped her book and fell asleep in bright daylight.

CHAPTER 8

Rescue

"Kate, open up. We've got an emergency!" Chipic shouted.

Kate ran to the door. "What is it?" she asked.

"Dr. Yu has been watching a mother bear with her cub on an ice floe through his telescope. This morning he saw a single cub, stranded on a smaller floe. Probably the same cub. The mother may have abandoned it, the floe could have split and separated them—or something could have happened to the mother."

"So what are you going to do?"

"Well, rescue the cub."

"I thought it was against the law to take marine mammals out of their habitat," Kate said.

"Dr. Yu has a permit to rescue cubs who've been abandoned. I've already contacted the Fish and Wildlife Service here and reported the rescue plan. But we do have to have someone willing to take care of the cub if we succeed. Are you willing to be that person?"

"You bet! Can I come with you?" Kate asked.

"We're going to rescue the cub in a umiak. There's no time to teach you about umiaks. You may be a wildlife biologist, but you'll never be an Eskimo," he said with a smile.

"And you think you can do this?" Kate asked.

"I do. The ice floe is close to the beach. So what do you think? Are you willing to take this on, at least until we can find out what's wrong?" Chipic asked.

Kate didn't hesitate. "Yes, yes, I will. Chipic, this is work I've dreamed of doing since I first saw a mother black bear with cubs," she said.

"And you understand that you can't change your mind. Once I bring the cub here, you're responsible for it."

"Chipic, you better leave right now and try to save that cub."

"Let me get this straight. You're willing to wake up several times a night to feed a baby bear?" Chipic asked.

"Yes, I am. Now go. Just do it!"

"OK, we'll give it a try. If we can rescue the cub, you're going to have a real adventure," Chipic said.

Then he ran out the door and headed across the tundra toward the shore. On the way, he stopped by his family's camp where they kept their sled dogs. Chipic's family used the traditional ways of travel—sleds pulled by dogs on the snow and ice and umiaks for travel on water.

Without explaining what he wanted, Chipic grabbed a large net on a pole, called to his brother Avik, and said quietly, "Follow me to the umiak and bring a large dog crate with you." Avik told their other brothers, who were building a sled, that he would be back soon. Then he followed Chipic across the tundra toward the sea.

"So what's up?" Avik asked.

"We've got a rescue job to do—a small polar bear cub is

stranded on an ice floe about a mile from here. No sign of the mother, but we'll have to be careful," Chipic said.

Umiaks can easily be forty feet long, but this one was less than twenty feet and weighed about 150 pounds. The two brothers lifted the boat and carefully walked down a path to the sea. They loaded the crate and the net into the boat and stepped in, with Chipic in front and Avik in the back. As they paddled quietly toward the west, fog began to roll in from the north. Chipic gazed into the fog, looking intently for ice. He used hand signals to indicate what was ahead, and Avik steered the boat. Soon they saw an ice floe and were able to make out the shape of a small bear.

Chipic signaled to his brother to stop paddling. As the boat silently floated toward the ice, he picked up the net and stood up in the umiak. With lightening speed, he jumped on the floe and with one motion tossed the net over the cub. At the same moment, Avik reached out with the grappling hook and held the boat steady against the ice. The next job was to lower the bear into the umiak and wrestle it into the crate. To their surprise the cub went limp, and in a matter of minutes, both Chipic and the bear were in the boat. No one was hurt.

A few hours after he left the research station, Chipic returned carrying the dog crate. Inside was a frightened polar bear cub. He put the crate next to Kate and watched while she looked into the eyes of this animal that was going to change her life in the Arctic.

"Chipic," Kate said excitedly. "You rescued the cub! Tell me what happened."

"Hold on, Kate. Let's talk softly. I think we need to take the cub out of the crate but not until we make a bottle of warm milk."

Dr. Yu kept baby bottles, dried milk, and canned milk in the field station just in case he needed them for a rescued animal. Chipic made a bed for the cub while Kate warmed some milk and put it in a bottle with a nipple. Then Chipic carefully lifted the cub from the crate and handed it to Kate. The little bear settled down in Kate's arms, drank the milk, and fell asleep. For a few moments, neither of them said a word as they watched the cub sleeping, each deep in thought about what would happen next. Kate spoke first.

"The cub's name is Delta," Kate said.

"What kind of a name is that?" Chipic asked.

"A good name for an orphaned bear cub," Kate said.

Chipic could tell that Kate had made up her mind, so he didn't remind her that Dr. Yu was opposed to naming animals that he was studying. At that moment, he was looking at her wavy brown hair and bluer than blue eyes.

"So tell me how you did this," Kate said.

"I will if you don't fall asleep," Chipic said with a smile. Then he told her about Avik, the fog, and the rescue.

CHAPTER 9

Decisions

Dr. Yu was always very formal, and he hardly ever joked or smiled. But when he returned to the research station, he was more excited than Kate had ever seen him. "Where is the cub?" Dr. Yu asked as he burst through the door.

"She's sleeping," Kate said, pointing to the bear.

"You already know this is a female bear?" Dr. Yu asked.

"Actually I don't know, but she seems gentle. Chipic told me that male cubs are more likely to fight than females. So I think it's a girl."

"Well, let's have a look," Dr. Yu said, settling down on the floor.

Dr. Yu turned the sleeping bear over and checked it out. "You're right. It's a girl."

He put the cub back on her blanket. She didn't wake up for a couple of hours. Kate got up and made a pot of tea for Dr. Yu and brought out some chocolate chip cookies. Chipic and Dr. Yu talked about the cub and what they would have to do if they kept it.

"If you save the life of a wild creature, you become responsible for that life, " Dr. Yu said.

"Responsible in what way?" Kate asked.

"In the case of this helpless cub, we have to feed it, take care of it, and eventually find it a home."

She noticed that Dr. Yu referred to the cub as "it." She knew better than to tell Dr. Yu that the cub had a name. "Most scientists do not name their subjects. We identify them with numbers," she remembered Dr. Yu saying to his students.

Dr. Yu stood up, cleared his throat, and began to talk. "The truth is, I don't think we can decide on the best course of action right now, and the cub may decide for us. It could weaken and die. Or it could do well. And if she lives and grows, we'll have many more problems to solve. This is one of those times when it doesn't make sense to plan for the future because we don't know what's going to happen." Kate and Chipic looked at each other and didn't interrupt Dr. Yu. They both had noticed that Dr. Yu had shifted from "it" to "she" and "her."

"Taking care of a wild animal is not easy, and this cub may have problems. We've got a lot of work to do to keep her alive," Dr. Yu said.

"I'm willing to do what it takes. I'll think of myself as her mother," Kate said.

"That's one of the things she needs," Dr. Yu said, "but a mother bear doesn't have to ask what her cub needs. Her milk is the perfect food, and we have to find out how to make a formula that's as close as possible to the mother's milk she's been living on. I know it's very rich and has much more fat than the powdered milk and water you're feeding her. We'll see how she does with that first, and then we could add oil and honey to increase the calories. In the meantime, you need to go on the Internet. See what you can find out about the best formula for feeding polar bear cubs."

"Is there anything else she might eat?" Kate asked.

"Well, mother polar bears mostly eat seals, giving the baby small bits to eat. But Max isn't going to find seal meat in the grocery store," Dr. Yu said in a serious manner.

Max had flown out that morning to buy supplies in Fairbanks. That was before Delta was rescued. Max didn't know to buy extra provisions for a bear.

Kate looked over at Chipic and saw that he was deep in thought. "What are you thinking, Chipic?" she asked.

"When I rescued this cub, I was only thinking of saving her life. And that's what I'd still like to do. But I have work to do and so do you, Kate. I'm thinking we'll need some help."

"You're right," Dr. Yu said. "We've got to find someone who will be comfortable in this small space with Kate and who is willing to spend hours every day helping with this cub."

"I think I know who could do the job, Dr. Yu," Kate said.

He looked at her with a questioning expression.

"This may sound crazy, but I think my eleven-year-old nephew, Joseph, would be just the person. He's a very mature boy—and really smart."

"I don't think so," Dr. Yu said. "I can't be responsible for a child. He would have to fly all the way to Barrow by himself. You won't be able to leave Delta long enough to go all the way to Georgia to bring him here."

"Dr. Yu, I'll be responsible for Joseph. When his mother was his age, she flew to Alaska alone to see her father," Kate said.

Dr. Yu couldn't think of anyone else to help. His graduate students already had jobs. "Actually an eleven-year-old boy might be the best we can do. He would find it quite an adventure. But he's going to have to come soon. How are we going to make that happen? Do you think his parents would be okay with this?"

Kate looked at Chipic and held her breath waiting for him to say something. For what seemed like a long time, he sat quietly looking at his feet. Then he looked up at Kate and said, "Do you think Joseph's parents will agree to his coming if I were to fly down to Anchorage to meet his plane and fly back to Barrow with him?"

"That's a good idea," Kate said. "When you go back to Barrow tonight, call my brother Ben—Joseph's father—and explain the situation. See how Ben and Joseph's mom, Rachel, feel about this. Tell them that if Delta is still doing well after a week, we'd like Joseph to come up here, and I'll be responsible for him. Meanwhile I'll send them an email."

Then Dr. Yu turned to Kate and said, "It's okay to mention the cub in your email so long as you don't give the location where it was found. Also, I don't want you to have high expectations for this cub. I know you've given her a name, and that's not consistent with scientific objectivity."

"How did you know I've given her a name?" Kate said surprised.

"Kate, you just referred to her as 'Delta.' I assume that's her name. But I'll refer to her as the cub. By the way, this one looks small to me."

"How much smaller is she than healthy cubs her age?" Kate asked.

"Much smaller than she should be. She looks bigger than

she really is because of all her fur," Dr. Yu answered. "On average cubs weigh a pound and a third at birth, and around twenty-five pounds when they leave their dens in April. I'd guess that's how big she is now. Imagine a chubby one-year-old baby. That's how big she is under all this fluffy white fur. It's June now, and she should weigh about fifty pounds; she's not even close to that. But I don't want your concern for her to keep you from doing the work you came here to do," he said firmly.

Dr. Yu had not yet told Kate what he expected her to do to help with his research. While the cub was sleeping, he explained how she would record data about the location of dens, and when the mother bears left the dens with their cubs. Some of the data had been collected by planes with infrared cameras, and some by Dr. Yu using a telescope in his tower. Most of this information was in handwritten journals collected over the previous year. Kate was curious and asked more about the details of Dr. Yu's research.

"Actually, Kate, it's not safe for me to tell you any more than I have. You know that we're collecting data about the location of dens. The rest has to be a secret. You might accidentally reveal what I've told you to someone who could tell the wrong person," Dr. Yu said.

"Who would I tell?" Kate persisted.

"I don't know. Your nephew perhaps?" Dr. Yu said. "Even he might meet someone who would like to know what I'm doing. Even Chipic doesn't know the whole story. Besides, you might not be safe if you know more than you do."

"I understand. I won't ask again," Kate said.

"Good. Let's change the subject. You haven't told me why

you chose the name 'Delta' for this cub," he said.

"It's a long story, and it's a secret," Kate said with a twinkle in her eye.

"Okay, I won't ask again either," Dr. Yu said, as he gave Kate one of his rare smiles. "Have a good night. I'll see you in a few days."

CHAPTER 10

Back in Georgia

While his aunt Kate was caring for the cub, Joseph was camping out in the Nantahala Wilderness with his good friend Carlos. Lisi, Joseph's grandmother, had taken the boys camping on the summer solstice. Joseph and Carlos liked to pretend that they were camping out by themselves, so they pitched their tent some distance from Lisi's tent. They all stayed up until about ten o'clock when the sky finally became dark and the stars came out, first one, then another, and eventually hundreds, thousands, and more.

The weather was perfect, and when the boys asked if they could build a campfire, Lisi said she thought that was a bad idea. The night was warm, and the fire would make it difficult to see the stars. The boys agreed reluctantly, but when they watched the stars appear, they were glad that there was no smoke or light.

When Lisi announced that it was time to crawl into their tents and go to sleep, Joseph tried to put off bedtime. "Lisi, let's stay up a little longer. Tell us the story about the time my parents and Kate tracked the black bear into its den."

The bear story was never the same. Joseph loved it that Lisi would change things around to make the story more exciting. Sometimes the bear would follow the children back to the house, sometimes with her cubs and sometimes not. In one version of the story, the cubs were lost, and the bear even came into the house looking for them.

"Mrs. Morse, I've never heard the story," Carlos said.

"Okay. I'll tell the story, and then we have to go to sleep. And Carlos, instead of 'Mrs. Morse,' just call me Lisi, like everybody in the family does."

After telling the story for about the hundredth time, Lisi said, "You know that was a very foolish thing they did. All bears can be dangerous. They usually run from people, but not always."

"In Ecuador where I was born, we have bears, too, but they live in the mountains and never bother people," Carlos said.

"I've read about those bears in the Andes," Lisi said. "They're called spectacled bears, but the bears here in Georgia are all black bears."

"Lisi, aren't grizzly bears and polar bears more dangerous than black bears?" Joseph asked.

"Not necessarily. They are just bigger and scarier," Lisi said. Then she looked over at Carlos and saw that he was wide-eyed. "What are you thinking about, Carlos?" she asked.

"I'm thinking about bears. I'm hoping none come around here tonight," Carlos answered.

"Well, I can't tell you that they won't. But I will say that we are not doing anything to attract them. We ate our dinner about a hundred feet away from the tent, and we hung our extra food between two trees," Lisi said.

"What if I get hungry during the night?" Carlos said.

"You'll have to wait until morning," Lisi said firmly.

Joseph went over to Carlos and whispered something in

his ear. Carlos looked down at his shoes and didn't say a word.

"Lisi, Carlos has something to tell you," Joseph said.

"You tell her," Carlos said.

"Wait a minute. What's going on here?" Lisi asked.

Both boys squirmed, and Lisi gave Joseph a suspicious look.

"Okay, we've got some food in our tent," Joseph confessed as he crawled inside and dragged out his pack where he had put a box of open cookies. Lisi insisted that they take the pack and hang it from a tree far from the campsite.

When they climbed into the tents, Carlos was still worried. "Joseph, I wish we had camped near the car instead of up here in the wilderness."

"You know what, Carlos?" Joseph said. "We shouldn't take cookies into the tent outside the wilderness either. There are bears all over these mountains, and you never know what they are going to do. If they smell food, they'll probably go for it."

"Still, I wish we were near the car," Carlos said.

The truth is the boys were just as tired as they were afraid, and after a while they finally fell asleep. At two o'clock in the morning in Georgia, it's ten o'clock in the evening in the Alaskan Arctic, and just as Kate was putting Delta back to sleep, Carlos woke to the sound of grumbling, snorting animals outside their tent.

"Wake up, Joseph, the bears are here!"

"You're dreaming, Carlos, go back to sleep," Joseph mumbled and slid further down in his sleeping bag.

"Joseph, wake up!"

Joseph sat straight up and listened intently as some large

animals rooted around the tent sounding for all the world like dogs with bad colds. Suddenly both boys were yelling. "Get out of here! Go! Lisi, we've got bears." But Lisi never woke up, and in a matter of seconds the boys heard the sound of what were surely bears crashing through the brush.

It was a while before Carlos and Joseph could fall back asleep, and when they did Kate was waking again to the squawking sounds of the polar bear cub she was caring for. When the boys woke up just after sunrise, they climbed from the tent and investigated the campsite. There were prints everywhere—huge prints of a mother bear, and the much smaller prints of her cubs. While the boys were measuring the tracks, Kate was sleepily measuring out the milk for what would be Delta's 4:00 AM bottle.

Kate had no way of knowing that her nephew was investigating bear tracks at the same time that she was feeding the polar bear cub. When he got back to Lisi's house, Joseph wrote Kate a long email about his adventure.

Dear Aunt Kate,

I wish you could have been here to camp out with us last night. You haven't met Carlos, but he just moved here last year with his dad from Ecuador. Lisi took us to her favorite place in the Nantahala Wilderness. Remember the ridge looking out over the river where we had a big family campout last fall? You won't believe what happened! Carlos woke up in the middle of the night shouting that bears were outside the tent. At first I thought he was dreaming, and I told him to go back to sleep. Then I heard something, too. Whatever was out there didn't seem happy. I don't quite know the words for what I heard, but there were grumbling and complaining sounds all at once. Must be bears, I thought. We made so much noise that they ran away.

We didn't go back to sleep for a long time. Instead we talked—whispered actually—and Carlos told me about the spectacled bears that live in Ecuador. The next morning when we climbed out of the tent, we saw tracks everywhere. We didn't go too far from the campsite that morning, and Carlos and I took turns looking out for the bears while Lisi cooked pancakes. I forgot to tell you that we think the bears may have come around because Carlos took a box of cookies into the tent.

Kate, I know how much you love an adventure. You would have loved this camping trip. And, by the way, all this happened on the longest day and the shortest night of the year, the summer solstice.

Please write to me about what you are doing in the Arctic. How long is the longest day there? I wish I could visit you.

Luv,

Joseph

CHAPTER 11

Kate and Chipic

Kate didn't know how to answer Joseph's email since there was so much happening that she couldn't tell him. So she sent off a quick message:

"What an adventure you've had. Very busy here. Not much sleep. Will write later."

The day after Kate's first night alone with the cub, Chipic came early to check on them. When he arrived, she was giving Delta a bottle. Before he did anything else, Chipic made a pot of coffee and took a cup to Kate.

"Thank you so much," Kate said, reaching for the coffee. "I need that as much as Delta needs her milk."

"Did you sleep well?" he asked.

"Not really. I got up to feed Delta several times," Kate said.

"Let me take her long enough for you to drink your coffee," Chipic said, reaching for the cub, who had already finished her bottle and was getting sleepy.

"Do you think I made a mistake giving the cub a name?" Kate asked.

"I think it's okay," Chipic said. "Maybe that will help you bond with her."

"Thanks," she answered, relieved that Chipic understood.

While they were talking, Delta had fallen asleep in Chipic's arms. Kate reached over and gently rubbed the cub's full belly, then stroked her soft white fur and touched her black nose. Then she examined Delta's small but sharp claws and gently pushed back Delta's lips to expose her teeth.

"Ouch," Kate said. "She could do some damage with those claws and teeth."

Chipic smiled and handed the sleeping bear back to Kate. "So how did you become interested in biology?" he asked.

"My mother is a herpetologist. She teaches biology and studies amphibians. When I was a child, she would take me in the woods to look for salamanders. I loved to snoop around streams and under leaf litter and to sit by the pond waiting for some creature to appear. I've watched birds build nests, a hawk take and eat a squirrel, a snapping turtle lay eggs, and a black bear with cubs—all of this and more in the forest that's just outside the house where I grew up."

"Tell me about your mother's research," Chipic said.

"For some time, she's been trying to find out how salamanders that lose body parts can grow new ones."

"Now that's interesting. She studies tiny amphibians, and you study one of the largest carnivores in the world. And the place where you grew up, what's it like?" Chipic asked.

"My mother has forty acres of forested land in north Georgia in the Appalachian Mountains. From the beginning she called our home place 'Paradise.' Her land backs up to national forest wilderness."

"You said your father died in a helicopter crash?"

"My father was a medical student, but he also worked as a rescue medic. He was on the way to bring an injured man off an oil rig when his chopper went down in a storm. That was just a month before I was born," Kate said.

"I'm sorry. It must have been hard growing up without a father."

"Well, yes, but I think it was harder for my brother, Ben," Kate said.

"So what does your brother do?" Chipic asked.

"He coaches high school soccer, but he does much more than that. He was a great player and even kind of famous when he played soccer in college, so he's also able to work as a trainer. Kids and even adults who play in soccer clubs hire him for private lessons."

While they talked, Delta woke up, rolled on her back and looked around. Then she began to play with her toes. "Look, that's the first time I've seen her playing. I've been keeping a record of her activities—mostly how much milk she drinks, how long she's awake, and how long she sleeps. I better add 'play' to her list of activities," Kate said.

After a few minutes, Delta turned over and fell back asleep.

"So tell me about your family, Chipic," Kate said.

"By the way, you can call me Chip."

"I don't think so. I like your Eskimo name."

"Actually, I like that better, too," Chipic said. He explained that he was born in Barrow, as were his parents, grandparents, great-grandparents, and ancestors as far back as he knew. His family worked hard to preserve the old traditions of the Eskimo people. Most of his family had never been anywhere beyond the north slope of the Arctic. They had never seen parks, farms, or forests.

"When I was seventeen," Chipic said, "I flew to Fairbanks with my father. He went there to have an operation. It was late June, and for the first time I saw trees and gardens. While my father was in the hospital, I walked all over the city. Each tree, each flower was amazing, but I couldn't tell one tree from another. I didn't know the name of anything I saw. I would ask people the names of trees, and soon I could identify them—quaking aspen, spruce, and a few others."

Chipic explained that while he was waiting for his father to recover, he visited the University of Alaska in Fairbanks. He talked to students there, and he decided to go to college. When his father got well, they returned to Barrow, but the next fall he came back to the university and earned a degree in wildlife biology. After graduating he came back to Barrow to work for scientists who do research on arctic animals.

"Did you miss your family?" Kate asked.

"Oh, yes. And I missed the life here—the sea, the whales, and the birds. Do you miss your family?" Chipic asked.

"I do, especially my mom and my nephew, Joseph. So do you think you'll stay here?"

"Not all the time. Now I miss the world outside. Somehow I'd like to live part time in Barrow and the rest of the time in a place with trees and seasons." For a moment, Chipic stopped talking, and they sat quietly. Then Kate broke the silence.

"I guess we're both torn between two worlds."

"I feel that way. Right now, I'm pulled to go outside."

"And where is outside exactly?" Kate asked.

"That's the word we use for the lower forty-eight. Outside Alaska. I've never been farther south than Fairbanks. I promised myself I'd go before my thirtieth birthday on September 21, the fall equinox. What's it like in Georgia? Is it hot there?" he asked, changing the subject.

"Oh, yeah. This time of the year it's very hot, but it's cooler in the mountains than across the rest of the state. It rains a lot, and we have amazing thunderstorms that cool things down. Still it gets hot, and it can be very humid. In the spring and fall, it's wonderful, and we do have snow in the winter, but it doesn't stay on the ground very long."

"What's fall like there?" Chipic asked.

"The forty acres my mother owns are mostly forested with hardwood trees. In October, before the leaves fall off, they turn beautiful colors—yellow, gold, red."

"I know more about sea mammals than I do about trees," Chipic said.

"Have you ever been whale hunting?" Kate asked.

"When I was sixteen, I was part of my father's crew, and we killed a bowhead whale. We don't want to take too many, but we need the whales to feed our way of life, our bodies, and our spirits."

About that time, Delta stirred, sat up, and began to make the yelps and shrieks that meant she was hungry. Kate warmed a bottle of formula and picked her up. While Delta drank the milk, and made the trilling purring sounds of a happy cub, Chipic and Kate continued to talk about their lives.

CHAPTER 12

Joseph in Alaska

The next time Chipic came to the field station it had been almost a week since the rescue. He found Kate standing over what looked like a bowl of mush. "I've been trying to get Delta to eat something other than her milk formula. I learned on the Internet that too much milk protein could be dangerous. Look at this," she said, showing Chipic a concoction of milk, oatmeal, olive oil and powdered eggs.

"I don't want to tell you what that looks like, Kate," Chipic said, turning up his nose.

"When I put it on the floor for Delta, she sniffed it and looked up at me as if to say 'Yuk,' and walked away," Kate said laughing.

"I don't think you can make her eat that. We have to find something she likes. For now, how about I make lunch for you?" Chipic asked.

"Sounds good to me," Kate said.

When they sat down to eat, Chipic said, "I think Delta is doing very well. Don't you think it's time for Joseph to come?"

"Actually I wrote him an email last night," Kate said.

"Have you checked your email this morning?" Chipic asked.

"No, let me do that right now. Yes, here's an email from

Joseph. He'll be here June 18. That's this Saturday!"

So the plan would be for Chipic to fly to Anchorage to meet Joseph's plane, and then fly with him back to Barrow. Since Chipic had never been to Anchorage, Dr. Yu suggested that he go a day early so he would have time to explore the city. He also asked Chipic to take a sample of Delta's blood to a lab, and to buy supplies and toys for her.

The day before he left, Joseph filled a duffle bag with his belongings. By bedtime he was feeling uneasy. When his mother came into the room to tell him goodnight, he was sitting on the side of his bed staring at his feet. "What's this about, Joseph?" she said, sitting down beside him.

"I don't know. I'm a little nervous. Alaska seems so far away."

"Most people feel this way before a trip. Remember the time we went to Florida, and I was so nervous that I forgot my driver's license? We had to go all the way back home to get it."

"Yeah, we almost missed the plane. I remember you were really upset," Joseph said.

Then his mother gave him a big hug and said, "I felt so stupid."

"Me, too. It's stupid to feel sad when I'm supposed to be happy," he said.

"Feelings are funny that way. They come and go and change without warning. Maybe you'll feel better in the morning," she said.

Sure enough, Joseph woke up very excited and happy. By mid-morning he had unpacked and repacked twice to make sure he had everything he would need. Right on top of his bag his mother put in his favorite snacks—walnuts, fruit, crackers, pretzels, and yogurt. For his dinner she put in a turkey sandwich and potato chips. "They may not give you much food on the plane," she said.

By early afternoon, Joseph and his parents were on the way to the airport. The plane was scheduled to leave at 5:30 in the afternoon, and they arrived in plenty of time. An airline agent named George stayed with Joseph through security and went with him all the way to the gate. Joseph's seat was by a window in the front of the plane. The seat next to him was empty, but at the last minute a woman wearing hiking boots sat down beside him.

"Hi," she said. "My name's Jane Oliver. What's yours?

"I'm Joseph Morse," he said.

"M-O-R-S-E?" Jane asked.

"That's right, just like the man who invented the telegraph," Joseph said, feeling proud to have the same name as a famous man.

"You traveling alone?"

"Yep," Joseph said.

"Me, too. Where're you going?" Jane asked.

"I'm going to Barrow to help with polar bear research," he said.

"Polar bears? By yourself?"

"Well, not exactly," Joseph said, and then he told Jane the story of Delta, how she was rescued and how he was going to help his Aunt Kate take care of her.

"So your bear is named Delta, and we're flying Delta Airlines. Any connection?"

"Not really. She was named for a toy bear. You know, a stuffed animal. A man named Chipic is meeting me in Anchorage, and I'm going to fly to Barrow with him," Joseph said.

"Well, Barrow is not going to be like anything you've ever seen before. I used to work there with the North Slope Wildlife Division studying the King Eider and other birds," Jane said.

"Chipic works for scientists like Dr. Yu, who studies polar bears. I'm going to Dr. Yu's field station," Joseph said.

"I don't know Chipic, but I've heard about Dr. Yu," Jane said. "People say he keeps to himself and stays out in his tower most of the time and that there's something secret about his research," Jane said.

Joseph told Jane that he wanted to be a wildlife biologist like his aunt Kate. Jane explained that her job studying wildlife in Alaska was not an easy life, but she loved it and wouldn't do anything else.

"So why are you going to Anchorage?" Joseph asked.

"I study birds. From Anchorage I'm going out to the Aleutian Islands where I'll be watching and counting birds. I've spent much of my life counting animals—whales and seals, but mostly birds," Jane told Joseph.

"You must be good at numbers," Joseph said.

"Well, at least I can count," Jane said, and they both laughed.

About that time, the flight attendant came down the aisle of the plane with a beverage cart. Joseph asked for a Sprite, and Jane had orange juice.

"I know orange juice is better for you than soda, but this is a special occasion," Joseph explained as he took out his sandwich and offered Jane half. "I can't eat it all," he said.

"Thank you. How would you like a piece of fruit?" she asked, handing him an apple. A few minutes later, Joseph fell asleep, and Jane began to read a book about migratory birds. Hours later, Jane nudged him, "Wake up, Joseph. Soon we'll be in Anchorage."

"That was quick," Joseph said.

"Not really. You slept about four hours. But look! It's still light. It's only 8:30 in the evening in Alaska."

"That means it's after midnight in Georgia," Joseph said.

"Look out the window," Jane said. "That's Wrangell-Saint Elias National Park, the largest wilderness in the United States."

"How big is it?" Joseph asked.

"Well, the park is more than twelve million acres, and most of it is wilderness."

"Wow! I thought my grandmother's place in Georgia was big, but it's only forty acres, and the Nantahala Wilderness where we went camping is only twenty-three thousand acres, and I thought it was huge," Joseph said. "So how much bigger is twelve million acres?"

Jane made a quick calculation and said, "More than five hundred times bigger than the Nantahala Wilderness. There are more than a hundred glaciers—one bigger than the state of Delaware."

Joseph looked out the window and saw mountains that he could not have imagined—huge jagged peaks, harsh gray stretches of bare rock, enormous rivers of ice cutting their way to the sea—but no trees, roads, or signs of life.

In a short while, the plane had begun its approach into

Anchorage. Below he could see boats in Cook Inlet, and for a moment it seemed they were going to land in the water. Then they were on the ground.

Joseph and Jane entered the terminal and walked down a long flight of stairs. A Delta agent followed behind to make sure that Chipic and Joseph found each other. Half expecting to see an Eskimo with a fur parka and a harpoon, Joseph saw instead a tall man in jeans and a red T-shirt. He had dark hair and light brown skin and was standing next to a glass case containing a huge stuffed polar bear. The man approached and said, "Are you Kate's nephew?"

Joseph nodded and asked, "Are you Chipic?"

"I am," Chipic said, smiling and offering his hand. Joseph turned to Jane and said, "Chipic, this is Jane; we sat together on the plane."

A few minutes later, Chipic and Joseph arrived at Susitna Place, a big house turned into a bed and breakfast inn. Linda, the owner, had left out a plate of sugar cookies, and Joseph ate them all and drank a glass of milk. It was still light outside.

They walked out onto the balcony overlooking Cook Inlet. Across the water they could see mountains. Chipic explained that one of them, Mount Spurr, was an active volcano, and it had erupted only twelve years before. There were no clouds and plenty of light to see Mount McKinley to the north.

"The native people call Mount McKinley 'Denali,' " he said.

"Then I'll call it Denali, too," Joseph said.

Early that morning, Chipic had taken Delta's blood to be analyzed. He had spent the rest of the day buying supplies and exploring Anchorage. He was as ready for bed as Joseph was.

CHAPTER 13

Off to Barrow

Joseph woke at eight the next morning and looked out the window. The sky was clear, and, for a moment, he didn't know where he was. Then he remembered. One of the mountains on the other side of Cook Inlet is an active volcano, he thought, half hoping to see smoke billowing from Mount Spurr. When he saw that Chipic's bed was empty, he pulled on his jeans and ran barefoot to the breakfast room.

"I thought you'd never wake up," Chipic said. "I want to see more of Anchorage before our plane takes off. I've never been here before either. How'd you sleep?"

"Great, I didn't even dream. I'm starving," Joseph said, helping himself to cereal and a bowl of fruit.

About that time Linda came over to the table. "Eat as much as you like and fill this bag with snacks for the flight to Barrow."

"Do you have any more sugar cookies?" Joseph asked.

"I do," Linda said. After breakfast Joseph filled a plastic bag with bagels, yogurt, bananas, sugar cookies, and chocolate-chip cookies—more than enough for himself and Chipic. Then he walked out on the balcony where Chipic was reading the *Anchorage Daily News*. Joseph was so excited he could hardly speak.

"Can we go now?" he asked.

"We don't have to leave for the airport for two hours. Our plane leaves at 12:30 PM. How would you like to walk on the path down by the water?"

"OK, but I'd really like to leave for Barrow right now," Joseph said.

A few minutes later Chipic and Joseph were walking on the trail along Cook Inlet. Joseph was leading the way. Across the water they saw two volcanoes—Mount Spurr and far to the south the top of Mount Redoubt. Joseph thought he saw a plume of steam coming from Mount Spurr, but he didn't have a chance to ask about it.

"Joseph, stop!" Chipic suddenly called out.

"Wow! Is that a moose?" Joseph asked, as he looked at the head and antlers of a huge animal standing in the willows at the side of the trail.

"That, Joseph, is a bull moose. Don't run," Chipic whispered while putting a finger to his lips as they backed up slowly until the moose was out of sight.

For the next few minutes, they walked in the opposite direction. "That was awesome. Do you think that moose would have attacked us?" Joseph asked.

"No, I don't," Chipic said. "But if he had decided to stomp us, he could have done some serious damage. Never approach a moose. That bull moose looked contented, but you never know. A cow with a calf is more likely to attack, especially if you get between her and her offspring."

Joseph felt safe with Chipic, but with active volcanoes threatening to erupt and a monster moose next to the trail, he was really ready to go to the airport. Back at the inn, Linda was sitting on the deck, and Joseph went out to tell her about their adventures.

"We have a lot of moose in this part of Alaska, and people often see them on the trail. Bears, too," Linda said, pointing down to the last place she had seen a big grizzly.

"Moose, bears, volcanoes," Joseph thought to himself, not wanting Linda or Chipic to know that he was uneasy. Trying to seem unconcerned, Joseph pointed at the cloud over Mount Spurr. "What do you think? Will that volcano erupt?" he asked.

"Someday. Nobody knows for sure when it's going to blow. There was a lot of activity last summer, and there were still rumblings a couple of months ago."

"So, what do you think?" Joseph asked.

"I don't think about it too much. Scientists say it'll blow in the next few years, but we usually have a warning. Don't worry. There are no volcanoes where you're going."

At the airport Chipic and Joseph had time to talk while they were waiting for their flight. Joseph asked about Eskimos, and Chipic explained that Eskimos in Alaska are also known as Inupiat. The same people in Canada are called Inuit, but they don't call themselves Eskimos.

"Except for my college days in Fairbanks, I've been in the Arctic all my life," Chipic said.

"Except for trips to North Carolina and Florida, I've been in Georgia all my life," Joseph said. "I can't believe I'm in Alaska on the way to the Arctic."

When they boarded the plane to Fairbanks, Joseph and Chipic both took window seats across the aisle from each other.

The plane was only half full when it landed in Fairbanks. There, at least fifty people boarded for the flight to Barrow, and the plane quickly filled. There were middle-aged men and women, mothers with babies, old people, and children. Joseph thought they must all be Eskimos.

Everyone seemed to know each other, and for a few minutes there was much confusion as people changed seats, called out to each other, passed babies down the aisles, and took off their coats. Only when the pilot announced that the plane was ready for takeoff did the passengers begin to settle down. At the last minute, an Eskimo girl about Joseph's age touched him on the shoulder and asked if she could sit in the empty seat next to him.

"Sure," Joseph said.

"My name is Ada Amatuk. What's yours?"

"My name is Joseph Morse. Are you going to Barrow by yourself?"

"Yes, I live in Barrow. I've been in Fairbanks, and now I'm going home," Ada explained.

Joseph thought that Ada seemed more grown up than the kids he knew back in Georgia. Just as he was wondering how old she was, Ada whispered, "I'm ten. How old are you?"

"I'm eleven. My birthday's in May," Joseph said.

"And I'll be eleven the first day of September," Ada said.

"So why were you in Fairbanks?"

"I went to the science fair for kids who won prizes for their science projects. My project was about global warming. Do you live in Fairbanks?"

"No, I live in Georgia. In the mountains."

"Georgia . . .hmmm. Where exactly is that?"

"Just north of Florida," Joseph said.

"Oh, I know about Florida . . . Sea World, right?"

"That's right. I've been there, and I saw the polar bears that were raised in the Denver Zoo after their mother abandoned them," Joseph said. "So, tell me about your science project. Global warming is really scary."

"I know it is. Where I live the polar ice is melting faster than it ever has before. Polar bears have to wait longer in the fall before they can go out on the ice and hunt seals." Ada paused before saying, "There's a lot we can do to stop global warming. That's what my project was about."

"Can we really stop it?" Joseph asked.

"First we have to slow it down. I think more people understand now what they're doing to cause global warming. Kids do. We learn about it in school," Ada said.

"Yeah, I agree. We can make a difference. So, how about a snack?" Joseph asked, changing the subject and reaching down for the bag of treats. "Now, let's see," Joseph said. "What will it be: chocolate-chip or sugar cookies?"

Ada chose the chocolate-chip cookies, and Joseph chose the sugar cookies. Then Ada asked Joseph why he was going to the Arctic. Joseph began to tell the story of the polar bear cub that had been rescued, how his aunt was taking care of it, and how he was coming to Barrow to help.

"Oh, I know about that! My dad and Uncle Chipic rescued that bear," Ada said excitedly. "Her name is Delta."

"Is your dad named Avik?" Joseph asked.

"Yes, he's Chipic's brother," Ada said.

Joseph pointed across the aisle and said, "Well, Chipic is

right over there, asleep under that blanket."

"He needs the sleep," Ada said. "He really works hard."

"So tell me about your dad," Joseph said.

"Well, he does some of the same work Chipic does, like helping the scientists, but in the summer, he's often out on the water doing inventories of orcas, belugas, and dolphins. He's a photographer, and he takes pictures of migrating animals. He once photographed three narwhals tusking."

"Narwhals?"

"They're small whales. I'll tell you about tusking later," Ada said.

For the rest of the flight they looked out the window together. As they flew over the Arctic, Ada pointed out the features of the changing scene below—the silvery ribbon of the Yukon River, the snow covered mountains of the Brooks Range, and the vast tundra dotted with hundreds of lakes both large and small. Joseph couldn't take his eyes off the scenes below. Ada, who liked to talk, told him about her school, her family, and their Eskimo traditions. She finally asked him what his home was like. Just as he started telling her about his life in Georgia, the pilot announced that they were about to land.

Still looking out the window of the plane, Joseph pointed at a town that seemed to be made of boxes. "That's Barrow," Ada said. As the plane banked out over the Arctic Ocean, Joseph saw an enormous dark oval shape in the water. "Ada, is that a submarine?"

"No, Joseph, that's a huge gray whale. They weigh almost forty tons," she said. "That one is really big, maybe fifty feet."

It was a bumpy landing, and as soon as the plane touched down, Chipic woke with a start. He looked around for Joseph, but the first person he saw was his niece Ada. She looked at her uncle and pointed to Joseph. "We decided to let you sleep," Ada said laughing.

As they got off the plane, they saw Max standing by the helicopter ready to take Joseph out to the station. Chipic explained that he would stay in town for awhile, but he would come out later to make sure Kate and Delta were okay. As Joseph started to say goodbye to Ada, Chipic said, "Don't worry, Joseph, I'll bring you to town for a visit in a few days. Ada has to go home now. Her parents are eager to see her." Ada was smiling as they waved good-bye.

Max quickly loaded the bags and boxes of supplies Chipic had bought in Anchorage. As he boarded the helicopter, Joseph felt butterflies in his stomach. Soon he would meet Delta.

CHAPTER 14

A Sitting Duck

THE DAY JOSEPH ARRIVED IN BARROW, Avik was out in his seal-skin umiak looking for any signs of beluga whales along the coast of the Arctic Ocean. Marine scientists were concerned that the beluga population was declining, and Avik was part of a team of Eskimos who were helping scientists at the National Arctic Research Laboratory (NARL) count the belugas as they passed through these waters. Avik's station was very near the spot where he and Chipic had rescued Delta. He always brought a camcorder along to document what he saw. But that day he hadn't used it. His watch was almost over when he saw a pod of about a dozen orcas—sometimes called killer whales—coming his way. Avik knew that belugas would probably avoid the carnivorous black-and-white whales, and to avoid a collision with them, he paddled closer to shore, giving them a wide berth. He grabbed his camcorder and began recording the approaching orcas.

When the orcas were out of sight, he noticed an ice floe drifting close to the shore. Through the lens he saw a polar bear riding the ice floe. As it drifted closer, Avik noticed from her size and the shape of her head that the bear was female. Then he realized that she was dead. Working fast, he attached one end of a line to the umiak and the other to a grappling hook. He paddled quickly to the floe and threw the hook toward the ice. He pulled alongside, jumped on the ice, and examined the dead bear. She had been shot in the neck. Using his hunting knife and a pair of pliers, he extracted the bullet and took enough hair and flesh for Dr. Yu to examine. Just as he was about to get back in the umiak, a shot rang out, hitting the dead bear in her front leg.

Avik looked back at the shore, but saw nothing. Terrified, he realized that the person who fired the shot had been watching him. "Anyone who could hit the dead bear could certainly hit me. I'm a sitting duck," he thought. "That must mean somebody wants to scare rather than kill me. Me, or anybody who messes with this bear." Gambling that the sniper had moved away, Avik took the time to remove the second bullet in spite of his fear.

Back in the umiak, he quickly stuffed the evidence in a sealskin bag. In the distance, he saw Quemik, his replacement, paddling toward him as the ice floe with its terrible cargo drifted away. Now Avik had a problem: how to let him know about

the bear and the shot without putting him at risk. He paddled as fast as he could so he would meet the incoming umiak out of the sniper's range. As the two boats approached each other, Avik signaled for Quemik to stop.

"Don't ask any questions," he said. "All you need to know is that there's a dead bear on an ice floe, and someone on the shore shot at me with a rifle—probably the person who killed the bear. Don't go any farther. Just watch for the belugas from here."

"I got it. No questions asked," Quemik said.

"I've got to get back to shore. Be careful," Avik warned.

It took Avik less than an hour to paddle the umiak to shore and make his way to Barrow. He needed to talk to Chipic as soon as possible, and he set out to find him. He went first to Pepe's Mexican Restaurant next to the Top of the World Hotel. As soon as he walked through the door, he spotted Chipic sitting in a booth talking with one of the scientists from NARL. He didn't want to interrupt business, but fortunately the scientist stood up just as Avik was about to sit at another table.

"Hey, brother," Chipic said. He was about to launch into a story about his trip to Anchorage when Avik interrupted.

"Something has happened," Avik said.

"Tell me," Chipic said, his smiling face turning to a frown.

"Let's talk quietly," Avik whispered, looking around to see if anyone might be watching them. "Remember how we thought the cub we rescued had been abandoned by its mother? Well, I don't think that's what happened. This afternoon I found a dead female bear on an ice floe with a bullet through her neck. I think the bear was the cub's mother."

"Whoa," Chipic said. "Who do you think killed her?"

"I don't know, but someone shot at me and hit the already dead bear, missing me by a couple of feet. I have the evidence—both bullets," Avik said, still whispering.

"Avik, you stayed on the floe long enough to retrieve both bullets? You're lucky to be alive."

"I figured the sniper left in a hurry as soon as he fired the shot."

"I think I would have done the same thing," Chipic said, remembering that his father had told him once that Eskimos had been living on the edge for thousands of years, making life-and-death decisions in a split second.

"I also got hair and tissue from the bear," Avik said.

"Great. That means that Dr. Yu can have DNA tests done and find out if the bear is Delta's mother," Avik said.

Before they left, they looked around the restaurant. They figured that the guys in brightly colored pullover sweaters and khaki pants worked for the oil companies. They recognized the men and women who worked at NARL. There was a scattering of children eating ice cream sundaes, and some tourists who were waiting to earn their membership in the Polar Bear Club by jumping into the Arctic Ocean. The only person they couldn't account for—a pretty woman wearing a gray-colored jump-suit—entered Pepe's hurriedly, took a seat in the back corner, pulled out a notebook and started writing.

"Maybe a journalist? Keep an eye on her when you're in town," Chipic whispered.

About that time Fran, the owner of the restaurant, came over and asked if they needed anything else.

"Glad you asked," Avik said. "What do you know about that woman in the gray jumpsuit?

"Well, she calls herself a writer. Says she's writing something about being a woman in Alaska."

Once they were out on the street, Chipic mentioned that he was sure Dr. Yu wouldn't want anyone to know about the dead bear and the mysterious sniper.

"I always figure that information we collect for Dr. Yu is secret," Avik said as he cautiously passed the bag of evidence to his brother. Then he handed Chipic what looked like a lunch box. "That's the camcorder," he said. "I think I got some good footage of the ice floe and the dead bear."

"Great job, brother, " Chipic said. "Tomorrow I'll take the camera out to the station so Dr. Yu can download the video. Kate and Joseph will have to know about this, but I'm not sure when. I'll let Dr. Yu make that call."

The brothers gave each other an Eskimo hug and went off in separate directions.

CHAPTER 15

Joseph and Delta

Kate had just finished giving the cub her bottle when she heard the familiar sound of a helicopter overhead. She opened the door and waited for Max to land. Soon he came down on the makeshift landing pad constructed on top of the permafrost. Kate watched excitedly as the door opened and Joseph climbed out. She ran out and gave him a big hug. "I am so-o-o-o glad you're here," she said as she took his duffle bag from Max.

"This feels like a dream," Joseph said, looking out at the tundra. "It's awesome!"

Max unloaded supplies Chipic had bought in Anchorage, carried them into the station, and in no time he had lifted off again. His helicopter was like an air taxi that people all over that part of the Arctic used to get themselves or supplies to places that were hard or impossible to reach by foot.

Once inside, Kate looked down at Delta and saw that she had fallen asleep. Then she motioned for Joseph to come over. At first he couldn't take his eyes off the cub, but at last he spoke, "How could she sleep with all that helicopter noise?" he asked, looking up at Kate.

"I guess she's gotten used to it."

"How long will she sleep?" Joseph asked, eager to see the

cub awake.

"She usually sleeps two or three hours after eating," Kate said.

Kate gave Joseph another big hug and said, "I can't believe you're here!"

"That's just what I was about to say. I'm going to take care of a baby polar bear! What can she do? What do I have to do?" he asked.

"I'll tell you in a minute. But first, I imagine you're hungry," Kate said.

"I don't feel hungry, but I could probably eat. Chipic said he bought toys for Delta and chocolate for you," Joseph said.

"We always have fresh fruit and milk when Max comes in." Kate said as she rummaged through the bags and boxes. "Here's something we'll both like: blueberries, sugar cookies, and milk."

Joseph and Kate sat down on the floor to eat their snacks and talk. Joseph told her about the moose in Anchorage and about meeting Ada on the plane. "So, tell me about Delta. What can she do?" he asked again, this time impatiently.

"Well, mostly she eats and sleeps. But she can walk. When a bear this age is with its mother, it would be out on the ice following her, watching her hunt, and probably eating bits of seal meat."

"How do you think Delta got separated from her mother?" Joseph asked.

"I don't really know. Delta is smaller than she should be at her age, so maybe her mother just left her. Sometimes a mother bear will abandon a cub if she knows it can't live in the wild. Also some mother bears are not returning to their dens, and Dr. Yu is trying to figure out why. But he doesn't want me to know more than that. I suspect that there're some bad guys up here who want to drive the bears away from their denning areas."

"Why would they want to do that?" Joseph asked.

"Well, I'm not exactly sure. Dr. Yu's on the job. I don't talk to him about my suspicions, and that's the way he wants it. My job is to enter his data into the computer and plot den locations on that map on the wall. But right now we have to take care of the cub and do everything we can to help her thrive."

"Does Delta play with toys?" Joseph asked.

"Well, we haven't had any here in the station. She plays with her toes and chews on my boots, and she bats at my face with her paws. Oh, yes, she takes the blanket out of her sleeping box and brings it to me. Then we play tug-of-war. That's about it. Tomorrow we'll look at the toys Chipic brought from Anchorage."

Joseph had no idea what time of day it was, but he was sleepy, very sleepy. When he asked Kate what time it was in Georgia, she said she'd have to figure it out.

"Remember your body is still on Eastern Standard Time. Let's see, if Alaska is four hours behind Georgia, and it's six o'clock here, what time is it there?" Kate asked.

"Let's see—seven, eight, nine, ten. I guess it's ten o'clock," he said.

"That's bedtime. Why don't you lie down and sleep for a while. You'll have plenty of time later to help with Delta," Kate said.

Joseph spread out his sleeping bag. In a few minutes he was sound asleep. Kate busied herself putting up the supplies and cleaning up the tiny space she called a kitchen. She left the box of toys out so that Joseph could find it in the morning.

Delta slept about four hours, and when she woke, Kate made her formula and fed her without waking Joseph. Then she fell asleep shortly after the cub did. The next time the cub woke up, she startled Joseph by making strange yapping sounds. He jumped up just as Kate opened her eyes.

"Time for another feeding," Kate said as she got up to make the bottle. "Do you want to give it to her?" she asked.

"Sure," Joseph said, settling down on one of the two chairs in the station.

"You're doing a good job," Kate said as she watched Joseph holding the cub firmly.

"You're not going back to sleep, are you?" he asked.

"Not yet. Delta's slept a lot, and she's acting like she may stay up for a while," Kate said, as she reached for the coffeemaker and pulled up a chair across from Joseph.

"A while" turned out to be about three hours—longer than Delta was usually awake. When she finished her bottle, Delta started squirming to get out of Joseph's arms. He gently put her on the floor. Kate handed him a granola bar. "Eat this and drink some orange juice. Then you can play with Delta," she said, handing him the box of toys. "I'll be working at my desk while you get to know her."

Inside the toy box, Joseph found a fuzzy wind-up mouse

for Delta to chase, a blue ball the size of a cantaloupe, and a bag of large foam blocks. Then he sat down on the floor next to the cub. For a few minutes, she was still as they looked into each other's eyes. Joseph wondered what could be going on in her mind. All he could do was stare back, almost hypnotized by her gaze. Slowly Delta moved closer to Joseph. She put a paw on his knee, pulled herself over, and settled between his legs. He placed the ball on the floor in front of her. She looked at the ball, back at Joseph, and then at the ball again. Joseph reached out and touched it lightly, rolling it slightly out of Delta's reach. She lunged forward and ended up on top of the ball for a few seconds before rolling off on her side. The games had begun.

For the next few minutes, Joseph and the cub played roll-the-ball, while Kate worked at the computer, occasionally glancing over at them. About that time, there was a knock on the door—Dr. Yu's secret knock. Kate got up to let him in, and the first thing he saw was Delta sitting in Joseph's lap with her blue ball on the floor in front of her. Dr. Yu rarely smiled, but when he saw the boy holding the bear cub, his whole face lit up. Still smiling, he looked at Kate, and without saying a word he dropped to the floor in front of the boy and the cub.

"I'm Dr. Yu," he said quietly. "You must be Joseph."

That was the beginning of their work together. From that moment, Dr. Yu spoke to Joseph as an adult, and he never treated him as a child. Dr. Yu had been a very intelligent boy himself in China, so bright that his teachers arranged for him to come to America to study when he was a teenager.

When Kate asked if he had heard from the lab in Anchorage, he said that everything was normal. At this point he was not concerned that she wasn't gaining weight. Only a short time had passed since the cub was rescued, and she was eating and sleeping well. As he observed her playing with Joseph, he could see that she was alert and responsive. More importantly, she seemed to be bonding with Joseph.

CHAPTER 16

Avik on the Tundra

About 4:00 AM the morning after the shooting, Avik set out for the place on the tundra where he figured the sniper had been the day before. He carried a camera with a powerful telephoto lens. Avik didn't expect to find the sniper or the gun. In fact he really didn't know what he was looking for. For sure he didn't want to be seen, and he didn't want Chipic to know he was snooping around where the sniper had been hanging out. That's why he came when almost everyone in Barrow was asleep. There was really no place to hide, no building, rock, or tree to get behind— no fog to obscure his passage across the nearly flat coastal plain.

To the person who doesn't know the terrain, the high Arctic tundra seems completely flat. But Eskimos know how to scan the ground and identify dips and rises called frost heaves caused by many centuries of freezing and thawing of the soil. Through his 400-millimeter telephoto lens, Avik saw a heave some hundred yards away that would be high enough to hide behind.

As he walked toward the rise, he suddenly stopped in his tracks. He had a spooky feeling that he was not alone. He dropped to his knees and studied the landscape. Some thirty yards beyond the heave, he saw something he couldn't recognize—not a rock, not a rise, not an animal, but what?

He walked a little closer and looked again through the lens. *It's a tent,* he thought—*a small one-person tent.*

Moving quietly over the tundra, he came to the heave, dropped to his knees, stretched out on his belly, and peered over the rim of his hiding place. There he stayed for about an hour watching as the lone camper emerged from the tent, made breakfast on a small one-burner stove, took down the tent, and packed it and other camping gear in a backpack. With the telephoto lens on his camera, he took pictures of the whole process.

Once the camper was out of sight, Avik crept over to the place where he thought the sniper might have fired the shot that penetrated the bear's leg. He dropped down on the tundra and stretched behind a grass-covered incline. Propped on his elbows he looked through the powerful lens on his camera. In the distance he could still make out the floe carrying the huge lifeless form of the polar bear—only just visible in the pictures he took.

Not until he took the camera home and loaded the pictures into his computer did Avik realize that he had been spying on a woman—a tall woman with dark brown hair, wearing a gray jumpsuit. Then he remembered seeing her at Pepe's. *No way she's the sniper. Just another crazy tourist who's come up here to learn about Eskimo life. Calls herself a writer. She's probably going to write about a woman camping out alone on the tundra.*

Avik felt uneasy and wondered why the woman had camped in the very place he thought the sniper must have been. Was it just a fluke that she had come there, or did she know something about the sniper? Was she writing a story for a newspaper?

When he zoomed in on the pictures of the ice floe, he could see the bloody spot on the bear's body. Chipic had warned his

brother not to get involved, because it would be easier to catch the sniper if he didn't know he was being pursued. This was why Avik didn't tell his brother or anyone else about his early morning adventure to the scene of the crime.

CHAPTER 17

Tracking the Bear Killer

Dr. Yu spent the whole day and night at the station. Chipic had given him Avik's video, and he was eager to see it. But he waited for Delta to get sleepy, and when she did, he asked Joseph to put her to bed.

"It would be a good idea for you to take a nap with her," Dr. Yu said. "You and Kate need to sleep when you can."

Joseph didn't have to be persuaded to take a nap. Soon after he curled up with Delta on his mat, they were both sleeping soundly. Dr. Yu and Kate sat in front of the computer and watched Avik's video. First they saw the pod of orcas surfacing and diving in unison. Kate was amazed that they seemed to come to the surface simultaneously and to dive back down all at once. "They're like dancers," Kate said quietly.

"Wait," Dr. Yu said, raising his hand. The orcas were out of sight, and the ice floe came into view. Gradually they were able to make out the lifeless body of the huge polar bear. Kate gasped and then remained silent, waiting for Dr. Yu to say more. To make sure he didn't wake Joseph, Dr. Yu took a scrap of paper and jotted down notes:

> *Killed with one bullet. Dead several days, Avik said.*
> *Avik shot at with same gun. Will send hair and tissue*

samples for DNA analysis.

Dr. Yu had already compared the bullets. He knew enough about firearms to think that the bullets had come from the same weapon, but still he wanted his conclusion verified by a ballistics expert. Kate looked at him with a raised eyebrow, silently asking for more information. Dr. Yu resumed writing.

Need sample of Delta's hair for DNA study.

Then they took turns, Kate asking the questions, Dr. Yu answering them.

Delta's mother?

Maybe. I think so.

Should Joseph know?

Not yet. I'll tell you when.

Who do you think did it?

Don't know, but whoever it is has committed a felony.

Poachers?

Don't think so.

Then who?

Maybe a hired gun.

Who's behind the hired gun?

People who have a lot at stake in this remote place.

Oil companies?

That's what I suspect.

Dr. Yu took the scrap paper they were writing on and stuffed it into his pocket. He would burn it later. He walked over to Joseph and Delta, who were still sleeping soundly. Dr Yu squatted down by the cub, cut off a small patch of her hair and put it in an envelope. Then he swabbed her mouth and sealed the saliva in a sterile tube. That woke Delta so he picked her up and brought her to Kate.

"I don't think Joseph will wake up anytime soon. I need your help taking a blood sample," he said, handing her an alcohol swab and a syringe. When Dr. Yu gently inserted the needle in the cub's leg, she squirmed but didn't make a sound.

"So the hair and saliva are for the DNA, and the blood. . .?" Kate asked.

"For more tests, especially hormone levels. I think I have all I need for Max to take to Fairbanks. Now it's time for one of us to sleep. You rest first, and I'll take care of Delta."

—

The next morning Max came to the station to pick up the shopping list and the package to take to the lab.

"Can you wait in Fairbanks for the results?" Kate asked.

"Well, I'll be out for a while, but I can circle back to Fairbanks before I come back to Barrow. I don't know for sure when I'll get back. It could be several days."

Pilots in Alaska are never definite about their schedules. There are too many variables. Sometimes Max would get to Fairbanks and find that he needed to fly someone out to the Arctic National Wildlife Refuge—sometimes scientists, sometimes reporters, and sometimes people just looking for adventure. And the changeable weather was always a consideration. Max was a careful pilot, and if there were any chance of fog or storms, he stayed put.

"Do you need anything special?" Max asked as he studied his shopping list.

"Plenty of milk, fresh salmon, raspberries if they have them, and whatever other fruit looks good," Kate said.

"And chocolate?" Max asked with a twinkle in his eye. Before Kate could answer, he waved good-bye, boarded the helicopter, and lifted it into the sky.

Back at the Barrow airport, the skies were perfectly clear. Usually the plane was full, but that day he had no passengers. Max had the plane and the sky to himself. He took off toward the north, flying out over the Arctic Ocean until he could see floating ice in the distance, then he banked the plane to the west, making a long curve until he was heading directly south. As many times as he'd flown this route, Max still was thrilled by the beauty and variety of the land below him: rivers, mountains, lakes, tundra—and from time to time a herd of caribou.

In Fairbanks, Max made the rounds—first a coffee shop, and after that the post office, grocery store, and a newsstand. Last he left the test sample at a medical lab. The lab technician explained that Delta's blood test would be ready in several days. The samples for the DNA tests would be sent to a lab in California, and the results would take longer.

While Max was gone, Kate and Joseph kept busy and concentrated on the day's work. The rhythm of Delta's days had changed from eat-sleep-eat-sleep to eat-sleep-play-eat-play-sleep. Sometimes she fell asleep after eating; other times she stayed awake to play. After a few days, Kate and Joseph had worked out a routine. When Delta was sleeping, one of them slept; when she was awake, they took turns feeding her. When Delta and Joseph were sleeping, Kate would work on the computer entering data for Dr. Yu.

Joseph's job was to work out games for Delta to get the exercise she needed to grow stronger. When the cub stayed awake after he fed her, he would get out the blue ball and sit on the floor with Delta in his lap facing the ball. When Joseph rolled the ball, Delta would scramble out of his lap and go after it. The ball would slip away from her, but she would follow behind it, always trying, but never succeeding in capturing it.

After his first few days in the research station, Joseph began to feel confident, and he really liked taking care of the cub. When Kate told him what a good job he was doing, he felt very proud. But Joseph didn't know that Kate was worried about Delta.

CHAPTER 18

Being in the Moment

Kate tried not to think about the future. Dr. Yu believed that good scientists were patient and that worrying about the future of their investigations was a waste of energy. "What is, is," he would tell his students. "If you're trying to find out if an animal is endangered, and you're hoping that it's not, then that hope can get in the way of good science. I've had students who've started out with a theory and twisted data around in order to prove it."

Joseph and Delta were sleeping when Kate was sitting at her desk remembering Dr. Yu's words. Then she heard a familiar tapping. "I thought you were spending the night in the tower," Kate said as she opened the door.

"Not tonight," Dr. Yu said, pointing at the window.

Kate looked out the window and saw a dense fog rolling in. That settled it. Max wouldn't be in that day and probably not the next. Sometimes fog settled in for days, and there would be no reason for Dr. Yu to be in the tower if he couldn't see. Kate made a pot of tea for Dr. Yu, handed him a cup, and poured one for herself. Delta and Joseph slept on.

"So, Kate, you look tired. Are you okay? " Dr. Yu said.

"I'm fine, except that I can't stop worrying about the blood test," she said.

"Kate, listen to me. The lab tests have already been done. Max will bring the results soon. But even then we may not know why she's smaller than normal."

"But we may. And then what?" Kate asked.

"We'll have to figure that out," he said.

When Kate talked about Delta's future, Dr. Yu suggested that she bring her mind back to the present. "All we have is this moment," he would say. "Every time we think about tomorrow, we miss out on today."

"Don't you worry about what's going to happen to Delta?" Kate asked.

"When thoughts come up about what's wrong with Delta," he told her, "I notice them. Then I let those thoughts go and bring my mind back to what's in front of me."

"I don't understand," Kate said. "You bring your mind back to what?"

"Well, to whatever I'm doing—making tea, writing a letter, watching the bears. Right now, I'm talking to you. Sometimes I'm just sitting."

"And you don't worry?"

"Of course I do. I'm human. But I don't worry for long."

Dr. Yu got up to check on Joseph and the sleeping cub and reported to Kate that for now, for that moment, there was nothing to worry about.

"You and Joseph are doing a great job with the cub," Dr. Yu said. "We've had very little time to talk since you got here. Let's take advantage of this foggy night to catch up. First fill me in on Delta's activities."

For the next hour, Kate told Dr. Yu about the cub's

progress, and for this short time, she was the teacher, and he was the student. Then they went over the data she had entered into the computer. There were charts about the location of denning areas, reports from the infrared cameras indicating whether dens were occupied during the previous winter, and records of the number of cubs that came out of the dens with their mothers.

"Do you think Delta was in one of these dens?" Kate asked.

"We may never know that, but there's a good chance," Dr. Yu said as he looked over at Kate just in time to see her trying to suppress a big yawn.

"You've got to be really sleepy," he said. "Tonight I'm going to take care of the cub when she wakes. This is a chance for you and Joseph to get a good long sleep." And that's what happened.

Dr. Yu rolled out a sleeping bag he kept in the station. When he got up to feed Delta neither Kate nor Joseph stirred. Dr. Yu had already left for his tower when Kate woke up. Joseph and Delta were still sleeping. Outside the fog had lifted, and the skies were clear as far as she could see. Surely Max would be coming soon. Kate opened the door, walked out to the landing pad, and spent half an hour scanning the skies for incoming aircraft. No Max. Back inside, she found Joseph feeding Delta her bottle. "Good morning," Kate said.

"How do you know it's morning?" Joseph asked as he looked at her with a teasing smile.

"Because I looked at the clock on the computer. It's 9:30 AM. And we went to bed around midnight. So how do you feel?" Kate asked.

"Great, " Joseph said.

"We both slept nine hours. Dr. Yu took care of Delta all

night," Kate said. Just then she heard the familiar hum of a plane. Max buzzed the research station, announcing his arrival. He would soon land the plane at the Barrow airport, load the supplies into the helicopter, and fly across the tundra to the station.

When Delta finished her bottle, she showed no sign of falling asleep. Joseph put her down. "Time to play," he said as he rolled the blue ball in her direction.

After a few minutes, Kate said, "Max has had enough time to load the supplies. Let's leave Delta inside and go out to watch for him." Once outside, they didn't have long to wait. Joseph, who had unusually good eyesight, was the first to see a spot on the horizon, which gradually came into full view. Then they heard the familiar sound of the chopper. By the time it was hovering over the landing pad, the noise was deafening. Max brought the chopper down, cut off the engine, climbed out, and carried a box of supplies across the ramp.

"It's the raspberry man, the chocolate man, the cookie man, and the salmon man," Max said as he walked up the stairs.

The first question Kate asked was whether Max had the lab results.

"I do, but I think Dr. Yu will have to read them first. They may not make any sense to us. I buzzed his tower. He'll come when he can," Max said.

"Can I help you?" Joseph asked.

"Yes, please. Take this in and unpack it," Max said as he turned to get another box of supplies.

Joseph busied himself carrying in boxes, and for a moment he forgot about Delta. After the boxes were all unloaded, Max and Kate came inside. Max looked over at Joseph. "So, kiddo, how's it going? And, where are you hiding the cub?"

"Oh, I forgot. She was playing with her ball when we went out." At that point everyone started looking for Delta. They looked in Joseph's bed, Kate's bed, behind the bathroom curtain, and in the plywood enclosures Chipic had made for her.

"She's got to be here somewhere," Joseph said. Then he looked at the stack of boxes against the wall. "One of these boxes was here before Max came," he said as he moved the boxes around, expecting the cub to be behind one. Still no Delta. Joseph was about to panic when Max noticed that one of the boxes was upside down. He lifted it carefully, and there was Delta sound asleep.

"I always say let sleeping bears lie," Max said jokingly. He was no longer in his "doing business" mode. For once he had some time off, and he didn't have to fly until the next day when he would take some people out to the Arctic National Wildlife Refuge. In the meantime, his plane would be serviced at the Barrow airport, and he would have time to relax, visit with Kate and Joseph, and maybe even play with the cub.

While Delta was sleeping, Dr. Yu tapped quietly on the door, opened it, and stepped inside. Max, Kate, and Joseph were sitting on the floor. Max was telling stories of his adventures taking visitors to remote places.

"You're not telling any secrets, are you?" Dr. Yu asked only half jokingly. Max stood up and handed Dr. Yu the sealed envelope containing Delta's blood test results and explained that the DNA test results wouldn't be ready for several more days. Dr. Yu sat down to read the report while Kate got up to boil water for his tea. Then she looked intently at his face, waiting for a sign.

"Be patient while I try to figure this out." Finally he looked up and said, "Let's all sit down while I try to explain this."

They all sat down on the floor in a circle. Expecting bad news, no one said a word. Still looking at the report, Dr. Yu waited before he spoke. "The bottom line is that Delta doesn't have enough growth hormone. Without it, she can't grow."

"What can we do about it?" Kate asked.

"I don't know the answer to that. People who don't have enough growth hormone can take a synthetic hormone, but it's expensive and controversial—and there can be side effects. Sometimes the hormones kick in, and the person will begin to grow, but it doesn't always work. But I don't know if anyone has ever given growth hormone to a wild animal, let alone a polar bear."

"Maybe we don't want her to grow," Kate said.

"Maybe not," Dr. Yu said. About that time Chipic arrived and joined the circle. Dr. Yu urged Max to stay. "We have decisions to make, and the sooner the better. We have to decide what to do with Delta as she is now. She isn't growing, so we need to talk about our options if she stays small. Let's go around the circle. You first, Joseph."

"How about we find a family who will take care of her," Joseph said.

"Some place in Alaska where she can have snow and cold weather," Chipic suggested.

Then everyone looked at Max. "How about a zoo?" he asked.

"I think a zoo is out," Kate said. "She's already adapted to us. She would be miserable being stared at all day by strangers.

112

Maybe a school that has a good wildlife biology program. There must be students at the University of Montana who would like to care for her," Kate said.

"I don't think that'll work," Dr. Yu said. "The building I work in is closed on the weekends, and everyone leaves the university for holidays—three weeks at Christmas break. I travel a lot. In fact, I'll be coming back up here in December after the bears have gone into their dens."

"Most of all we need a permanent place for her to stay and someone to take responsibility for her," Chipic said.

"You're right," Dr. Yu said. "The problem is we don't have a place for Delta."

"I've got it!" Joseph said suddenly. "I know the perfect place for her. My grandmother Lisi loves animals, and she's a biologist. Maybe Lisi would take Delta, and we could build a habitat in her house."

"You know, that's a possibility," Kate said. "My mother might be able to care for her."

"Wait a minute, Kate," Dr. Yu said. "Help me understand. Why would Lisi want a wild bear living in her house? I thought she was a herpetologist."

"She is, but she's interested in all kinds of animals, including bears. She might very well like to take this on."

"This is hard for me to believe. It's going to be a big job. You know Delta can't just live in a house. She'll have to have a special habitat," Dr. Yu said.

"First of all, Lisi lives in a rambling old farmhouse," Kate explained. "There are rooms that she's never used. Maybe Chipic could come to Georgia and help build Delta's habitat."

"There's another problem," Chipic said. "A habitat is going to be expensive. Where will we get the money?"

"I think I can find the money," Dr. Yu said. "I know of a foundation that gives grants for educational projects about climate change and the Arctic. Delta could help people understand the seriousness of global warming. She could help people see how polar bears won't have a place to live if the ice melts. But a grant would only help us get started, and there'll be other challenges—medical care, for example."

"Oh, I forgot to tell you. My other grandmother is a veterinarian. She lives in town, and Lisi's place is out in the country. She and Lisi are best friends," Joseph said.

"Okay," Dr. Yu said. "I think we have enough ideas for today. Kate, Joseph, and the cub will be right here in the research station for another six weeks, and that'll give us enough time to figure out what Delta needs and how to take care of her when we close down the station for the winter. Kate, I want you to email your mother. Make sure she understands what's involved before you ask her if she'll take the cub."

CHAPTER 19

A Day in Barrow

Joseph woke to the sound of Max's helicopter. He jumped up and was ready in five minutes. This was the day he was going into town to see Ada. They would start the day having breakfast at Pepe's North of the Border Mexican Restaurant, and after that Ada promised they would have an adventure.

"Kate, are you sure you can handle Delta by yourself?" Joseph asked as he was leaving.

"Not to worry. Chipic is coming sometime today," Kate said.

Max brought the helicopter down at the airport. He let Joseph out and yelled the directions, "Go straight down Momegana and take a left at Agvik. Less than a block, and you're there."

Twenty minutes later Joseph was climbing the steps leading to Pepe's. Inside he saw Ada sitting alone in a booth reading. Joseph tiptoed to her table. "Do you like that book?" he asked, surprising Ada.

"Joseph! It's you. Sit down. I've got so much to tell you."

"I was about to say the same thing," said Joseph as he slid into the other side of the booth. "You're not going to believe all I have to tell you."

Ada marked her place and passed her book—*Harry Potter*

and the Sorcerer's Stone—over to Joseph. "Have you read this?" she asked.

"Yeah, I like books about magic, but mysteries are my favorite," Joseph said.

"Mine too!" Ada said. "And I might have discovered a mystery of our own—and it's real, not fantasy. I want to hear about Delta, and I want to tell you what I learned. If anyone comes to the table, I'll change the subject. Follow my lead."

About that time, Fran Tate, the owner of Pepe's, came over. "Hey there, Ada, who's your friend?"

"This is Joseph. He's visiting his aunt Kate. He lives in Georgia. I met him on the plane from Fairbanks."

"Welcome to Barrow, Joseph. Are you going to join my club?" Fran asked.

"Fran, don't tell Joseph about the club yet. I want that to be a surprise," Ada said with a smile.

"Whatever you say, Ada. I suppose it's okay to tell him about the pancakes. You can have a stack of three, or just one," Fran said.

"Do you have blueberry pancakes?" Joseph asked.

"Nothing special, no blueberries, no strawberries. Just butter and syrup. We also have French toast, eggs, bacon, ham, the usual, but Ada always gets pancakes. Is that okay with you?" Fran asked.

So Ada and Joseph both ordered the large stack of pancakes, and Fran took the order back to the kitchen. Ada leaned forward and whispered to Joseph that she had overheard her dad, Avik, and her uncle Chipic talking about a polar bear being shot and left dead on an ice floe. She explained that she had been

116

reading curled up in a big chair nearby. Either they didn't know she was there or didn't think she was listening.

"Whoever shot the bear, also shot at my dad. The bullet that killed the bear probably came from the same gun. They want to find out who did the shooting, but they don't want anyone in town to know about it. It could be anybody."

"Anybody?" Joseph asked.

"I mean anybody who has a motive. It could be someone hired by one of the oil companies. It could be someone who killed the female to capture her cub," Ada said.

"I don't understand. Why would an oil company want a polar bear dead?" Joseph asked.

"I'm not sure, but I heard Chipic say something about denning sites being in areas where they think there's oil and want to drill. A dead bear can't go back to her den," Ada said.

"And why would someone capture the cub?"

"Maybe to sell it to a zoo—but, here comes breakfast," Ada said when she spotted Fran coming their way with two plates of pancakes. While they ate, Joseph looked at the notes she took when she eavesdropped on Chipic and Avik:

Bullets match?
DNA
Delta's mother?
Sniper hired by oil company?
Poachers after cub?
Hunters?
Keep dead bear secret.

"So why did you keep quiet? Why not tell Chipic and Avik you heard them talking?" Joseph asked.

"They don't want me or anyone to know about the dead bear or about someone shooting at my dad. I'll tell them I overheard them talking if we have some clues and can help find the perpetrator."

"The perpetrator? Do you mean the person who shot the bear? The killer?" Joseph asked.

"You got it. I mean the one that did it."

"What can we do?" Joseph asked.

"First we're going to listen in on conversations. I'm good at eavesdropping. Sooner or later everybody comes to Pepe's. This is a good place to spy on people. We'll pretend to play a game," she said pulling a backgammon board and two small notepads out of her backpack.

"Good, my friend Carlos likes this game. I can play, but he always beats me," Joseph said.

While Fran cleared the table, Ada asked her if they could stay and play games. "Sure," Fran said, "I'll bring milkshakes when you get hungry. My treat."

"Look around at the other customers. Anybody seem suspicious?" Ada whispered.

"Well, there's that woman in the last booth writing in a notebook," Joseph said.

Ada turned around and craned her neck to get a good look at the woman. She was wearing a gray jumpsuit. "I don't think so. Maybe she works for a newspaper. I'll call her Ms. New York Times—NYT for short."

"What about the man and woman sitting in the booth in

front of NYT?" Joseph asked.

Before Ada could answer, the door opened and two men entered the restaurant and sat down in the booth behind them. Fran came to the table with menus and coffee. One of the men said loudly, "We don't need menus. Just bring us the works." Ada gave Joseph a knowing smile, and without words they both knew that they would spy on the new customers.

Ada laid out the backgammon board, handed one of the notebooks to Joseph, and kept one for herself. "You're white; I'm red," she said, referring to the checkers.

"Well, not exactly," Joseph said, referring to the color of their skin. They both laughed as Ada handed Joseph a pair of dice.

"Roll 'em," she said in a voice loud enough for the suspicious-looking men to hear. From where she sat, she could see the men. She handed Joseph a pencil, indicating that he should write down what he heard the men say. Then she began to write in her notebook:

> Tall white man
> Age: 50?
> Language: English
> Build: lean, muscular
> Clothes: worn dark green jacket,
>   polar fleece, worn jeans and
>   hiking boots
> Hair: gray, shaggy
> Rings: none
> Mood: confident, serious
> Voice: normal, not loud, not soft

Medium height white man
Age: younger, 35-40?
Language: English with funny accent
Build: stocky, not fat, not thin
Clothes: new gold colored parka
Hair: blond, short
Rings: wedding ring
Mood: nervous, excited
Voice: louder than the other man,
    talks fast

Joseph looked at the notes. He wasn't able to hear everything they said, but he caught enough of the words to get an idea of what they were talking about. The words he jotted down included:

dinosaur, skeleton, prices, Colville River, fossil tracks, rifles, camera, and Fairbanks

Phrases included:

no one must know, not even your wife; partly buried skeleton; enough provisions for a week, equipment flown in; beat Dr. Rob to the draw

"Here, Ada, what do you think?" Joseph whispered, passing his notes to her.

Ada studied the list and shook her head. Then she told Joseph in a whisper, "They may be doing something illegal, and they're talking about guns. Obviously whatever they're up to is a secret."

Joseph frowned and looked puzzled. "I didn't know there were ever dinosaurs up here," he said.

"I'll tell you more about that later."

Joseph resumed eavesdropping just as Fran came to the men's table with an enormous breakfast and left without saying anything. Fran either didn't know the men, or she didn't want to talk to them, and they didn't seem to know her. Once their food arrived, the men concentrated on eating. There was no more talk until after Fran came again to refill their coffee cups. The taller man grumbled that this would be their last real breakfast for a week. The shorter man said something about sleeping on the ground near grizzly bears and wolves. He never said he was afraid, but Joseph and Ada thought he was.

After the men left, Fran came to the table with milkshakes—chocolate for Ada, vanilla for Joseph. "So, kids, how's the backgammon?" she asked, noticing that the checkers had not been moved.

"Have you seen those guys before?" Ada asked.

"The tall one, yeah. He was in here yesterday for dinner. I haven't seen the other one before," Fran answered.

"Do you know what they are here for?" Ada asked.

"Nope. They sure don't seem very friendly."

When Fran left them with their milkshakes, Ada studied

121

Joseph's notes and tried to put a story together. "I don't think those guys killed Delta's mother," she finally concluded.

"Why not?" Joseph said.

"They may be up to something illegal, but it doesn't have anything to do with polar bears. And, by the way, there were several types of dinosaurs in Alaska. Most of the fossils found here are along the Colville River. Maybe they are going there to steal fossils."

"Why would anybody steal fossils?"

"Money. People all over the world buy fossils. Some dinosaur bones are worth a lot," Ada said.

Before they left, they went up to the cash register to pay and to ask Fran one more question. "What about the woman in the back?" Ada asked quietly.

Fran bent over the table and whispered. "She's here off and on at different times of day. Says she's a writer and that her name is Sally Poling or something like that. She asks me questions from time to time—about whales and walrus. The other day she wanted to know about bear dens around here and if I've ever seen a polar bear. She seemed real interested when I told her we had one in the garbage back of the restaurant a couple of years ago."

"Instead of Sally, I'm calling her NYT. Like the newspaper," Ada said.

Fran went along with the snooping. Ada gave nicknames to strangers, and made up stories about them. Fran assumed it was a harmless game. After all, Ada was a curious child who was very interested in other people, especially visitors to Barrow she'd never seen before.

Ada wanted to pay for their breakfast, but Joseph explained that Kate had given him spending money, so he would like to pay. To avoid an argument, Ada suggested that they split the check, each paying half. That's how they did things from then on. The truth is, there wasn't much to spend money on in Barrow. There was a gift shop at the Top of the World Hotel next door, in the King Eider Hotel, and in the Inupiat Heritage Center. Other than the "Big Store," also called Stuakpak, which had groceries and basic clothing, that was about it.

Out on the street, Ada told Joseph that she would take him on a tour of Barrow. It was a cool, windy day. They zipped up their jackets and began their adventure. First they walked through the streets lined with wooden houses built on pilings buried in the permafrost. Under most houses was a cellar or "icehouse," dug into the permafrost to keep whale, seal, and caribou meat frozen even in the summer. Outside many of the houses were snowmobiles and four-wheelers along with assorted animal skins and bones.

Next Ada took Joseph to see Joe's Museum. Joe Shultz was Fran's son, and for many years he had been collecting artifacts, animal skins, and numerous oddities that had washed up on the beach. The museum was in his house. Joe met them at the door and for almost an hour he talked about his collection of northern treasures: knives, spears, ivory combs, carvings from ancient mastodon tusks, and baleen baskets. Joseph had never seen such things, and Ada had to pull him away. Back on the street, Joe went back to Pepe's, and Ada announced that they were going to another part of Barrow called Browerville where they would see the Inupiat Heritage Museum and the Big Store.

On one side of the road to Browerville was the Isatkoak Lagoon; on the other was the Arctic Ocean. The wind was blowing from the north, and Joseph pulled up the hood to his jacket. Still he was cold—very cold—but he didn't complain. Ada showed no sign of discomfort. He didn't want her to think he was a wimp. Finally they were on the other side of the lagoon, and Ada pointed to a big, modern building, unlike anything he had seen in Barrow.

"That's our new post office," she said. "Let's go in."

It was warm inside and people were milling about, checking their mailboxes and socializing as if they were at a party. Most seemed to be Eskimos. Ada explained that the post office was a community gathering place. Many people came there to see their neighbors and to catch up on the news.

Back outside, the wind seemed to have died down, and Ada and Joseph headed for the Inupiat Heritage Museum. Also a modern building, the museum had a large collection of Eskimo artifacts. Joseph loved museums, and he spent a long time looking at skin boats and models of a bowhead whale and a narwhal, which is also known as the unicorn whale because of its single spiraled tusk.

"Remember I told you my dad once photographed three narwhals tusking," Ada said. "Well, nobody knows if they rub their tusks together to clean them or just because it feels good."

Before they left, an Eskimo man came over to where they were studying ivory carvings made from antique walrus tusks. He said his name was Luther Leavitt, and that he was an artist. He invited them to visit the traditional room, a large studio space where artists and elders were creating sculpture from fossilized ivory, masks from caribou skin, and baleen baskets. Luther explained that baleen is a flexible material that comes from inside the jaws of some whales.

"I have a gift for you," he said as he handed Joseph what looked like a piece of string. "It's animal gut. We Eskimos use it for dental floss."

Joseph didn't know what to say, but he felt he should give Luther a gift in return. Reaching into his pocket, he pulled out a buckeye and handed it to Luther. "Here is a buckeye. It's a gift for you."

"Do I eat it?" Luther asked.

"No way," Joseph said. "The nuts inside are poisonous to eat, but the Cherokee Indians believed they had magical powers. Some people still collect them. Keep a buckeye with you, and it'll bring good luck."

Luther and Joseph smiled and thanked each other for the special gifts. Luther put the buckeye in his pocket and tied the gut around Joseph's wrist like a bracelet. "I don't think you will use this to clean your teeth. Wear it, and maybe it will bring you good luck, too."

Back on the street, Ada suggested they go to the library, which was next door to the Heritage Museum. Once inside Ada showed Joseph the computers she used to search the Internet, the periodical section, and the newspapers. "I come here whenever I can," she said, "usually about twice a week."

"This is a really cool library. I'd like to come back here just to read newspapers and magazines," Joseph said, eager to know what was happening in the outside world.

"Sure," Ada said. "I like the *New York Times*. We get the Sunday edition. I'm getting hungry. How about you?"

"Definitely," Joseph said. "It must be way past lunch time." Since the sun was always shining low in the sky, it was hard to know when it was time for lunch.

"We can get a snack at the Stuaqpak," Ada said. "That's the Inupiaq word for the 'Big Store,' the only place in town to shop for food and clothes. It's just across the street." Inside they walked down the aisles and Joseph saw many of the same products he saw at home—cereal, candy, and chips—but the prices were much higher. They paid more than ten dollars for pretzels and dried fruit.

"Now we're going to the beach," Ada said. Instead of sand, the beach was covered with tiny, smooth rocks, about the size of sunflower seeds. Joseph sat down and swept the stones into a pile with his hand. *No way to make a sand castle with these.* Then he walked to the edge of the beach and saw a long row of jellyfish a few feet out in the water.

Ada kept quiet as Joseph explored this strange place that was so different from the sandy beaches of the Georgia coast. There were no shells, no crabs, no beached fish or seaweed. And, no sand. Joseph was examining the pelt of a young ringed seal when Ada pointed to a flock of beautiful pale gray birds. They were following a school of fish and then hovering in mid-air almost like a helicopter before diving into the sea. As the fish swam closer to shore, the birds followed, and up close Ada and Joseph could see their long forked tails, black caps, and bright red beaks. They stood fascinated watching the feeding frenzy, as one bird after another hovered, dove, and came up with a fish.

"Joseph, those are Arctic terns. They migrate from the Arctic all the way to the Antarctic."

"Wow! That's halfway around the world," Joseph said. "And next spring they turn around and come all the way back?"

"You got it—more than twelve thousand miles. And they can live more than twenty years. An Arctic tern that lives that long flies more than half a million miles in its lifetime."

Joseph was about to say something when Ada suddenly brought her finger to her lips.

"What is it?"

"Listen," Ada suddenly said. "Listen for a shrill, squealing sound." At first Joseph only heard the sound of the sea, the wind, and the terns that were following the fish farther out to sea. Then from offshore he detected a high-pitched sound. The sounds were spooky and not like any he'd ever heard. He waited for Ada to explain what they were hearing.

"The belugas are coming," she finally said. "What you hear are the sounds they make. Watch carefully, and you'll see them swimming from the west." It wasn't long before Joseph saw the white backs of the whales swimming along the shore, one behind another. As the wind settled down, the squeals, grunts, and whistles grew louder, and Joseph stood still, listening and watching. After the belugas had passed, Joseph and Ada looked at each other. "Awesome," Joseph said.

"You're really lucky," Ada said. "Most people never get to see what we just saw—migrating whales lined up one after the other."

"Ada, you're so smart. You know so much, and I hardly

know anything about the Arctic," Joseph said.

"Well, this is my home. I've known about belugas since I was little. Many kids here learn Eskimo ways as well as what's taught in school. In class I learned about geography and global warming; my father has taught me how to set up a hunting camp and butcher a caribou, and my grandmother taught me to make Eskimo ice cream and a coat out of seal skin."

Joseph was surprised that Ada was allowed to be on her own, that she could meet him at breakfast, walk over to Browerville, go to the Heritage Center, and walk along the beach—all without being with an adult. He and his friend Carlos roamed the woods around Lisi's house, but they were never very far away, and from time to time they came back to the house to check in with Lisi. Ada and the other children of Barrow seemed to have more freedom than kids he knew back in Georgia.

Back at Pepe's at the end of the day, Joseph ordered food to take back to the station. He and Ada agreed to meet for breakfast on days that Max could pick him up in the helicopter. That turned out to be about twice a week. When he met Max at the airport, Joseph was carrying a large bag of tacos, burritos, chips, and salsa. He offered Max a bean and cheese taco.

"Only one?" Max asked, only half joking.

"Yep," Joseph said. "The rest are for Kate."

"None for you?" Max said as he loaded the bag on board.

"Well, maybe one burrito," Joseph said with a smile.

CHAPTER 20

Secrets

While Joseph and Ada were eavesdropping on customers at Pepe's, Kate worked on the computer, and Chipic played with the cub. Delta had become much more active. After a lengthy game of roll-the-ball followed by hide-and-seek, she finally fell asleep.

Chipic had not yet found any solid food that Delta would eat. It was time to prepare lunch for the humans, and Chipic went to the grocery cupboard and picked up a can of salmon, olive oil, breadcrumbs, and other ingredients to make salmon cakes. He opened the salmon and spooned it out into a bowl. Then he noticed that Delta was sitting up sniffing the air. Next she made a shrill, loud noise. She was smelling the salmon. When he held out a piece of the fish, she walked over to Chipic and took it in her mouth. Kate looked up from the computer and watched Delta eat a small amount of salmon.

"That's enough, Delta. Let's see how you do with that," Chipic said.

"I think you've found something for her to eat," Kate said as she reached for the can and read the label out loud: "Wild Alaskan Red Salmon."

"That's very good salmon. Luckily, you have five more cans. That may be enough to last until Max brings us more,"

Chipic said.

"Isn't all salmon wild?" Kate asked.

"Well, not really. If it comes in a can, it's wild. But most salmon sold in supermarkets in the lower forty-eight is farm raised and has antibiotics and chemicals that come from the food the fish are fed."

Soon, they sat down to a plate of hot salmon cakes, canned peaches, and nuts. "What's the hardest part of what you're doing?" Chipic asked.

"I don't know. I love it all. I never get tired of taking care of Delta, and I've gotten used to having my sleep interrupted. Dr. Yu's research about polar bear dens is interesting, too."

"There must be something you don't like," Chipic said.

"Well, I'm used to being outdoors much of the time, so sometimes being inside these four walls gives me cabin fever. Usually I'm too busy to notice. But when Joseph's gone, Dr. Yu doesn't stop by, and Delta's sleeping, I get the urge to go wandering through the tundra," Kate said.

"We'll plan a trip to town. I'd like to show you my family's summer camp and Point Barrow," Chipic said.

"I'd love to go out to NARL to meet other scientists," Kate said, referring to the National Arctic Research Laboratory.

"I'm not sure about that. You might be asked questions you don't want to answer. Remember, nobody knows about Delta as far as we know. Dr. Yu wants to keep it that way," Chipic said. "If the person who killed Delta's mother knows we have a cub, he might figure we know about the killing and he certainly knows he's committed a serious crime."

"You said 'he.' How do you know the killer's a man?"

Kate asked.

"Well, I guess I don't know. There are women in Alaska who can do anything. Many women build houses, drill for oil, and operate large fishing boats. It's not unusual for a woman to hunt and field dress moose or caribou. My mother helps butcher whale when one's killed and dragged up on the beach."

"But what about breaking the law?" Kate asked.

"Probably there's nothing that's been done by a man in Alaska that a woman hasn't done."

"So the sniper could be a woman," Kate said.

"Could be, but I doubt it," said Chipic. "The important thing is that we don't want the sniper—whether a he or a she—to know about Delta, and that means we can't take Delta outside the research station."

"I know that, but I wish we could," Kate said.

"We have to give her what she needs right here, especially exercise and the right food. I'm thinking that polar bears eat seals in the wild. When a mother takes cubs out on the ice, she gives them small pieces of seal meat," Chipic said.

"Dr. Yu doesn't think Delta will ever be able to return to the wild."

"I don't think so either, Kate, but she probably would like seal if she likes salmon. If you run out of salmon before Max returns, I could bring you some seal meat. My father hunts seal as well as whale."

"That's really kind, Chipic," Kate said, "but Max will go for supplies soon. You'd better get back to your other projects. I appreciate your help."

"Okay, I'm off. You can offer Delta some more salmon tomorrow," Chipic said as he told Delta goodbye and patted her on the head.

Several hours, one nap, one play session, and two feedings later, Kate heard the familiar sound of a helicopter. Delta was sleeping. Kate opened the door just in time to see Max bring the chopper down on the landing pad. Joseph scrambled out and rushed up the stairs carrying a bag of Mexican food.

"I brought your dinner!" he said excitedly. Once inside, Joseph got out plates and forks and set the small table where he and Kate ate.

"Wow, this is super!" Kate said, surveying the feast that Joseph had spread out. "I love Mexican food. This is so much better than peanut butter sandwiches and canned salmon. I never thought I'd have food like this in the Arctic. Let's save the chips and salsa for later," she suggested as she served herself a taco and a burrito.

Joseph was glad that Kate was preoccupied with the meal, as he was afraid he might accidentally give away what Ada had told him. Before they left Pepe's, she reminded him not to tell anyone about the dead bear and the sniper. He had to keep quiet about her eavesdropping on her father and Chipic and also their plans to spy on Fran's customers.

He wanted to tell Kate about the dinosaur fossil hunters, but he stopped himself. If he told her about them, she would know he'd been listening to other people's conversations. He wondered if eavesdropping was wrong. Not if spying was necessary to find out who had done a very bad thing, he told himself. Besides, he thought, they would only be listening to people in a public place who were talking loud enough for them to hear.

Then there was the matter of secrets. If a friend tells you a secret, it's a good thing to keep it to yourself, isn't it? Joseph thought so, but then he didn't like having secrets from Kate.

"Joseph," Kate said, interrupting his thoughts, "Tell me about your day."

"It was a great day," he said, telling her about Joe's Museum, the walk to Browerville, the Inupiat Heritage Center, the whale models, the dental floss Luther gave him, the library, and the walk on the beach.

"What was the best?" Kate asked.

"That's easy," Joseph said. "The best was watching and listening to a pod of beluga whales. I counted fifteen, but there may have been more."

Kate listened quietly while Joseph talked about the whales—the amazing sounds they made, their white bodies, the excitement he felt watching them migrate past Barrow.

"Ada asked me to come back whenever Max can bring me," Joseph said, afraid that Kate would say "no."

But she didn't say "no." Instead she told Joseph that she thought it was a good idea for him to spend time in town. She never asked what he and Ada talked about, and Joseph never told her that they were on their own all day—no adults, no checking in.

Joseph went to bed that night thinking that no one would suspect that he and Ada were hoping to find out who killed the polar bear and who shot at Avik. When he woke a few hours later, it occurred to him that Kate might already know about the shootings. Maybe she had a secret, too. But one thing was certain; stuck in the research station, Kate wouldn't be able to track down a suspect. That was a job for Joseph and Ada.

"Kate, I think you should let me take care of Delta tonight," Joseph said, as Delta began to show signs of waking.

"Well, I'll let you take the first shift," Kate said.

That was just what he hoped would happen.

CHAPTER 21

The Best of Two Worlds

For the rest of the summer, Joseph's time was divided between what he and Ada called their undercover work in town and his official work as Delta's caretaker.

Once a week, Chipic took Kate away for a day to explore Barrow. He took her to town, to Pepe's, to Joe's Museum, to Point Barrow, and to Browerville. They visited the high school where there was a heated indoor swimming pool. At the Big Store, Kate bought a swimsuit for Joseph to wear for his initiation into the Polar Bear Club, but she didn't tell him about it.

The first day Kate went to Barrow, she left Joseph alone with Delta until Dr. Yu arrived. They were playing roll-the-ball when Delta suddenly startled and made a guttural huffing sound Joseph had never heard her make. "I wonder what that's about," he said out loud. Still making rapid huffing sounds, Delta turned to the door just as Dr. Yu walked into the research station. Joseph brought his finger to his lips, and he and Dr. Yu listened quietly. Then Delta fell silent and climbed into Joseph's lap.

"I didn't hear you coming, but I think Delta did," Joseph said.

"What does this sound mean?" Dr. Yu asked.

"She's not happy, and she seems upset. Maybe frightened."

"That's not good for her. Has she made this sound before?" Dr. Yu asked as he lowered himself to the floor next to Joseph.

"I don't think so. I've only heard her make baby sounds. When she wakes up, she whimpers. Then if she doesn't get what she wants right away, she shrieks and squalls until we give her a bottle. When she takes her bottle, she purrs. She also likes to suck my fingers, and she purrs then—it's not exactly like a cat's purr, but it's closer to that than to anything else."

"With all the research I've done with polar bears, I've never spent time with a cub, so I've never heard the sounds they make. I know the adults growl, bellow, and even roar, but I don't know about cubs," Dr. Yu said as he reached out and picked up the blue ball. With that Delta whirled around and hissed at him.

"Whoa! Now what is she doing?" Joseph asked.

"I think that's clear. She's angry, and she doesn't want me to touch the ball," Dr. Yu said as he rolled it toward Delta. The cub rolled it over to her bed, scampered after it, and sat with both paws resting on the ball.

"Looks like she's guarding the ball. I think she wants to be alone," Joseph said.

"That's good. We need to talk," Dr. Yu said. "I have three important jobs for you. First, I want you to keep a record of all the sounds she makes—how long Delta makes each sound and what it seems to mean. I'll ask Max to buy a tape recorder the next time he's in Fairbanks. Your second job is to play with her each day until she gets tired and then record how many minutes she was active. Try to increase her activity each day. Finally, keep up with how much formula she takes and what she eats."

"Are you going back to your tower?" Joseph asked.

"Not now. I'd like to spend some time with Delta. I'll give you a break," Dr. Yu said.

"Good," Joseph said. "I need to email Lisi."

"Be sure to tell her what it's like to take care of a polar bear cub," Dr. Yu said. "Also remind her we'll need a veterinarian with experience taking care of wild animals. Your other grandmother will probably qualify."

CHAPTER 22

Email to Lisi

Dear Lisi,

So much has happened here, and some of it's a secret that I can't even tell you. Dr. Yu is here today taking care of Delta. He's a very important polar bear scientist, but he's never been around a cub. Can you believe that?

I know that Kate has already written to ask if you would be willing to take Delta when the summer is over. Dr. Yu wants me to explain what taking care of a cub is like. Getting her to take formula is easy. At first she was fed powdered skim milk, but after that Dr. Yu prepared a much richer formula with canned milk, cod liver oil, and honey. Delta has been able to digest this formula from the beginning, but she's not growing. Dr. Yu ordered some lab tests and found out that she doesn't have enough growth hormone. Otherwise she's healthy.

Delta also loves to eat small amounts of canned salmon. We feed her about every three to four hours. That's about six to eight times a day. Sometimes after she eats, she likes to sleep, and sometimes she plays.

Playing is the only way she can get exercise, so I spend several sessions a day playing tug-of-war, roll-the-ball, hide-and-seek, and find-the-salmon. The last game is new. I hide a can of salmon somewhere in the research station, and she can usually find it in less than two minutes. There are not many places to hide in the research station, but Delta doesn't seem to mind. It's easier to hide a can of salmon than to hide myself. Sometimes I put a towel over my head or cover myself in my sleeping bag. She loves this game and will grab the towel and pull it off my head. When I'm hiding in the sleeping bag, she tries to climb in with me. When I laugh, she seems happy.

Lisi, I don't want you to think that you will have to play these games. I'll come every day to play with her. Once she's in Georgia, Delta will be able to go outside. We don't know for sure, but Dr. Yu thinks she'll sleep longer at night when she's older. When we get to Georgia at the end of August, she'll experience dark and light for the first time since she was rescued. I think we can teach her to sleep at night and stay awake in the daytime.

Taking care of Delta is not always fun. She is definitely not housebroken. Chipic made a container for her to use when she poops, and we put her there after she eats. Most of the time she poops there, but not always. Then we have to clean up her messes all over the room. I have to remember that she's a wild animal, but she can't live without humans to take care of her.

Dr. Yu already has a scientific research permit that will allow us to take her out of Alaska. If Amy agrees to be her veterinarian, all we have to do is build a habitat that meets the requirements for a captive bear.

If you agree to do this, I'll not only come over every day to play with her, but I'll also help clean up and feed her. I think you'll have as much fun as I do.

Luv,

Joseph

The day was steaming. The thermometer in the shade of the broad porch of Lisi's house read 88 degrees at five o'clock in the afternoon. Two women, long-time friends, sat under the ceiling fan sipping iced tea. Amy was reading Joseph's email.

"So what do you think?" Lisi asked.

"I don't think you can turn down an opportunity like this. You know I'll help with the cub. I wouldn't miss it for the world," Amy said. She was the only veterinarian in town. She worked long hours, but Amy always had time to help people she cared about.

"I knew you'd want to help," Lisi said, "but we have to be realistic. We don't know what's wrong with her. She's not growing, and she has a deficiency of growth hormone. She may have other problems."

"Seems to me that she's thriving in spite of not growing," Amy said. "Look, just say 'yes,' and we'll figure out the 'how' later. Sometimes you have to dive off a diving board and invent the water on the way down."

"Okay, we'll do it. Let's go inside and write to Joseph," Lisi said.

———

While Joseph was writing to Lisi, Dr. Yu was getting to know Delta and trying to win her trust. He sat without moving on the floor near where she was guarding her blue ball. Then slowly he moved toward her an inch at a time until he was sitting about three feet in front of her. Delta didn't take her eyes off Dr. Yu, and she still acted as if she didn't trust him. Finally Delta rolled the ball toward Dr. Yu. He pushed the ball with one finger and rolled it back. Delta squealed and rolled it again. At last, they were playing roll-the-ball.

In the meantime, after Joseph finished the email to Lisi, he settled down on his mat with a book. Minutes later he was asleep, but he woke with a start when he heard the words "You've got mail." He rushed to the computer and found a short message from Lisi and Amy. Then he went over to Dr. Yu and Delta and sat down with them.

"There's good news," he whispered quietly. "Lisi says she'll make a place for Delta, and my other grandmother, Amy will help."

"That is good news," Dr. Yu said just as Delta crawled into Joseph's lap. For one moment the man, the boy, and the cub sat in silence, content and untroubled about the challenges that lay ahead.

CHAPTER 23

Back in Barrow

Joseph stepped off the helicopter at the airport, waved good-bye to Max, and took off at a run through the streets of Barrow. He made it to Pepe's before Ada got there. Fran seated him in the same booth they'd had the last time. Joseph got out his notebook and looked around to see who was there.

In front of him was a booth full of men, all Eskimos and all eating pancakes and drinking coffee. The talk was about whales—migrating belugas that passed by Barrow eight days before, the melting ice, warmer temperatures, and the location of the bowhead whales. Joseph could hear most of what they said, and he quietly jotted down key words—

whales, belugas, bowhead, melting ice, permafrost

and on and on. Joseph was trying to hear the details of a story one of the men was telling about a baby walrus washed up on shore in Kivalina, an island village west of Barrow. The walrus was taken to the Alaska SeaLife Center in Seward to be rehabilitated.

Joseph loved listening to the talk of life in the far North, but all the while he was glancing at a copy of *The Arctic Sounder*, Barrow's local newspaper. There on the front page was a picture of the seventy-pound baby walrus that the men at the next table were talking about. Looking at the picture of the whiskered, wrinkled baby, Joseph was glad he was taking care of a polar bear cub instead of this strange looking creature.

All the customers that morning seemed to be regulars. Fran called them by name and joked about how much they were eating. By ten o'clock the last customer had left, and Joseph was alone. He told Fran he was waiting for Ada, and that he would order after she came. Fran went back into the kitchen and returned with one pancake. "This will hold you until Ada gets here," she said, putting the plate in front of him and pouring a glass of orange juice.

As Fran was heading back to the kitchen, the door opened and in came the men Ada thought might be dinosaur thieves. They sat in the booth next to Joseph, and before Fran could ask what they wanted, the taller of the two men called out, "Bring us a lot of everything—eggs, bacon, pancakes, whatever."

"No coffee?" Fran asked with a smirk.

"Do I look like a man who doesn't want coffee?"

"I'm not sure what you look like," Fran said as she filled their cups and walked briskly back to the kitchen. Almost everyone from Barrow who came into Pepe's called Fran by name. She knew about their families and the names of their children. When a group of tourists came in, she found out where they were from. Before they left, she knew their names, too.

But not these guys. They were rude to Fran, and she had nothing to say to them. Except for Joseph, they were the only customers, but they acted as if he were not there. He thought of them as bad guys—maybe dino thieves. They never called each other by name, so Joseph decided they would be "Mr. Green" and "Mr. Gold, " after the colors of their jackets. He listened carefully as they talked. It never occurred to the men that a kid might be interested in what they were saying, and they didn't bother to speak softly.

"So you think we can trust this guy Max?" Gold asked.

"Trust him how?"

"Well, to keep his mouth shut. Not to talk about what we're flying to Fairbanks," Gold said.

"I told you the word on Max is that he doesn't talk. He'll take anybody anywhere he can land safely in this part of Alaska. No questions asked. I told him our cargo may weigh up to a thousand pounds, that we didn't want any other passengers, and that we'd pay for the whole plane. He'll take us out tomorrow morning," Green said.

Joseph couldn't believe what he was hearing, and before Ada came, he had heard enough to be certain that he was listening to incriminating evidence. He heard them say that from Fairbanks they would truck the goods to Valdez, where they would load them onto a ship.

Joseph looked up from the notebook he was scribbling on and saw Ada come through the door. He raised his finger to his lips and mouthed the words "be quiet." Ada looked over at Green and Gold and recognized them as the suspicious looking men they'd seen the first time they met at Pepe's. Ada slipped into the booth quietly as Joseph passed her a note with only two words—

dino thieves

Fran came out from the kitchen carrying a tray loaded with practically every item on the menu. "That ought to do the job," she said gruffly, placing the food in front of her rude customers.

"So, kids, what'll it be?" Fran asked, turning to Joseph and Ada.

"I'll take the usual pancakes," Ada said.

"I'd like to try the French toast," Joseph said.

Green and Gold ate silently, and when they had cleaned their plates, they began to talk in normal voices, as if they were alone. Joseph and Ada wrote key words on paper they passed back and forth as they picked up fragments of the conversation: *fossil, Colville River, worth more, six figures,* and *danger.*

"We need to go," Joseph said as he stood up to leave. About that time, Fran walked up carrying the swimsuit Kate had bought for him at the Big Store.

"Joseph, you're not going anywhere yet. It's time for you to join the Polar Bear Club. All you have to do is run into the sea and dive completely under the water—that means the head, too," Fran said.

"Fran, it's not a good time. Ada and I have some very important work to do," Joseph said, thinking he could talk his way out of this ordeal. He'd never seen anybody jump into icy Arctic waters. But Fran wasn't smiling. Joseph looked at Ada, who had a funny expression on her face.

"You're not going to get out of this, Joseph," Ada said.

"Ada, I'm not an Eskimo. I live in a place where it only snows a few times a year, and the snow melts as soon as the sun comes out. Maybe I don't want to belong to the Polar Bear Club," Joseph said.

Ada crossed her arms and stared at Joseph. She didn't have to say a word. He knew she was thinking he was a wimp. Joseph looked back at Fran, who still had a stern expression on her face. Okay, Joseph thought, this is not a joke.

"Joseph, go back to my office and change," Fran said, handing him the swimsuit. "You can wear your sneakers."

Joseph looked down at the rubber soled cloth shoes that he wore outside in Georgia. "They're not going to keep me from freezing to death," he protested one last time.

The next thing he knew he was wearing a swimsuit and running out to the Arctic Ocean. Ada and Fran were cheering him on as he ran to the edge of the ice-cold water. Still unable to make himself go further, Joseph looked down at his shivering legs. He was about to turn around when he heard Ada shout, "You can do it Joseph!"

Then he was running and running and plunging under the freezing water. His muscles stiffened, but somehow he was able to keep moving. Rather than turning around and getting out of the water, Joseph began swimming—five, ten, almost fifteen yards. Only then did he turn around and swim back, thinking nobody would call him a wimp now. Back on the beach, Fran wrapped him in a bright blue towel, and Ada clapped her hands.

"So what do you think, Fran?" Ada asked.

"Well, for sure he's a full-fledged member of the Polar Bear Club. Hardly anybody swims, and nobody goes that far," Fran said.

"And, he's an honorary Eskimo," Ada said, leaning over to give him an Eskimo kiss. Joseph was too cold to resist.

By the time Joseph was dressed, Green and Gold had paid their bill and left. Ada was waiting for him, and they walked outside together. They both were so excited by the morning's events that they could hardly stop talking—about the Polar Bear Club, the price of dinosaur bones, and the fun of solving real crimes.

"If we can solve this mystery, maybe we can figure out who killed Delta's mother," Joseph said. "But I don't think the killer's going to meet with someone at Pepe's and talk about what he's done."

"You never know," Ada said. "I listened to a conversation between my dad and Chipic a couple of days ago. Dr. Yu told Chipic that he thinks the killer is working for an oil company that wants polar bears eliminated from the area they want to prospect. They think the sniper may still be here in Barrow. The DNA test was a match. The bear that was shot was Delta's mother. They've got the bullets. All they need is the rifle and the person who fired it."

They stopped by Chipic's house and left a note on the door explaining what had happened at Pepe's and asking him to come to the research station as soon as possible. Joseph headed for the airport, and Ada turned back to the beach. She had promised to help Fran initiate some tourists into the Polar Bear Club.

Joseph found Max working on his plane. "Max," he said, "we have to get back to the station now. Something has happened you need to know about. I'll tell you after we get there."

In less than thirty minutes, Joseph and Max were landing on the helicopter pad. Dr. Yu was feeding Delta, and Kate was making tea. Max asked everyone to sit down. Kate brought cookies, the teapot, and cups and sat them on the floor, and everyone helped themselves. Joseph was still cold from his plunge into the icy sea, and it felt good to wrap his fingers around the warm teacup. Max was the first to speak. "Joseph has something to tell us," he said.

"Well, Ada and I have found out that two guys we've seen at Pepe's are out to steal dinosaur fossils," he said.

"How do you know this?" Dr. Yu asked.

"I'll tell you the story," Joseph said. He began with the first time he and Ada had been to Pepe's and listened to the men talk about going out to the Colville River. They couldn't hear everything the men said, but they did hear the words *dinosaurs*, *skeletons*, and *fossil tracks*. Joseph explained how he'd heard one of them warn the other not to tell anyone what they were doing, not even his wife.

"Do you know their names?" Dr. Yu asked.

"No, I don 't. I just call them Mr. Green and Mr. Gold after the color of their jackets," Joseph said. "But the first time I did hear one name. They talked about beating Dr. Rob to the draw."

"Rob?" Dr. Yu said. "I don't know him, but I've heard about him. His real name is Robert Thomas. He teaches at a university, but some people suspect he might be taking fossils without a permit and selling them for big money. "

"Joseph, we can't go chasing after thieves in Barrow," Max said. "Many people come to Alaska because they're running from the law. Some of them make it all the way to Barrow. Some of them are here to commit crimes they can't get away with anywhere else. Stealing fossils from federal land is one of them."

"Max is right," Dr. Yu said. "We have to focus on what we're here for. We have nothing to do with dinosaur bones."

"Dr. Yu, with all due respect, I don't agree," Joseph said. Kate had told him to speak politely in this way if he ever disagreed with Dr. Yu. "We learned today that these guys have hired Max to fly them and their cargo to Fairbanks tomorrow morning. One of them wonders whether they can trust Max. The other told him that Max will take anyone anywhere in northern Alaska—no questions asked."

Kate, Dr. Yu, and Joseph all turned to Max with questioning looks on their faces. "Wait a minute, guys," Max said. "It's true that I don't like to get involved in my clients' business. I don't really need to know what they are up to. I carry scientists like you, oilmen, backpackers, hunters, and fishermen. I believe most people are good and that they aren't here to do any harm."

"But these guys are here to steal fossils, and now you know it," Joseph said.

"We could call the FBI," Dr. Yu said. "After all, if they're guilty, they've broken federal law."

Kate, who had remained silent until now, finally spoke. "Suppose the FBI is already on to these guys. If they're arrested, wouldn't they arrest Max too?"

There was a sudden knock on the door, and Chipic burst

in. "I know what's going on," he said. "Ada and Joseph left me a note explaining how they figured out that two men in town have stolen dinosaur fossils. They said they've hired Max to take them to Fairbanks tomorrow."

Dr. Yu stood up, still holding Delta. She'd fallen asleep, and he put her down on her bed. "Max," he said, "before you fly out tomorrow, ask these guys to list the contents of the cargo you're carrying."

"I won't mention the cargo until we're already on the plane ready to go," Max said.

"Chipic, I know an FBI agent in Fairbanks who's worked with me on crimes against marine mammals," Dr. Yu said. "Here's his phone number. When you go back to town, call him, explain the situation and ask him to meet Max's plane and have it searched. If these two guys have lied to Max about their cargo, he'll be safe, but they'll be arrested."

CHAPTER 24

Secrets Revealed

Before Max left the research station, he asked if there was anything else he could do in Fairbanks. "Give this to the agents," Dr. Yu said, handing Max a package. "Remember: no questions asked."

The next morning Green filled out the cargo form, indicating they were carrying heavy equipment for testing the permafrost. He listed his name as "Robert Thomas," without even thinking that Max might have heard of the infamous paleontologist. And, in fact, Max had not heard of him until the day before when Dr. Yu said he knew about Dr. Rob.

Late in the afternoon of the same day, Max returned to the station. He jumped out of the helicopter, giving the victory sign with two raised hands. To everyone's surprise, Chipic and Ada climbed out behind Max.

Back in the station, Max handed an envelope to Dr. Yu, who walked over to his private space, pulled the curtain behind him, and read the letter from the FBI. When he came out, he announced that it was time to have a meeting. Kate, Chipic, Joseph, and Ada joined him in a circle on the floor. Ada had never seen Delta, and she asked if she could hold the cub and give her a bottle.

"You can hold her, but she may not be very hungry. She just had some salmon," Dr. Yu said. "Now I want everyone to listen carefully. What I have to say is important."

Delta seemed to understand that what was happening was not about her. She sat quietly in the middle of the circle with her blue ball and rolled it to Joseph, who rolled it back. Then she crawled over to Joseph and settled down in his lap, where she stayed until the meeting was over.

"Tell us what happened in Fairbanks," Dr. Yu said, nodding to Max.

"To tell the truth, I was really afraid when I learned that my passengers might be thieves and their cargo contraband, but the FBI had everything under control. There were three agents dressed like ground crew. They had a warrant and everything they needed to make an arrest. Before Gold and Green knew what had happened, one of the agents was reading them their rights, and in no time, they were handcuffed. The cargo was confiscated and taken inside to be examined. Each item was carefully wrapped in bubble wrap. Some looked like rocks, but others were clearly dinosaur fossils—a jawbone, a rib, and a tooth."

"Can you tell us what was in the envelope?" Kate asked.

"Well, I'm going to have to tell you, and I'm swearing you to secrecy," Dr. Yu said. "In fact there's more that I have to tell you that I've kept quiet about up until now."

"About what you're doing in the tower?" Joseph asked.

"That, and a lot more," Dr. Yu said. "You need to know that Avik was out in the umiak when he discovered a dead polar bear on an ice floe. The bear had been shot. While Avik retrieved the bullet and a tissue sample, another shot was fired, probably to scare him."

Joseph and Ada gave each other a knowing look. "Do you

think the dead bear was Delta's mother?" Ada asked.

"We know she was. The DNA testing proved it," Dr. Yu said.

"And the envelope?" Kate asked again.

"The message from the FBI had to do with the bullet that killed Delta's mother and the one that was shot at Avik. They're 338 caliber bullets fired from the same big game rifle, most likely using a sniper scope. There probably aren't that many 338 rifles in Barrow, Dr. Yu explained."

"So you think the killer is still in Barrow?" Max asked.

"I have a hunch the killer is still here and that he has more work to do with that gun."

"Dr. Yu, what does this have to do with your work?" Kate asked.

"Only Chipic knows what I'm about to tell you," Dr. Yu said. "My official research has to do with the denning habits of polar bears in this area—those that den on land instead of out on the ice. I've been watching the dens for several summers now—that's what Kate is helping me with. Every year at least one den seems to have been disturbed. Whoever killed Delta's mother has eliminated one more breeding female and her den. The denning sites that I've been watching are in an area that oil companies want to drill. And that's why I think one of them has hired this sniper. We need to know who did the shooting and who hired the killer."

"So is there anything else we need to know?" Joseph asked.

"Again, I have to remind you that everything I say is top secret," Dr. Yu said. "I'm also gathering data for environmental organizations. They are looking for data that they can use to block oil drilling permits where polar bears den."

"So can you tell us where your tower is now?" Ada asked.

"Let me answer that question," Chipic said. "Dr. Yu doesn't

want any of you to know where it is because if you talk about it in the Big Store or at Pepe's, someone might overhear your conversation."

"Well, I do know people eavesdrop on conversations," Ada said.

"It's true. Everything has changed in Barrow and on the whole North Slope since the oil companies came up here in the early seventies. Many people are here just to spy on others, to find out who's after what."

"How can you keep the location of the tower a secret?" Joseph asked.

"The tower is not always in the same place," Chipic said. "I designed the tower so it could be moved. Max helps with that. The dens are spaced far apart so in order to observe disruption of den sites, we have to move from one area to another. In the summer, Dr. Yu is looking for evidence that the denning areas have been disturbed or even destroyed. When he comes back in the winter, Max will be flying over denning areas with infrared thermal imaging equipment to detect heat given off by bears in their dens. That's how we'll know which dens are actually occupied."

"How are you going to find the sniper?" Ada asked, thinking that with a little work, she and Joseph could do the job.

"Now, here's some really good news," Dr. Yu said. "We don't have to find the sniper alone. The FBI has agreed to take the case, and they're sending two undercover agents to Barrow next week, but they'll need help from us. Max met the agents, and they believe that if the sniper and his gun are still in Barrow he can be caught. It's important that no one else in Barrow suspects that the FBI is on the job."

"So what's the cover?" Chipic asked.

"The guys will be on the plane from Fairbanks next week. They'll be dressed as hunters. Their names will be Pete and Gordon. Their story is they're from Texas, and they both have Texas accents. This is their first trip to the Arctic, and they're here to meet with guides to set up trips into the National Petroleum Reserve around Lake Teshekpuk. They want to learn about grizzly and caribou hunting. They'll seem serious about hunting but a little naïve about this part of the world."

Ada and Joseph gave each other knowing looks. Each knew the other was thinking that they could do some more spying. When Ada raised her finger to her lips, only Joseph saw her. He knew that she was telling him to keep quiet.

"Are there any questions?" Dr. Yu asked.

"Yeah, what can Ada and I do?" Joseph asked.

"Well, first I'll talk about what you won't do," Dr. Yu said as he looked sternly at Joseph and then at Ada.

"You won't ask any questions about guns. If by chance you overhear talk that might be important to the case, you tell Pete and Gordon. But don't go looking for trouble," Dr. Yu said.

"So how do we find Pete and Gordon?" Ada asked.

"Since almost everyone goes to Pepe's, nobody will be suspicious if you meet there for breakfast twice a week. Around four o'clock in the afternoon, you'll come back, maybe for an ice cream. Whenever you're there, Pete and Gordon will come in. If you've heard anything that might be helpful, write a note and secretly slip it to them."

"We can do that," Ada said.

"If for some reason they don't come to Pepe's, or if you

think anyone is watching you, we'll need a fallback plan," Dr. Yu said. "Here's an idea. Go to the library, walk to the reference books. I believe it's the first row on the left. Take the "A" volume of the Encyclopedia Britannica to a desk. Read for a few minutes and leave a note for Pete and Gordon on page 222 and then return the book to the shelf. You'll be the only contact between the agents and me. Remember just act like kids having a good time hanging out in Barrow. Except for the two of you, nobody in town will know that Pete and Gordon are FBI agents."

"Chipic, Max, and Kate know," Ada said.

"Yes, but they won't have any contact with the agents," Dr. Yu said. "We don't want anyone to suspect that there's a connection between the agents and our research. Are there any other questions?"

"You forgot something, Dr. Yu," Joseph said.

"What's that?"

"What about Delta?" Joseph said as he pointed to the cub sleeping in his lap. Everybody looked at Delta and laughed.

With mock seriousness, Dr. Yu said, "I don't think she'll talk, Joseph."

The next two weeks of the summer went smoothly. Kate and Joseph shared what they called "Delta Duty"—preparing her food, feeding her, holding her, bathing her, and cleaning up after her. Playing with her was Joseph's job, and every day he staged games of roll-the-ball, hide-and-seek, and find-the-salmon. There was just enough room in the research station for Delta to get her exercise. Joseph would sit holding her at one end of the room and roll the blue ball to the other. Then Delta would tumble out of his lap, run the length of the room, and pounce on the ball. They would play this game until the cub was exhausted. Joseph would time the games, and each day they lasted a couple of minutes longer. Delta was thriving. She was definitely getting stronger, but she still was not growing.

Dr. Yu had a permit that allowed him to take rescued animals from Alaska for research purposes, and he had to fill out some forms agreeing that he would provide Delta with the standard requirements for a polar bear habitat. Max took the forms to the U.S. Fish and Wildlife office and made arrangements with the airlines to transport Delta from Barrow to Anchorage and from there to Georgia.

Chipic continued to take Kate on a weekly adventure. They took long walks on the beach and talked about Chipic's trip to Georgia where he would build a habitat for Delta. One day they went to the family summer camp to meet Chipic's brothers and their sled dogs. Avik and Chipic took Kate along the shore in the umiak. At their house in town, Chipic's mother prepared a meal of muktuk and Eskimo doughnuts. Kate surprised herself by eating a large plate of raw whale blubber and traditional fried bread. She took enough back to the station for Joseph to have later.

On the second day of August, the sun set for the first time since the tenth of May. Winter and twenty-four hour darkness would come by the middle of November, and the first sunrise at the end of January. Dr. Yu would return in early December to monitor the infrared photography of the denning sites.

CHAPTER 25

Back in Barrow

Ada and Joseph had just about given up on identifying any suspects for the FBI when they heard two men in a booth behind them at Pepe's talking about a gun. Joseph picked up their conversation first.

"It's a custom 338 Remington with a Bushnell scope," said the man sitting with his back to Joseph.

Ada was starting to tell the story about her father's first whale hunt when Joseph crossed his two index fingers, the signal they used for "silence." He scribbled words on a scrap of paper—

> Two men – Big ears selling gun.
> Skinny Guy wants to buy. Maybe
> gun used to kill Delta's Mother.

Ada, listening intently, didn't say another word.

"Here's the deal: $1,000 cash with the bag and scope," said Big Ears.

"I can't come up with the cash before Monday, and I can't pay more than $800. Can you hold it for me?" the other guy asked.

"Can't promise without some earnest money, and if I get

a better offer this weekend, I'll sell her," Big Ears said.

"That's the best I can do," Skinny Guy said.

When the men stood up, Joseph could see the face of the man selling the gun. He was older than the other man—maybe sixty—and he wore glasses with thick lenses. "So what do you think?" Joseph asked Ada when the suspects walked by their booth.

Ada crossed her fingers to silence Joseph. As soon as the men paid for their coffee, Ada got up and gestured for Joseph to stay put. The men headed out to a red Ford pickup truck parked in front of Pepe's. Ada ran to the door to get a good look at both men and the truck.

"Great job, Ada," Joseph said as she came back to the booth and wrote down the license number. "So now what do you think? Is Big Ears the sniper?" he asked.

"Well it makes sense that the sniper would want to get rid of the evidence, and it's the right kind of gun, but I don't think he's the right kind of guy," Ada said.

"Why not?" Joseph asked.

"Well, what do you think it would take for somebody to be a good sniper?" Ada asked.

"Let's see. The sniper who killed Delta's mother and shot at Avik would be mean—a really bad guy—one who didn't care about animals or people either," Joseph said.

When Ada asked if Big Ears looked like a bad guy, Joseph said he couldn't tell.

"I couldn't tell either, but I did notice two things that would keep him from being a good shot," Ada said.

"I give up, Ada. Just tell me what you saw," Joseph said.

"First of all, the glasses. They were thick. He had trouble reading the check. Held it up close to his eyes, and when he did, his hands were shaking. Bad eyesight and unsteady hands. He can't be the sniper."

"Okay. I agree Big Ears is not the sniper, but what is he doing with the 338? And why is he selling it?" Joseph asked.

"I'm thinking about possibilities. He may be selling it for someone else, or he may have stolen it or found it," Ada said.

"And it may not be the gun that the sniper used. May not have anything to do with killing Delta's mother," Joseph said. "So what's next?"

"We'll wait for Pete and Gordon to show up," Ada whispered. "They should be here any minute."

When the two agents arrived, they did what they always did. They sat in a booth across from the kids and paid no attention to them. After a few minutes, Ada got up and dropped her bag on the floor, spilling the contents under their booth. Pete helped Ada pick up her belongings. He kept a scrap of paper that looked like trash.

In Ada's handwriting were these words:

Custom Remington 338 for sale $1,000
with scope. License tag of seller's red
Ford pickup is DMK 386. Cash only
sale next Monday. Seller middle
aged, wears thick glasses, has big
ears and shaky hands.

Pete and Gordon left a ten-dollar bill on the table and took off in the old Subaru they had rented. There was no place to hide a red Ford pickup truck in Barrow so they figured if they made a tour of the town, they'd find it. First they drove by houses where they mostly saw four-wheelers, both new and junked snowmobiles, and the bones of whales and seals. They checked the license numbers of any trucks they saw. Some were so old and rusted that it was hard to tell if they had ever been red. In Browerville they rode past the post office, the Big Store, and any place a truck could be parked. Back on Stevenson Road, they passed the Naval Arctic Research Laboratory (NARL) and continued out toward Point Barrow, passing the huts of the shooting station, where natives stay while they hunt during the summer. They drove to the northern-most house on the North American continent. Still no truck.

Back on the other side of the lagoon, they drove by the airport and finally they spotted the truck parked in front of the King Eider Inn. Pete and Gordon went inside and looked around. Pete strolled over to the receptionist and asked to see the ivory carvings of Arctic animals that were for sale; Gordon settled in a rocking chair near a brown leather sofa where a middle-aged man with thick glasses and prominent ears and an attractive young woman were talking in low voices. He would do the eavesdropping, while Pete kept the receptionist occupied with questions about two polar bear carvings.

The woman had taken off her jacket and cap. She was wearing jeans and a black T-shirt. "It's been two weeks," she said. "I can't wait much longer."

"Sally, this guy wants the gun, and he's willing to pay $800 on Monday morning when the bank opens."

"Go back and tell him I want $1,000 cash. Twenty percent is yours," she said loud enough to be heard before lowering her voice again.

Gordon recognized the woman as the one Ada called "NYT" and that Fran said was a writer. He wondered how she could be the sniper. A Remington 338 was too powerful for a woman to handle, he thought at first. The recoil is enough to create a serious flinch, enough so the bullet could go off course.

Just as he was about to give up on the idea that Sally could be the sniper, Gordon caught another snippet of conversation. They were talking about the gun, ". . . not just any 338, but a custom-made Remington." And then later he heard her say, "It takes good eyes, a steady hand, and practice, practice, practice."

Gordon looked closely at this woman Big Ears had called Sally.

He noticed that she was tall and muscular. She wore her long dark brown hair in a single braid down her back. If she didn't have such an unpleasant manner, she would be almost beautiful. Gordon kept an eye on her as she stood up and walked outside without saying a word. *Yep, she could be the sniper*, he said to himself.

Coffee was always available in the lobby of the King Eider Inn. Big Ears poured himself a cup, picked up *The Arctic Sounder*, sat back down on the leather sofa, and skimmed through the paper. When Big Ears stood up, Gordon followed him outside. Pete bought a small polar bear carving and sat down to wait.

"Excuse me," Gordon said as he approached Big Ears. "I overheard you talking about a 338 Remington. I might be interested in buying that gun. Could I see it?"

Big Ears looked at Gordon, gave him a once over, and motioned for him to get in the truck. He reached behind the seat and pulled out a moose-hide rifle case. "Okay, here she is. A thousand bucks with the case, the ammo, and scope. The case alone is worth two hundred."

When Gordon took out the rifle, he noticed a hairbrush and sunscreen stuffed into the bottom of the case. This might be just the evidence he needed to arrest Sally, and he was careful to keep it out of sight. Then he took his time and carefully examined the gun, "I'll take it," he said.

"You got the dough? I can only take cash."

Without saying a word, Gordon reached into his pocket and pulled out a wallet. He counted out ten hundred dollar bills, and handed them to Big Ears, who carefully inspected each bill before surrendering the rifle. Neither man wanted to delay the sale, for fear that the other would change his mind. Gordon locked the gun in the back of the Subaru, and Big Ears went back into the King Eider. A few minutes later, Pete came out carrying a bag of ivory carvings—a polar bear, an arctic fox, and a baby seal. He looked at his buddy and raised an eyebrow.

"It's a done deal," Gordon said as Pete climbed into the passenger seat.

"Now what?" Pete asked as they drove toward Pepe's and the Top of the World Hotel.

"Well, we have to make some ballistics gel, find a test site, shoot into the gel, retrieve the bullet, and send it off to the lab for tests," Gordon said.

"You're the expert. Making the gel is your job. I'll set up the test site and line up a lab that'll do the testing right away. If we can get a commitment to turn this job around in three days, we should have the evidence in less than a week," Pete said.

"I'm pretty sure this Sally woman is the sniper, but we gotta have proof. If the tests show we have the rifle that killed the bear, we still have to make that gun smoke," Gordon said.

"You mean we have to prove she did the shooting," Pete said.

"Yep. But I think I have an ace in the hole. There was a hairbrush in the rifle bag with dark brown hair in the bristles. If the kids can get hair directly from her, we'll do a DNA test, and then we'll have the smoke. And we can't let her slip away," Gordon said.

The two FBI agents posing as bumbling Texas hunters looking for adventure had succeeded in creating a convincing cover. They were already known around town as inexperienced, not very bright, and harmless. Nobody paid them much attention, and they wanted to keep it that way. As experienced FBI agents, Pete and Gordon knew the shadowing had to be done by someone else.

"Ada and Joseph would be better spies than most adults. No one would suspect them," Pete said.

"You're right. Let's let them keep an eye on Sally," Gordon said.

Before they stopped at the hotel, Gordon turned onto

Stephenson Street and headed toward the Big Store to buy a container for making the ballistics gel. In less than ten minutes, Gordon was climbing into the car with his purchase. "I've got everything I need to make the gel, including a candy thermometer, and I can have it ready to use in about a day and a half," Gordon said.

Gordon would heat water, mix the gelatin in the right proportions, and then cool it to just the right temperature. All this he would do in the room where he and Pete were staying. Their room was the only one at the Top of the World Hotel that had a kitchen with a stove and a full-sized refrigerator, He would need both to make the gel.

When they pulled up to the hotel, Gordon wrote a note on a scrap of paper:

Do what it takes to get a sample of Sally's hair. Seal it
in the bag. Need it for evidence.

"Give this to Ada," he said, handing Pete the note and a Ziploc bag. Pete went into Pepe's while Gordon grabbed the gun case and disappeared into the hotel.

As he entered Pepe's, Pete saw Sally and Big Ears sipping coffee and talking in low voices. In the booth opposite them, Joseph and Ada appeared to be playing backgammon. Pete sat in a booth as far away from the others as possible, and ordered a plate of burritos and a Coke. When Fran brought his order, he asked her if she would sit down for a minute.

"Sure," she said. "I've been on my feet all day, and it's still a couple of hours before I can go home."

"That's a good looking woman sitting over there with that old guy. Is that her husband?" Pete asked.

"No way. He's a local. I'm pretty sure she's single—no wedding ring."

"I've seen her around. Do you know how much longer she'll be in Barrow?" Pete asked.

"She told me she's going to stay until she finishes a chapter for the book she's writing about the Arctic—probably another couple of weeks," Fran said.

"I'd like to meet her—maybe take her out on a date—but I don't know how to do that in Barrow—no movie theater, no concerts, no place to dance, no nightlife, not even any night this time of year," he complained.

"Well, you could bring her here to Pepe's for dinner, but I really don't think you want to get involved with her. She's not very friendly. She goes around interviewing people for her book, but when she's in here she acts like she doesn't want to be bothered. I better get back to work," Fran said.

As Fran walked away, Pete took a deep breath and smiled to himself, satisfied that he had the information he needed. Halfway through his plate of burritos, he stood up and strolled toward the door, motioning with a slight nod to Joseph to follow him outside. Pete lit a cigarette and pretended to smoke. Joseph stepped outside, stood in front of Pete, and pretended to be looking for someone.

"The woman inside who calls herself a writer may be the killer. She goes by the name Sally. You and Ada follow her tonight and find out where she stays. She was in the lobby of the King Eider Hotel this afternoon, but we don't know if she has a room there," Pete said just loud enough for Joseph to hear him. Then he passed the note and bag to Joseph and tossed away the cigarette he was pretending to smoke before returning to his table.

Joseph waited a few minutes before coming back inside. As he sat down, he slipped the note and bag under the table to Ada, who was carefully watching what was going on at the next booth. Then they saw Big Ears pass an envelope to the woman. She picked it up, counted the bills inside, and gave two back to him. They noticed that when Big Ears got up, he didn't say good-bye or shake the woman's hand.

Sally signaled for Fran to bring her a cup of coffee. Then she gathered her belongings—sunglasses, jacket, notebook—and moved to the booth in the back where she usually sat to write. Ada read the note from Gordon. Then she looked across at the now empty booth and saw that Sally had left her baseball cap. Ada stood up, quickly grabbed the cap, and sat back down, all without saying a word. In less than a minute, she had examined the cap, found hair attached to the Velcro fastener, and carefully sealed it in the Ziploc bag.

"Good job," Joseph said quietly as Ada tossed the cap back across the aisle. All the while, he kept an eye on Sally and noticed that she was writing intently, as if she wanted anyone who saw her to assume that she was a writer.

About that time Chipic walked in the door and came over to Joseph and Ada. "Hey, kiddo," he said to Joseph. "It's about time for you to go back to the station. Max will be at the airport in an hour or so. He'll take you back."

"I'll come to the airport as soon as we finish up some stuff here," Joseph said.

Chipic looked at Joseph with a questioning expression.

"How about continuing this game the next time you're in town?"

"Chipic, this is not a game, and what we have to do can only be done tonight," Ada added.

Ever since Ada and Joseph had solved the dinosaur fossil robbery, Chipic had gone along with their spy games. At least he thought they were games. He sat down at the table with them and ordered a chocolate sundae. Without giving any details, Ada whispered to Chipic that she and Joseph had helped find the gun that may have been used to kill Delta's mother.

"Ada, you're serious, aren't you?" Chipic asked.

"She's really serious," Joseph said. Then he looked at Ada and raised an eyebrow, which was his way of asking if he should say more.

"I don't have time to tell you the details now. But I can say that a woman called Sally might be the sniper and that Gordon believes that he has the gun that killed the bear. He's running tests to be sure," Ada said.

Chipic was quiet at first. Finally he said, "Sounds like we all need to get together after the tests are finished."

"Everybody?" Joseph asked.

"Yes, everybody—the two of you, Pete, Gordon, Kate, Dr. Yu, Max, Avik and me. That's nine people," Chipic said as he looked at his watch.

It was almost 10:00 PM, closing time at Pepe's. Chipic left first, urging Joseph to be at the airport in an hour.

Several minutes later, Joseph and Ada put on their parkas, went outside, and tossed around Ada's yellow Frisbee while they waited. Then Sally came out of the restaurant and almost bumped into Ada.

"Excuse me," Ada said.

"Watch what you're doing," Sally said, scowling at Ada before turning to march down the street. She never even looked at Joseph.

Ada and Joseph continued to toss the Frisbee as they moved on down the street, making sure they didn't lose sight of their quarry. In a short while, they had followed her to the King Eider Inn. Keeping their distance and crouching behind a parked truck, they watched as she went inside. Minutes later, Joseph peeped in the door of the inn and saw that there was no one sitting in the lobby.

"She's not coming out again tonight," he said as Ada set out for her house and Joseph walked over to the airport, less than a hundred yards away.

CHAPTER 26

Back at the Station: One Week Later

"So how many people are coming?" Kate asked as she brewed coffee for the group that would be gathering at the station around 10:00 AM.

"Well, there's you and me, Ada and her dad Avik, Chipic and Dr. Yu, and Pete and Gordon. That's eight. Add Max, and we're nine," Joseph said.

Max came in carrying lab reports and bags of bagels and doughnuts that he bought in Fairbanks early that morning. Just behind him were Pete and Gordon. "Kate, this is Pete and his partner Gordon. People in Barrow know them as two Texans who want to set up a hunting business and who don't know much about how to do that. Kate is Doctor Yu's assistant," Max said.

Pete and Gordon nodded to Kate, who was sitting on the floor giving Delta a bottle. Kate patted the floor and motioned for them to sit down. When Dr. Yu entered the room, the two FBI agents—dressed as hunters—were sitting next to the cub, stroking her fur and listening to the strange sounds she made as she drank her breakfast.

Joseph met Dr. Yu at the door and introduced the two agents on the floor petting the cub. Finally Avik, Ada, and

Chipic arrived. Dr. Yu asked everyone to sit in a circle on the floor and one at a time to introduce themselves and to explain their part in searching for the polar bear killer. Pete and Gordon had never met Kate, Dr. Yu, Avik, or Chipic. Only Joseph and Ada knew everybody. In less than an hour, everyone had their say—all, that is, except Avik, who asked if he could talk later. Everybody figured his part in this mission ended the day he risked his life by jumping on the ice floe and retrieving the bullets from the dead bear.

"So, let me get this straight," Dr. Yu said. "The bullets Avik took from the bear were shot at different times, and the ballistics lab report showed that they came from the same gun. Joseph and Ada have been spying on suspicious people, listening in on conversations, and communicating what they learn to Pete and Gordon. Joseph and Ada overheard a local man trying to sell a 338 rifle to a man who couldn't pay the asking price. Then what?" he asked, looking at Pete.

"After that we were on a roll," Pete said. "Ada got the license number of the truck driven by the guy selling the gun. Gordon and I located the truck and found the seller talking to the woman folks around here know as Sally. She calls herself a writer."

"Do you think that she's the sniper?" Chipic asked.

"Well, Gordon bought the gun, prepared ballistic gel, shot bullets into it, and we sent them off to the nearest ballistic lab. Joseph witnessed Big Ears giving the cash that Gordon paid for the rifle to Sally and he also saw her pay him back a two-hundred-dollar commission," Pete said.

"Wait a minute," Dr. Yu said, interrupting Pete's summary

of events. "Did I miss something? Who is Big Ears?"

"Your turn, Gordon," Pete said.

"The man who was selling the gun for Sally," Gordon said. "We don't know his real name; Joseph and Ada named him Big Ears. We don't know Sally's real name either. When they thought she really was a writer, probably a journalist, Ada named her NYT for *New York Times*. Now we just think of her as the woman who calls herself Sally, or the woman who calls herself a writer."

"And we don't know your names either," Kate said. Gordon and Pete kept straight faces and didn't say a word.

"Okay, go ahead with the story," Dr. Yu said, frowning at Kate.

"When Sally left her cap on the table, Ada grabbed it and found a few long brown hairs. The next day we sent off hair samples for DNA analysis: one sample from a hairbrush we found in the rifle bag, the other from Sally's cap," Pete explained.

"And the ballistic test results?" Dr. Yu asked, nodding to Gordon.

"Positive. The bullets shot from the rifle I bought match the ones Avik took from the bear," Gordon said.

"And the DNA?"

"Likewise, Dr. Yu. Positive. The DNA from the two hair samples match."

"So-o-o—the woman is the sniper. Do you have enough proof to arrest her?" Kate asked.

"Not necessarily," Gordon continued. "We know she sold the gun, and that she must have used it since her hairbrush was found inside the rifle case. But, it's possible that she was selling it for someone else. We have enough evidence to show 'probable cause' for an arrest, but what we really need is someone who saw her in the vicinity of the crime."

"I have something to say about that," Avik said mysteriously.

Everybody looked at Avik as he took his laptop computer from his backpack and turned it on. The entire group gathered around to watch a sequence of photos of a woman taking down her tent and packing up her gear. Then Avik went back through the pictures, pausing and zooming in on each. There was no doubt that they were looking at the woman who called herself a writer.

"That's her. No doubt about it," Gordon said. "What is she carrying?"

"Camping gear, that's all," Avik said.

About that time Chipic noticed a detail he hadn't seen before. The last picture in the series was taken as the woman called Sally was walking east back toward Barrow. "Look at this," Chipic said, pointing to a bag strapped to her backpack. "The bag is just the right shape and size to hold a dismantled rifle."

"So when were you out there, Avik?" Gordon asked.

"I figure I was on the ice floe and heard the rifle shot about 4:00 in the afternoon. It was around 5:00 when I met Chipic at Pepe's. Brother, I know I said I would stay out of this, and I mostly did, except for going to the crime scene at 4:00 AM the same night. I knew that's the time most Barrow folks are sleeping. I thought I might find something, and, besides, I'm the one who could have been killed."

"That's twelve hours from the time of the shot until you photographed the suspect," Gordon said. "And by the way, you not only found something, you found and photographed exactly what we needed to wrap up the case."

"Avik has been taking pictures since he was Joseph and Ada's age," Chipic said proudly. "Whenever he got some spare cash, he bought camera gear. Now when other people are buying four-wheelers and snow machines, he goes for the latest camera or lens."

"Don't forget the camcorder," Dr. Yu said. "It was Avik who made the video of the dead bear on the ice floe."

"The video will be Exhibit A and the still photos Exhibit B, and Avik will be the hero of the day!" Joseph said.

"Absolutely," Gordon said. "But to me, you're all heroes—Max for flying back and forth across the Arctic, carrying everything from DNA to dinosaur thieves; Chipic for helping scientists like Dr. Yu and Kate, who are trying to save the polar bear; and you, too, Joseph and Ada. You turned a game into real work."

"Don't forget Delta," Joseph said. "If Chipic and Avik hadn't rescued her, I wouldn't have come to the Arctic or met Ada," Joseph said.

Dr. Yu finally spoke up. "And if Joseph and Ada hadn't figured out about the dinosaur thieves, we may never have had the FBI step in to help. That's the way it is in science, too. It's like detective work. One thing leads to another, and without that one thing that leads down a particular road, everything would be different."

"Pete, you forgot to mention Gordon and yourself," Kate said. "You're the ones who came up here to track down the sniper."

"Thanks, Kate. FBI undercover agents don't usually expect praise for their work because much of what we do is secret. But remember, without you guys, we wouldn't be able to make an arrest," Gordon said.

"How do you know Sally's still in town?" Kate asked.

"Well, she goes to Pepe's every morning for breakfast, sits in the same back booth, and writes in her notebook. Sometimes she talks with Fran about how she plans to stay here until she's finished the first draft of her book," Gordon said.

Then Pete chimed in. "Here's what I figure. She's staying here to create an identity as a writer, so if later anyone comes after her, the locals will remember her and verify that she was here writing a book. And, I happen to know that her bill has been paid at the King Eider Inn through the end of the week."

"How do you know that, Pete?" Kate asked.

"You know, Kate, I can't tell you everything. But trust me, I know. She thinks that she's safe. She probably intends to leave next Monday."

"I'd really like to know what she's writing in that notebook," Ada said.

"If we're able to, we'll seize the notebook at the time of the arrest," Pete said. "We may be able to use it in court, but we won't be able to show it to anyone before then."

"Will she go to jail?" Joseph asked.

"I think so. But how long she stays there will depend on whether she's willing to say who hired her," Pete said.

"So when will you arrest her?" Kate asked.

"Tonight, after she leaves Pepe's," Gordon said.

"Suppose she's not there," Kate said.

"I can't afford to think about that now, but I'd bet money that she'll be there," Gordon said.

As it turned out, Gordon was right. He and Pete arrested the woman called Sally that night; she was booked and spent the night in the Barrow jail. The next day, she flew with the agents to Fairbanks to be charged before a federal judge.

The last night that Delta, Kate and Joseph spent in the research station was very different from the twenty-four hour sunlight of June and July. On August 25, about an hour after sunset, the three of them fell asleep in the arctic twilight and they were still sleeping when the noise of the chopper woke them on August 26, just in time to make the only direct flight to Anchorage. They had slept through twilight, darkness, and dawn, and at last Delta had slept through the night.

Chipic came with Max in the helicopter to help get Delta in the travel crate he had built for her. Ada, Avik, and Dr. Yu were waiting at the airport to say good-bye. No one spoke. Even Delta was quiet. Everyone felt that the end of something wonderful had come, and no one wanted the summer to be over. Chipic, Kate, Joseph, and Delta would fly to Georgia, and Chipic would stay as long as it took to build Delta's habitat. Kate would stay until she had to go back to the university for her last year of graduate school. Dr. Yu would take a later flight to Anchorage and leave for Montana the next day. Max, Avik, and Ada would stay in Barrow.

The Alaska Airlines flight arrived on time, and as it

approached the one room airport, Joseph broke the silence. "Ada," he said, "You have to come to Georgia to visit Delta."

Ada looked at her father with a look that said, "Please let me," and Avik looked at Joseph and smiled. "As long as you don't open a detective agency in Georgia," he said. With that the serious mood was broken, and everyone laughed.

"I can't promise," Joseph said, "We may need to do a little snooping around."

Avik and Ada gave everyone Eskimo hugs. Just before they boarded the plane, Dr. Yu said, "This may be the end of the summer, but it might also be the beginning of something big for all of us. I have a feeling that Delta could make a difference in how people understand the Arctic, and our job is to figure out how to make that happen."

PART III

CHAPTER 27

Taking Delta Home

BEFORE ANYONE ELSE BOARDED, THE CREW of the Alaska Airlines direct flight to Anchorage settled Joseph and Delta in the front row of the passenger compartment. They strapped the cub's crate securely to the aisle seat. Chipic and Kate would sit across the aisle, and there would be as much privacy as is possible on such a plane.

Joseph felt both happy and sad at the same time. He wanted to see his family and show them the orphaned polar bear he had been caring for. He looked forward to helping Chipic plan a habitat for Delta with everything she would need to survive and have a good life. But he was very sad to be leaving the Arctic. He wasn't ready. In the two months since he arrived in Barrow, the northernmost community in the United States, he had begun to feel at home.

As soon as the plane was airborne, Joseph scrunched down between the bear crate and the window and looked down at the rapidly shrinking boxlike houses. As the plane

banked out over the Arctic Ocean and flew back over the town, he caught a glimpse of Pepe's where he and Ada met to plan their adventures. The houses below, the museum, the library, and the post office quickly contracted to the size of toy buildings. In minutes Barrow was left behind, and Joseph was looking down at seemingly empty tundra. He felt his eyes sting and a lump in his throat.

To improve his spirits, Joseph did what he always did. He reached for a book—this time his own personal journal that his grandmother Lisi had given him to record his experiences and what he was learning. On the first blank page she had written these words:

Keep this with you at all times. Use it whenever something special happens or when you want to remember names of people and places. You may want to write about your own feelings, what you like, and what you dislike. You don't have to show your writing to anyone unless you want to.

179

Inside the cover of his journal, Joseph had written these instructions: "If found in Barrow, AK, please take this book to Fran at Pepe's. She will return it to the owner." Leafing through his journal, Joseph read the notes he had jotted down while waiting for Ada at Pepe's or just before falling asleep. Before the plane landed in Anchorage, Joseph had read through his journal twice, writing notes in the margins to indicate the significant parts of his time in the Arctic. As it turned out, almost everything that happened seemed important.

When he came to the end of his journal entries, Joseph scribbled these words:

Nobody at home will believe what I've done and seen. Maybe Lisi will, but definitely not Carlos. I still have to keep some things secret, especially what I learned eavesdropping. Sometimes it all feels like a dream.

Joseph closed his journal, pushed it into the bottom of his backpack, and sure enough, he felt better. Then he lifted the blanket covering Delta's crate and peeked inside. She was still sleeping.

In Anchorage, Delta Airlines arranged to meet the flight from Barrow and transfer Delta and Joseph to the plane to Atlanta. They were quickly settled in the front row of the first-class section; Joseph gave the cub another bottle of formula mixed with a drug that would keep her sedated for several hours, just as he had done before he left Barrow. He had the window seat and again Delta was strapped into the aisle seat with a blanket over her crate. Before the other passengers boarded, the pilot checked to make sure everything was okay. He reassured Joseph that nobody except the crew would know that there was a polar bear on board.

"Got everything you need for the bear?" he asked.

"As long as she keeps sleeping," Joseph said.

"How about you? I bet you're hungry."

"Food would be good," Joseph said.

Once they were in the air, a flight attendant brought Joseph a turkey sandwich, a banana, cookies, and a Sprite. Next came pillows and a blanket. Before settling down, Joseph looked out the window at the glacier-covered mountains of Wrangell-Saint Elias National Park. He peeked into Delta's crate and saw that she was still sleeping, pulled his feet into the roomy seat, laid back against his pillows, and covered up with the blanket. "First class is great," Joseph thought as he closed his eyes and fell almost instantly asleep.

Kate and Chipic had two seats together on the left side of the plane on an exit row, so they had more room than most other passengers. They were in the coach section of the plane, where all the seats were occupied. There were families with children, sports fishermen, soldiers in uniform, college students, and a large group of retired people traveling together on a tour. There were a few business people bent over laptops, and the occasional lone man or woman who didn't seem to belong in any category. Somehow Kate and Chipic managed to talk continually, stopping only to check on Delta and Joseph and to walk around the plane for exercise.

"Being in Barrow has changed my life. Before coming to the Arctic, I thought I would finish my Ph.D., live in Montana, and work with the Department of Fish and Wildlife," Kate said.

"And now?" Chipic asked.

"All I know for sure is that I want to go back to the Arctic and do what I can about global warming. Being here has brought the reality of climate change home to me. Now I know that polar bears are suffering as the ice melts earlier in the spring and freeze-up comes later in the fall. Taking care of Delta sometimes feels like taking care of her Arctic world," Kate said.

"In a way you are. If we can provide her with what she needs to be a healthy polar bear, and if she stays small, then she can play a big part in helping people understand what's happening to the world and what we have to do to turn things around" Chipic said.

"Chipic, you seem so calm. I've never seen you lose it. Sometimes I get so upset I could scream. How do you stay so cool?"

"I don't always. Sometimes I'm steaming on the inside, but I've learned to control my feelings. And that's not always easy. I talk to myself. 'Okay, Chipic,' I say, 'don't yell. Keep your mouth shut; wait 'til you can speak calmly.' That's what I did when I learned that my brother had been shot at by the person who killed Delta's mother."

"So, you wait until the anger cools?" Kate asked.

"I do. As soon as I calm down, I let the anger go and start trying to get to the bottom of a bad situation," Chipic said.

"Like who might be killing polar bears?"

"Yeah, like that. So what makes you angry?" Chipic said.

"Greed, and the attitude that the earth belongs to humans but not to other creatures—crickets, salamanders, raccoons, and polar bears," Kate said.

"And then there are the oil companies," Chipic said. "All they seem to want is more oil, more markets, and higher prices. Dr. Yu believes that some of them are willing to kill mother bears to free up denning areas for drilling, and he suspects there are those who are feeding false data to the Environmental Protection Agency for the same reason," Chipic said.

"So you can talk about this now?" Kate asked.

"Dr. Yu asked me to explain to you what we're up to, and, yeah, now that we're outside Alaska, we can talk. But only to each other."

Kate turned and looked out the window, riveted by the mountains of Wrangell-Saint Elias National Park. "We're still over Alaska," she said, pointing to the scene below.

Chipic had flown over the Brooks Range on the way to Fairbanks and over the Alaska Range on the way to Anchorage, but he had never seen the peaks of the Wrangell and Saint Elias mountains. In fact he'd never been on the ground in any mountains, and now he looked down at the largest collection of peaks higher than 16,000 feet in all of North America, at glaciers beyond number, and the huge Bagley Ice Field that was more than 4,000 feet thick and ninety miles long.

"I'd really like to climb a mountain, but not one of these," Chipic said. He continued to gaze out the window until they had left Alaska and were above the vast forests of

183

Canada. "It's all green down there now. I'll do a walk around to check on things," he said, taking off his safety belt and standing up.

As he walked the aisles, Chipic listened to the passengers talking among themselves about seeing whales, landing on glaciers in helicopters, watching grizzly bears in Denali National Park, and fishing for halibut and salmon. One boy was showing people his junior ranger badge and telling about almost being run over by a caribou, and another kid was talking about riding on a dogsled. When he passed by Kate again he told her he was going up to see Joseph and Delta.

Chipic had permission to keep an eye on Joseph and Delta in the first class cabin. Sitting in the seat directly across from the cub in her crate was Diane, an airline employee with special training in emergency medicine. She had agreed to be available in case the cub had problems. When Chipic approached, Diane stood up and reported on Joseph and the cub. "Both sleeping. Two hours. No sound from Delta. No one has asked about the crate, and I don't see anyone who looks like they'll give us problems," she said. "Remember you have a legal permit to transport the cub as long as you're in compliance with all the rules and regulations."

"Well, let's hope no one asks," Chipic said softly with his back to the other passengers.

"Don't worry; we'll handle it," Diane said. "The last thing we want is for people to know there's a polar bear cub in first class. Everybody would want to see it."

"You're right. I don't think we'll have a problem . . . that is if she stays asleep," Chipic said. Then he lifted up the blanket and verified that Delta was still sedated and sleeping soundly. Back in his seat, he reported to Kate that all was well.

Meanwhile Joseph slept and dreamed: about Delta being rescued from the ice floe, about playing roll-the-blue-ball with her at the research station, about feeding her a bowl of wild salmon, about listening to her whimper when she woke from a nap. He was still sleeping when the dinner service for first class passengers began. In addition to asparagus and a stuffed potato, the menu included salmon—wild Alaskan salmon.

Delta, like all polar bears, had a very acute sense of smell, one that allows an adult bear hunting on the ice to smell a seal twenty miles away. Joseph woke with a start to the sound of Delta's whimpers as she got a whiff of the salmon all around her. He was afraid that other passengers might have heard her, but when he peeked into her crate he saw that she was only making soft noises in her sleep. Joseph looked around at the other passengers, but they were preoccupied with the meal they had been served. No one was paying any attention to him or to the soft sounds coming from the crate he was guarding.

The passengers were not happy when they landed at the Atlanta airport. All were required to remain in their seats—seatbelts fastened—until Joseph, Delta, Kate, and Chipic had disembarked and boarded a cart that would move them rapidly through the airport, bypassing the train system and using elevators and back corridors that led to the transportation area where Lisi was waiting in her Subaru station wagon.

185

Chipic's first day outside Alaska went by like a dream as he was bombarded with unfamiliar sights and sounds—a continuous stream of planes landing and taking off as Lisi negotiated a maze of roads leading away from the airport. There were deafening sounds of multiple jet engines, and blurring colors created by vehicles zipping from one lane to the other. As they headed north through steadily increasing morning traffic, he was mesmerized when the sunrise changed from pale pastels to deeper shades of purple, lavender, orange, and yellow streaming across the sky. Then he was stunned as the sun seemed to erupt above the clouds.

"This sunrise is as amazing to me as the aurora borealis would be to you," Chipic said.

"You mean the Northern Lights?" Joseph asked.

"Yep," Chipic said. "They're only visible when the sky is dark and clear. Late September and October are good times."

Kate and Lisi chatted nonstop, while Chipic stared at the changing light reflecting off skyscrapers. He assumed Lisi was a good driver, but he felt uneasy when she changed rapidly from one lane to another. Finally they were outside Atlanta and past the morning traffic. Kate and Lisi were still talking quietly in the front seat. Chipic and Joseph fell asleep, and Delta was quiet and still in her crate in the back of the Outback. It had been ten hours since the plane took off in Anchorage when they turned down the narrow dirt road that ended at Lisi's house. "Welcome to Paradise," she said as she turned off the engine and lowered the windows.

At ten in the morning the temperature was already in the seventies. There had been rain the night before, and the air was fresh and clear. "Hey guys, wake up," Kate said, "You really are in paradise. It doesn't get any better than this." Then she grabbed a box of Delta's supplies and hurried into the house to set them up in the new habitat.

Chipic rolled out of the back seat, looked around, and said, "I must be on another planet. I've seen trees and forests, and ponds, and gardens in movies and on television, but I had no idea what it would be like here—the smells, all the birds, and so many different shades of green." He stood in amazement trying to take in this world that to him was so foreign and to the others so familiar. Then he remembered Delta and why he was here.

Joseph and Chipic lifted the crate and carried it to Delta's habitat that Lisi created by closing in the back porch. About the size of the research station, the room was empty except for Delta's bed, a blue ball, and a counter with bottles, prepared formula, and a stack of unopened cans of wild salmon. There was a window air conditioner that cooled the room down to 60 degrees even on hot days.

When Joseph opened the door to the crate, Delta slowly crept out, looked around, and with stops and starts crawled over to Joseph who was sitting on the floor next to Lisi. Joseph picked her up, held her in his lap, and offered her a bottle of formula. Lisi stayed close by, but she didn't approach the cub. She wanted Delta to get to know and trust her. But that would have to be done gradually.

Chipic tiptoed quietly out of the room and found Kate in the big porch swing looking out on Lisi's vegetable garden. He sat down with her, but they were too tired to talk, and in a matter of minutes they were dozing. Kate leaned her head on Chipic's shoulder. They slept like this for a while, and at some point without waking up, Kate had pulled her feet up into the swing and slumped down, resting her head on Chipic's knee, while he rested his arm around her waist. Kate woke first and startled Chipic when she tried to sit up. Coming out of a deep sleep, they looked at each other first with surprise and then embarrassment.

Neither said anything until Kate offered to make lunch. Pointing to the garden, she said, "You pick tomatoes, and I'll cook the bacon for the BLT."

When Chipic gave Kate a questioning look, she added "That's short for bacon, lettuce, and tomato sandwich."

Chipic had seen vegetable gardens at the University of Alaska at Fairbanks, but he didn't even recognize some of the vegetables in Lisi's garden. He knew green beans, squash, cabbage, and peas, but he didn't recognize the eggplant or cucumbers. As for the tomatoes, he wasn't sure which ones to pick, so he chose two large, nicely rounded red ones, and a far-from-perfect gnarled one with purple splotches. Chipic walked into the kitchen and put the tomatoes on the counter. Bacon was sizzling in the pan, and Kate was laying out two plates with lettuce leaves and Lisi's country wheat bread ready to be made into sandwiches.

"That's perfect, two Better Boys and one scrumptious heirloom," she said, picking up what Chipic thought of as the ugly tomato.

"I didn't know whether to pick that one," he said. "It looks so bad."

"Wait 'til you taste it."

When Joseph came to the door, Kate and Chipic were sitting across from each other eating sandwiches. On the table was a tall pitcher of iced tea mixed with lemonade, and Kate kept refilling their glasses.

"This is really good. What is it?" Chipic asked.

"It's called an Arnold Palmer," Kate said, explaining that a mixture of lemonade and tea was the famous golfer's favorite beverage. We call it an AP for short."

"I got it. I'm having a BLT with an AP. When we go back to the Arctic, we'll bring lemons, tomatoes, lettuce, and some of Lisi's bread. I'll make you a WBLT with an AP," Chipic said, with a twinkle in his eye.

"Let me guess. I don't suppose it could be whale bacon, lettuce, and tomato sandwich," Kate said breaking into laughter.

"You got it. And I'm not kidding. And for dessert, we'll have whale ice cream," Chipic said, joining her in laughter.

Joseph had a funny feeling. Kate and Chipic seemed different, not so serious as they were in Barrow. Everything one said made the other laugh, or at least smile. *Happy*, he thought. *Chipic and Kate are happy.*

"Hey, you guys," he said, still standing at the door. "What's so funny?"

"I'm not sure," Kate said, still laughing. "I think we're punch-drunk."

"Is that what an Arnold Palmer does to you?" Joseph asked.

"No, no, no, an Arnold Palmer is nothing but lemon juice, sugar, tea, and water. Here, have some," she said handing him a tall glass of AP.

"And punch-drunk?" Joseph asked, feeling left out of the joke.

"Let's see. Punch-drunk is a serious brain condition caused by injuries to the head. So it's not really the right word. Truth is, we're just being silly."

"I need some lunch, and Lisi will want some as soon as she wakes up. She fell asleep with Delta," Joseph said, still feeling left out.

"How about I make you a smoothie?" Kate asked.

"Sounds good to me," Joseph said.

Kate opened the refrigerator and took out orange juice, blueberries, and a cantaloupe. "Trust me, Joseph, you'll like this," she said.

In the late afternoon, Rachel and Ben came to pick up Joseph and take him back to their house so he could spend the night in his own bed. As they pulled up to the house, Joseph rushed out to greet them, shouting, "Mom, Dad, you're not going to believe all I've seen and done."

After giving Joseph a big hug, Rachel said, "You look older, and you've grown an inch or more."

"I don't think I've grown that much, but maybe," Joseph said.

"So do we get to see Delta?" Ben asked.

"Not tonight, Dad. We want her to settle down and get used to her new home. She's only seen a few people in her whole life. Let's see, Avik and Chipic rescued her, that's two; Kate and I have been her primary caretakers, so that's two more. Then there's Dr. Yu, Max, and Ada. That's seven altogether. Mostly she's only been with me and Kate," Joseph said.

"She's bound to be stressed out after traveling so far." Ben said.

"Yep, Dr. Yu told us not to introduce more than one person at a time. Tomorrow Amy's coming out to examine her. Mom, you can come a couple of days later. After that, Dad can come," Joseph said, smiling to himself. Never before had he told his parents what to do.

That night when he was settling down to sleep in his own bed, Joseph had a strange feeling—it was like being homesick, but it couldn't be that because he was at home. When he turned the light off in his room, it was completely dark, and he had not slept in the dark all summer. That was strange, but there was something more. The window was open, and instead of the silence of the Arctic, he heard the night sounds—crickets, tree frogs, and the occasional car passing on the nearby road. The only sound he was accustomed to hearing while he slept in the Arctic was the whimpering of the hungry cub and the purring sounds she made as she took her bottle of formula. Still he felt strange, lonely, sad. There was something missing, something he wanted but didn't have any more.

Joseph slept soundly, but just before dawn, he had a dream—he and Ada were walking along the beach at the edge of the Arctic Ocean. Ada pointed out to a pod of beluga whales swimming one after the other just a few yards offshore. Then as only happens in dreams they were suddenly sitting in Pepe's North of the Border Mexican Restaurant, spying on two men in a nearby booth. Ada was telling him that they worked for an oil company, and she had heard one of them say, "Our job is to make sure all the pregnant females are dead before they go into the dens." The dream shifted again, and Ada was at the tiny Barrow airport telling him good-bye. "I'll come to Georgia during

Christmas holidays," she said.

"And I'm coming back to the Arctic," Joseph said, as he woke up suddenly, realizing he had said these words out loud. Then he knew. Ada was the best friend he'd ever had. They had secrets and had solved mysteries. He had never known that it was possible to be good friends with a girl. She had taught him so much about her world. Now he wanted to teach her about his.

"Joseph," his mother said as she entered his room. "Do you know you're talking in your sleep?"

"I do. I was dreaming about whales, about spying on people who did dirty work for oil companies, and about my Eskimo friend."

It had been many months since Chipic had slept in total darkness. That evening he sat in a rocking chair on the porch and watched the sun sink behind a mountain, leaving a rosy, flame colored afterglow spread out against the western sky. After dinner while the family was gathered in Lisi's sitting room, Chipic excused himself and went to his bedroom. On his bedside table he found a book with the title *Trees of Georgia and Adjacent States*. He fell asleep studying the types and shapes of leaves.

Chipic woke up as light came through the east-facing window of his room. The house was quiet. He slipped outside to watch the sunrise and look more closely at the trees he'd been reading about.

Kate slept on a mat next to Delta, just as she had in the Arctic, and she woke only once to give her a bottle. The sun was up over the horizon when she was awakened again by the sounds of a hungry cub. When she carried Delta down to the kitchen, Lisi had already made a pot of coffee and warmed a bottle of formula.

"It's your turn to feed her," Kate said as she handed Delta to Lisi.

Kate poured herself a cup of coffee and sat down for some quiet time alone with her mother. For the next few minutes, Kate talked about her time in the Arctic—about how much of what Dr. Yu does is secret, how no one knows exactly where his tower is, and how the tower is movable.

"Dr. Yu didn't want me to know the details of his work, and he didn't want me to write about what I did know in an email. He was afraid that spies for the oil companies would be able to hack into the computer system and find out what we're doing. That's why my emails to you were so sketchy."

"How does he move a tower?" Lisi asked.

"Well, the tower has to be broken down into parts," Kate said. "Max carries the parts to a new location with the helicopter, and Chipic helps reassemble it."

Kate drained her second cup of coffee and said with a start, "Oh, I forgot about Chipic. Is he awake?"

"Look out the window," Lisi said.

There was Chipic, sitting by the pond and watching a snapping turtle. As they stared in silence at each other, man and turtle seemed frozen. While Kate and Lisi watched Chipic watching the snapping turtle, Delta began to squirm. Kate finally turned to the restless cub.

"I think she may be ready to go to her room," Kate said to

Lisi. After placing Delta in her litter area, Kate suggested that they leave her alone to do what she needed to do. When Lisi checked on her a few minutes later, the deed was done.

"She used the litter!" Lisi said excitedly, as she came back to the kitchen.

"She doesn't do that every time," Kate said as she poured a cup of coffee for Chipic and took it out to him. For the next few minutes, they sat together by the pond and looked across at the turtle.

"I've never seen one before," Chipic whispered.

"I used to watch a snapping turtle from this same spot when I was a child," Kate said.

"Could it be the same one?" Chipic asked.

"Actually, it could. Snapping turtles live between thirty and forty years. They spend much of the time in the water. In the winter they live in the mud on the bottom."

"Do you think I could pick it up?" Chipic asked.

"Not a good idea. There's a reason they're called snapping turtles," Kate said, laughing.

That day Kate and Chipic spent several hours exploring. They collected leaves, bark, seeds, conifer cones, and acorns. Kate pointed out the places where she had first seen a red salamander, a rattlesnake, a turtle laying eggs, and a hawk capturing a squirrel. Then they went further into the woods and climbed up the rock where so many years ago, Kate, Ben, and Rachel sat watching the mother bear make her den. There Kate spread out a picnic of fruit, nuts, and cheese.

After lunch, Kate took Chipic further into the wilderness, all along pointing out the differences in common trees. Chipic learned to recognize trees by the leaves: red and sugar maple; umbrella magnolia and tulip poplar; redbud and flowering dogwood. They would have gone still deeper into the wilderness, but Chipic was eager to begin planning the habitat for Delta.

"Kate, Let's go talk to your mom. I love being in the woods, but we need to make a plan for how we're going to bring Delta's habitat up to the standards that her permit requires," Chipic said.

Back at the house, they found Lisi resting on the porch under a ceiling fan. She was drinking ice tea and making notes in a notebook she called the "Delta Journal."

"So what's happening?" Kate asked.

"Delta is getting to know Amy," Lisi said, reminding Chipic that Joseph's other grandmother is a veterinarian who has had some experience with wild animals.

"But not with bears, I'll bet," Chipic said.

"Well, some years ago Amy helped rehabilitate a black bear that had been shot in the leg. She won't even try to examine Delta until they're comfortable with each other. Then she'll give Delta the equivalent of a complete physical—she'll take blood and hair samples, urine samples, stool samples, and I don't know what else. One of us will help her with that," Lisi said.

"Something smells good. What's for dinner?" Kate asked.

"I made a southern meal for Chipic," Lisi said. "Ben, Rachel, and Joseph are coming over. As soon as they get here, we'll sit down to dinner."

Soon they were all seated at the table—Ben at one end, Rachel at the other, Lisi and Joseph on one side, Amy, Kate, and

Chipic on the other. "So this is a traditional Georgia meal," Chipic said as he surveyed the abundant table set out family style, with heaping bowls of vegetables and a platter of fried chicken. There were butterbeans, fried okra, corn-on-the-cob, tomatoes, collard greens, and corn bread. All the vegetables were organic and grown in the garden. The free-range chicken came from a nearby farm.

"Chipic's mother prepared a traditional Eskimo meal for me," Kate said. "There was muktuk, caribou stew, wild rhubarb, sourdock greens, and fry bread. Everything came from right there on the North Slope—all except the flour for the fry bread. I ate some of everything. That means Chipic has to eat some of everything on the table," Kate said smiling.

"You forgot about the dessert. Kate ate her share of Eskimo Ice Cream," Chipic said.

"How do you make it?" Ben asked.

"Ingredients vary, but this one was made from seal oil, dried caribou fat, berries, sugar, and probably some other things, maybe even fish," Chipic said.

"If Kate ate that, you have to eat our dessert," Ben said.

"Don't worry, Chipic," Lisi said. "You'll like it—Ben's hand-churned peach ice cream and Rachel's chocolate brownies."

That was the last festive family meal Lisi would cook for a while. Kate would leave in a few days to return to the University of Montana but would come home at Thanksgiving for a visit. Chipic would stay behind to finish working on Delta's habitat and to build her an enclosed pool behind the house.

CHAPTER 28

Delta in the Wild

It was a couple of days before Thanksgiving when Kate came back to Georgia for a visit. She and Lisi spent the whole next day preparing the Thanksgiving feast—a wild turkey given to her by a neighbor, sweet potatoes and winter squash from the garden, cranberry sauce, and apple pies.

The day after Thanksgiving, Joseph woke just after sunrise. He had spent the night in Delta's habitat on a cot in a sleeping bag covered with a blanket. The room was never heated but was kept as cool as possible for Delta, so whoever slept with her had to bundle up to stay warm. He crawled out of his winter sleeping bag and walked to the window to check the thermometer—thirty degrees outside, and thirty-five inside. Chipic was already up and putting the finishing touches on the outdoor pool. Lisi and Kate were still sleeping.

"Lisi, wake up," Joseph said as he knocked on her door. "This may be the day." That's all it took to get Lisi out of bed and into the kitchen. She had promised that they would take Delta on a camping trip as soon as the weather was cold enough and likely to snow.

"Meet you in the kitchen," he heard her say.

"Let's see, eggs, milk, bread, butter, cinnamon, orange

197

juice," Joseph said as he was lining up ingredients for breakfast. In the Arctic Joseph usually made breakfast for himself and sometimes for Kate, and when he came back home to Georgia, he liked to prepare breakfast on weekends.

"Looks like French toast to me," Lisi said as she came into the kitchen carrying Delta and giving her a bottle.

"So what do you think, Lisi?" Joseph asked. "Is it going to snow?"

"I think so," she said, looking out the window at gray skies. "Check the weather on the computer."

"It's a go," Joseph said. "Storm coming into the north Georgia mountains tonight—wind, snow, maybe heavy snow."

"We'll pack all the winter gear and leave as soon as we can," Lisi said. "I'd like to make camp before the storm comes in."

Joseph put out the French toast, maple syrup, powdered sugar, and strawberry jam. Lisi had set up the coffee pot before going to bed, so all he had to do was press the start button. "Go ahead and eat," he said as he reached for Delta, put her on the floor, and went to the back door to call Chipic in from the cold.

"This is so nice of you to make breakfast," Lisi said as she sat down at the table and poured her first cup of coffee.

"Eat as much as you like," Joseph said. "I've set aside a plate for Chipic. He'll be here in a few minutes."

"The French toast is really good," Lisi said.

"I'm glad you like it. Fran taught me some things about cooking," Joseph said.

"Fran?" Lisi asked.

"You know, I told you about her. The woman who owns

198

Pepe's. There were days when I had to wait for Ada, and Fran would let me come back into the kitchen to watch the cooks," Joseph said.

"I'll never understand everything you did in the Arctic, but I do know you seem much older since you came back," Lisi said.

"Well, it's been almost six months since I left for the Arctic, so I am older. But mostly I know a lot I didn't know then. I know that kids can do more than some adults think they can," Joseph said.

"Okay, you pack our food and gear while I do Saturday morning chores. I don't want to come back to a dirty house," Lisi said.

Joseph divided what they would need into categories—food, shelter, cooking gear, emergency supplies, and clothing. First he packed the food—energy bars, freeze-dried meals, trail mix, marshmallows, graham crackers, and chocolate bars. To make sure there would be enough food Joseph put in oranges, pancake mix, bananas, bread, tea bags, oil, eggs, catsup, chips, walnuts, and peanut butter. At the last minute he added formula and two cans of salmon—one for Delta, the other for salmon croquettes

He packed a large tent, two winter sleeping bags, and three mats, a camp stove, matches, a knife, spoons, forks, cups, bowls, one pot, one pan, and several gallons of water. For emergencies he packed a first aid kit, flashlight, map, and compass.

Then he packed his clothing—rain gear, heavy jacket, warm hat, extra wool socks, extra pants, shirt, sweater, and long thermal underwear. Finally he went back to the habitat to check on Delta.

Soon she was in her crate in the back of Lisi's Subaru. The gear and supplies were packed. It was early afternoon before they got on the road, and by the time they reached the campground, the temperature was below freezing. Lisi and Joseph pitched the tent and put the mats and sleeping bags inside. Joseph made a bed next to his bed for Delta. The campsite they had chosen was near the river.

"Looks like we're going to have this campground to ourselves," Lisi said.

This would be no ordinary camping trip. If the weather report was right, they would be able to introduce the cub to snow. Delta was restless. She paced up and down in front of the tent and looked back and forth from Lisi to Joseph.

"Are you ready for an adventure, Delta?" Joseph asked as he began to walk toward the woods behind the campsite. At first Delta didn't move. She sniffed the air and then slowly turned the other way and walked toward the river. Joseph changed his direction and followed Delta. Every few steps, she stopped to sniff the air. Then she resumed her walk straight toward the river. When Delta paused, Joseph stopped and waited for her to take another step. He let her lead the way. Finally she came to the edge of the river and sat down.

She was fascinated by the water, and for a long time she didn't move anything but her head. She watched it flowing over rocks and listened to the gurgling, swishing sounds it made. She sniffed the air. Finally she lay down on her belly, lowered her head, and put her paw into the cold water. She brought it to her mouth, tasted it, and then tasted it again.

When Joseph called to Delta, she didn't even look at

him. She didn't take her eyes off the water, and from time to time, she reached down, scooped up the water and brought it to her mouth. Joseph could see that Delta was puzzled. There was something she was supposed to be doing, but she didn't know what.

"Delta, come away from the river," Joseph said, hoping she would follow him back to the campsite.

Still she stared at the river, ignoring Joseph. When he reached down to pick her up, she made a growling sound and batted his hand away with her paw. About that time, Lisi came down to the river with a snack for Joseph and Delta—a sandwich for him and a bottle for her. Joseph ate his peanut butter sandwich, but Delta didn't even look up.

Lisi and Joseph stayed by the river, watching Delta watch the water. As the light faded, the temperature continued to drop, and Joseph and Lisi were getting very cold. Finally they lured Delta away from the river with the can of salmon, but after taking a bite, she refused to eat more.

Back at camp Lisi built a fire for warmth and began cooking supper on the camp stove. She made salmon croquettes, thinking that both Delta and Joseph would eat them. As it turned out, Joseph ate a big plate of croquettes with catsup and potato chips, but Delta wasn't interested. She was restless, and she paced around the campsite while Lisi and Joseph ate and cleaned up. After supper Lisi put a plastic bottle filled with hot water in each sleeping bag to keep them warm during the cold night ahead. Still Delta had not eaten. When it became dark, Joseph carried her into the tent.

Sitting by the fire that night, wrapped in blankets and sipping hot chocolate, Lisi and Joseph talked about all that had happened since he'd returned from the Arctic—but mostly about the enclosed pool and other things that Chipic had built for Delta.

"The spring made all the difference," Joseph said, remembering the day that Chipic uncapped the spring to fill Delta's pool.

"I always knew there was a spring house where the Paxtons kept food cool before there was electricity, but I didn't know that the water would be cold enough to keep a polar bear happy," Lisi said.

Chipic had spent nearly three months in Georgia working on Delta's habitat, making sure it met all the federal requirements for a polar bear. Because Delta was a cub with growth hormone deficiency, her habitat could be smaller than that for full-grown bears, but Chipic made it as large as space and money—mostly money—would allow.

He rented a Bobcat to dig a hole for the pool where she would play and swim. He lined the pool with heavy, flexible plastic, and then laid an underground pipe that fed a constant supply of clean, cold water from the springhouse to the pool. Lisi would use the overflow to water her garden.

Chipic poured concrete around the pool, and on top he placed different sized rocks ranging from small pebbles to boulders for Delta to climb on and play with. Over all of this, he built an enclosure with walls of heavy animal-proof screen and a metal roof. This was all in addition to Delta's indoor habitat, which Chipic upgraded, completing what Lisi had started. The plan was to introduce the new outdoor space to Delta after the camping trip.

Delta woke up several times during the night, and finally about dawn, she got up for good. Joseph and Lisi were sleeping soundly, but Delta was restless and eager to go outside. She put her paw and then her head through a small opening in the door of the tent and pushed until she had made a space big enough to wiggle through. There was a cold wind blowing, and she lifted her nose into the air and sniffed. Snow was falling.

An hour passed before Joseph stirred in his sleeping bag. He rolled over and sat up, expecting to see Delta staring back at him. Her bed was empty. He looked around the tent, behind his backpack, and in the duffel bag. No Delta. There really was no place for her to hide.

"Lisi," he shouted. "Wake up! Delta's gone."

Joseph and Lisi quickly put on their boots and climbed out of the tent. They looked around and saw a blanket of fresh snow covering everything. Snow was still falling, and the air temperature was below freezing.

"Look for tracks," Joseph shouted.

There were no tracks, no sign of Delta. Joseph was frantic, afraid that the cub was lost and he wouldn't be able to find her.

"Joseph," Lisi said, "Let's calm down. I think we can find Delta, but we have to make a plan. It's been snowing for a while, and this heavy snow would have covered her tracks."

"That makes sense. But what do we have to go on?" Joseph said.

"Let's think about what she might do," Lisi said.

"She might have an instinct to build a shelter out of snow," Joseph said. They looked around the campsite for anything that looked like a snow cave. Joseph searched in one direction, Lisi in another. Then after a few minutes, they met back in camp.

Joseph was miserable. "This is hopeless. There are a thousand places she could be out here," he said to Lisi.

"But only one place where she is. I don't think she's too far away, but we have to be careful," Lisi said. "We don't want to disturb a hibernating black bear in her den."

Joseph hadn't even thought about black bears. "Do you think a black bear has hurt Delta?" he asked.

"Actually I don't think black bears would come out in this weather. Mother black bears are probably hibernating in their dens with their cubs, but we don't want to wake one."

Then Joseph remembered that Delta was fascinated with the river. She hadn't wanted to leave. What's more, she hadn't eaten the night before.

"I know she's hungry. Let's take a can of salmon down to the river," Joseph suggested.

Lisi grabbed a can of salmon and a can opener, then she and Joseph walked slowly toward the river, tapping on the can and calling Delta's name. When they reached the place by the river where Delta had been the day before, they looked around. There was no sign of her, only the soft white snow covering everything—except for something dark on top of the snow near the river.

"Look Lisi," Joseph said, pointing to a pile of fresh scat. "She's been here. And it's fresh."

"She must have done this a few minutes ago."

"Do you think she could have fallen in the river and drowned?" Joseph asked.

"No way," Lisi said. "But she may have gone swimming."

About that time, they heard a splash downstream and then another splash. They walked toward the sound, and in a matter of minutes, Delta came into view. She was sitting on a rock in the middle of the river. And she was eating a fish.

"This is amazing," Joseph said quietly. Without speaking to each other, Lisi and Joseph lowered themselves to a sitting position on the riverbank and watched the cub totally absorbed with the business of eating the rainbow trout she had caught. When she finished eating, the little that was left of the trout slid into the river and floated downstream.

The polar bear cub sitting on a rock in the middle of the Tallulah River in north Georgia surrounded by a snowy landscape seemed to belong there. Sometimes snow would come down so hard Joseph had trouble seeing her. But he was able to see her stand up and begin watching the water again.

"Oh, no. She's going fishing again," Joseph whispered.

"We've got a problem," Lisi said. "Delta is neither wild nor tame."

"Sometimes I think I want to be wild with her," Joseph said. "But I know that's not possible."

"When we're in the woods, we feel our wildness," Lisi said, "but for now we better focus on getting Delta back on this side of the river."

Joseph called to Delta in the same voice he used to get her attention inside. At first she seemed to ignore him, but the third time she looked up at Joseph, jumped in the river, and swam straight for him. Up on the bank she shook herself dry like a dog.

The purpose of the trip was to give Delta a chance to be

in the wild in conditions similar to the Arctic. Except for the trees and up-and-down terrain, Joseph could imagine that he was outside Barrow in the snow. For the rest of the day, he played with Delta near the campsite. This time he dug a snow cave with her, and when she crawled in the cave, he followed her. But Delta was not satisfied with one snow cave. When one was finished, she would rest in it for a few minutes and then crawl out and start all over again. At the end of the day, Joseph and Delta were both exhausted. He carried her into the tent and pulled his sleeping bag in front of the door to make sure she couldn't escape.

The next day was even colder than the day before. While Lisi was packing up, Joseph watched Delta carefully. When she made a break for the river, he ran to catch her. Delta thought Joseph was playing, and she turned around and started chasing him. This went on for a while as Delta went back and forth to the river. Sometimes she chased Joseph, and at other times he chased her. Finally, exhausted, they both plopped down on the riverbank. Joseph put an arm around her to make sure she didn't break away, and together they watched the water flowing over and between the rocks. There were no fish in sight.

When they returned to Paradise, Chipic and Kate greeted them in the lane before they pulled up to the house. "It's done," Chipic said, "The outdoor habitat is complete. We'll introduce it to Delta tomorrow." He had worked all day to finish the job.

As soon as Kate told him that his mother was inside waiting to take him home, Joseph ran into Lisi's house shouting, "Mom, you're not going to believe what happened."

"Again?" Rachel said as she gave her son a big hug.

"I want to come back early tomorrow when Chipic takes Delta to her outdoor habitat," Joseph said.

"You know I'm leaving tomorrow and so is Kate," Chipic said. "Maybe Joseph could come stay with Delta while Lisi takes us to the airport."

And so it was settled. The next day, the Monday after Thanksgiving, Kate would fly back to Montana, and Chipic would return to Alaska. That afternoon Lisi would drive them to the airport, and after school Joseph and his friend Carlos would come over to stay with Delta. But the morning was for the cub.

Chipic stuck his head in the kitchen where Lisi and Kate were having breakfast. "Bring your coffee and come outside. It's time for the grand opening of the only polar bear pool in Georgia. Delta is still sleeping," he said.

Scrambling into their coats, they followed Chipic through Delta's inside space, out the back door, and crossed the ramp that led to the pool enclosure. Just inside, Chipic had placed a split log bench for them to sit on while they watched what happened. Under the roof was a sprinkler system to simulate rain on warm days, and at the far end was a fan to create wind. The ramp led to the pool.

"I might cool off out here myself on a hot day," Lisi said.

When Chipic went inside to get Delta, he picked her up from the mat where she was still sleeping and brought her out

207

and sat her down near the shallow end of the pool. For a few minutes she didn't move. Kate and Lisi sat quietly on the bench, and Chipic sat cross-legged next to the cub.

Eager for Delta to do something, Lisi started to go inside to get the blue ball, but Chipic raised a finger to stop her. "This will take as long as it takes," he said in a whisper. He wanted Delta to explore the new space when she was ready. And finally it seemed that she was.

After almost twenty minutes of sitting quietly, Delta began to make the whining sounds she made when she was hungry. Then she got up and walked toward the pool. Just as she had stared at the river, she looked down at the water. But it didn't move, and there were no fish. She didn't seem to know what to do.

"What do you think, Kate, should I go in with her?" Chipic asked. She shook her head and said emphatically, "No. It's too cold."

"Well I am an Eskimo, and I do belong to the polar bear club. Besides, the water temperature is about fifty-five degrees. That's warmer than the air," Chipic said. But after waiting another fifteen minutes, he scooped Delta up and brought her back to her inside habitat.

"We'll let Joseph bring her back to the pool this afternoon," Kate said.

Chipic looked around at Delta's space. It was about the same size as the research station in Alaska, but there was no desk, no kitchen, no bathroom, and no chairs. There was an old-fashioned tub with running water where Delta was able to have a bath. Sometimes they filled it with blocks of ice for her to lie on. There were a few floor pillows and one sleeping mat. Someone had slept with Delta every night since she came to Georgia.

Chipic had researched habitats for captive polar bear cubs on the Internet. He hung a rubber tire from the ceiling with an adjustable rope. Sometimes he raised it a foot, sometimes two feet from the floor, and sometimes he untied the rope and rolled the tire on the floor. Chipic had made two foot square wooden cubes with one side open. Delta could hide inside or behind the cubes. Of course there was the blue ball brought from Alaska, and a soccer ball that Ben brought to Delta the day he met her. In the corner of the room was Delta's den, a small, enclosed space.

Chipic spent the next hour or so playing with Delta. They played hide-and-seek, roll-the-ball, and swing-in-the-tire. Last they played a rather strange game with the soccer ball, with Chipic on his hands and knees pushing the ball with his head and Delta batting it back with her paws. Just as Delta backed herself into the wall, Lisi came in with a salmon snack.

"Chipic, what would your brother say if he could see you now?"

"I think this should be our little secret, Lisi," Chipic said with a chuckle as he picked himself up off the floor.

"We have to leave for the airport in about an hour. I've made sandwiches for you to take on the plane. We want to get there early," Lisi said.

CHAPTER 29

Surprise

Carlos had waited a long time to meet Delta. Dr. Yu and Amy had warned against introducing her to too many people at once, and so one by one they came to meet the cub—first Lisi, who often spent nights with her; then Amy, who came to examine her and take blood and urine samples. Joseph's mom Rachel came next, spending only an hour or so at a time. Ben was last, and since he came every weekend to help Chipic build the outdoor habitat, he visited Delta both on Saturday and Sunday. So by the time Chipic returned to Alaska, Delta had only met four new people—Lisi, Amy, Rachel, and Ben. That day Carlos would make five as he was coming home with Joseph after school.

About three thirty that afternoon, Rachel dropped Carlos and Joseph off at Lisi's place. Rachel was a fifth-grade teacher, and she had to go back to town to a PTA meeting. Lisi would return from the airport around seven that evening. That would give Joseph and Carlos more than three hours to be with Delta and to take her back to the outdoor habitat.

This would be the first time for Joseph to be alone in Lisi's house without adults nearby. When he was younger, his dad had told him stories about the house being haunted—how he and his sister Kate heard noises during the night in the attic, and how even after the noises turned out to be raccoons, they thought there might be ghosts as well. Ben only told ghost stories on Halloween and around a campfire. Still Joseph remembered them and told them to his friend Carlos.

But ghosts were the last things the boys were thinking about when they climbed the front steps. Taped to the door was a note:

Joseph, there's a surprise for you on the dining room table.

Once inside Joseph and Carlos went straight to the dining room, and there in the middle of the table was an aluminum case about the size of a large briefcase. It was locked. There was a note beside it.

For Joseph: Do not open until Delta has eaten and played in her outdoor habitat.

"So what do we do?" Carlos asked.

"We do exactly what Chipic tells us to do," Joseph said. "We take care of Delta. I'll get her a bottle."

When the boys entered the cub's indoor habitat, Delta was sleeping in her den lying on her stomach with her legs spread out. They sat on the floor and waited for her to make the "feed me" sounds that meant she was waking up. They didn't wait long. First Delta rolled over. Then she opened her mouth, stuck out her tongue, and began to smack her lips and suckle her own paw. Finally she began to raise a ruckus, screeching in a rasping, hoarse cry.

"Wow, she's loud," Carlos said. "She sounds like a cross between a human baby and a toucan, a bird we have in the rainforest in my country."

"She doesn't usually carry on like this," Joseph said in a low voice. "She must have gotten up when no one was here and realized she was alone, and now she's determined to wake the dead."

When Joseph reached inside the den and touched Delta, her shrieks gradually subsided. In no time she was sitting in Joseph's lap taking her bottle, producing the purring sound that she made whenever she drank her formula. Carlos sat a few feet away and spoke to Joseph in a whisper. He knew not to approach the cub.

"Meet you outside," Carlos whispered. Then he rose from the floor and tiptoed out the back door leading to Delta's outdoor space. This is really cool, Carlos thought to himself as he looked at the outdoor habitat—the gravel paths, the rock formations, the boulders, and the hiding places.

Then something on the path caught his eye. Every three feet or so was an arrow (/|\ ) made from sticks. He followed them to the other side of the pool where the last one pointed to an opening between two rocks. Reaching into the opening, Carlos pulled out a small, flat object.

About that time Joseph came through the door carrying

the cub. At first he didn't see Carlos perched on a large rock with his arms folded over his chest and his head between his knees, he looked very much like a boulder himself. Both boys remained silent, not wanting to upset the cub. Joseph put her down, and walked on the gravel toward the deep end of the pool. Delta was right behind him, and when he stopped in front of Carlos, she tried to climb up his legs.

Still Carlos didn't lift his head, and so Joseph began exploring the rocks himself. Again the cub was right behind him, doing whatever he did. But when it seemed they had explored all the rocks on one side of the pool, Joseph sat down near Carlos, and Delta went off alone to investigate the other side of the pool.

"Sorpresa!" Carlos said, holding out two clenched fists. "Which one has the llave?" He liked to use Spanish words that Joseph didn't know.

"Llave? What does that mean?" Joseph asked as he tapped his friend's left hand.

"What do you think?" Carlos said as he opened his hand revealing a small brass key.

"I think Chipic is playing with us. This must be the key to the box. Let's go check it out," Joseph said, for a minute forgetting about the cub. Just then, they heard a splash as Delta threw herself into the deep end and began swimming across the pool.

"Not quite yet," Carlos said. "I think we better stay here

a while longer."

For some time they watched the cub pull herself up on the side of the pool, walk around looking down at the water, then belly flop again. She paid no attention to the boys. After about an hour when she was resting on the side of the pool, Joseph wrapped her up in a towel and took her inside. A bowl of salmon and another bottle was all she needed to fall asleep.

CHAPTER 30

Treasure

"You unlock it," Joseph said to Carlos. They were sitting at the table. Using the key he found, Carlos opened the case. Inside was a letter from Chipic:

Dear Joseph,

I found all of the objects in this container in the springhouse and in the ground where I dug the hole for Delta's pool. There are Indian arrowheads, two spearheads, fragments of pottery, and some other items you may find interesting. I found the wide-mouthed brown bottle sealed with cork and wax in the springhouse. Don't open it until we're all together at Christmas, and be careful not to damage the wax seal. I suspect that there's something important inside.

I wish I could watch you open this box. See you at Christmas.

Love, Chipic

Joseph and Carlos spread the objects out on the table, starting with a human jawbone and ending with the skull of a small animal. In between were other bones, pottery shards, coins, and a few unfamiliar items. Joseph held the mysterious, sealed bottle up to the fading late afternoon light as he wondered what it contained. As he examined the wide-mouthed bottle carefully he noticed four numbers pressed in the wax—1863.

"Look at the wax seal," Joseph said as he handed the bottle to Carlos. "It's a date. Two years before the Civil War ended."

"That's spooky," Carlos said, noticing for the first time that it was getting dark.

"Yeah, that is spooky. I feel like a rabbit ran over my grave," Joseph said.

"What does that feel like?" Carlos asked.

"You know, that chills-up-and-down-the-spine feeling."

"Oh, yeah, I felt it too," Carlos said.

Without saying any more, Joseph stood up to turn on the lights. He flicked the switch. Nothing happened. "We've got a problem," he said. "No electricity."

"Not many people had electricity where we lived in Ecuador. We had it, but it went out a lot," Carlos said.

"Yeah, it goes out here in the country, too—especially during storms," Joseph said.

"I think it is storming," Carlos said. "I just heard thunder."

Neither wanted to say to the other that he was afraid. Besides, something about the approaching darkness seemed right. Joseph walked out on the porch. Only then did he notice black clouds in the southern sky. A bolt of lightening struck nearby, followed almost immediately by deafening thunder.

"I think we should light the room with a lantern while we think about what to do. All of the objects in the treasure box were made and used long before any houses had electricity, and this bottle was probably sealed by the light of a kerosene lamp," Joseph said as he went into the kitchen to bring back one of Lisi's lanterns.

While lightning crackled, thunder roared, and a wall of rain blew against the old house, Carlos and Joseph examined the objects by lamplight. They decided that the dark color on an arrowhead was a bloodstain and that one object must have been a tool used to sharpen arrowheads. When they held the brown bottle up to the light, they could see what looked like a roll of paper inside.

"I wish we could open it now," Carlos said. "My mother knows how to cut glass."

"We have to follow Chipic's directions. He has his reasons," Joseph said.

"He probably just doesn't want us to cut ourselves."

"There's more to it than that," Joseph said, just as the lamp began to flicker and go dim as it ran out of kerosene, then went out. "It's really dark now."

"Maybe we should check on Delta?" Carlos asked.

"Let's do it. There's a flashlight in the kitchen drawer." Joseph said.

But before he could get it, the boys heard a noise outside. Someone was walking up the outside stairs and onto the porch. Joseph and Carlos scrambled to their feet. By the time they heard the doorknob turn, they were down the hall heading for Delta's habitat. Once inside, they found their way in the dark to the cub's den where she was sleeping.

Crouching in the back of the den, they were hidden from view as they heard the footsteps come closer. The door opened and light from what they thought was a flashlight flickered around the room. In a few minutes the sound of footsteps slowly faded away, just as Delta began making her "feed me" sounds.

The boys crawled out of the den with Delta following Joseph. Wide-eyed and shaken, the boys stared silently at each other. "I don't believe in ghosts," Carlos said, just as Joseph was about to ask him if he did.

"Do you think we imagined that someone or something came into the house?" Joseph asked.

"Maybe. It happened pretty quickly. But I know I saw light," Carlos said.

"Maybe we saw lightening," Joseph said.

"Maybe, maybe not," Carlos said.

"Well, let's don't tell Lisi. Whatever—I mean whoever—it was, is gone," Joseph said.

Ever since the bears visited their campsite, Joseph knew that Carlos was easily frightened.

An Email from Ada

Dear Joseph,

I can't believe I'm coming to Georgia for Christmas. Dr. Yu, Chipic, and I will travel together. We'll fly from Barrow to Fairbanks, from there to Anchorage, and then we'll board the Delta Airlines flight to Atlanta. Remember I've never been any farther south than Fairbanks, so this trip is a really big deal for me.

My last day of school is Friday, December 16— two weeks from today. We leave Barrow the next morning. Fifteen hours later we're in Georgia. Dr. Yu has something important to report about his research when we're all together in Georgia. Give Delta a hug for me.

Your partner in solving crime,
Ada

PART IV

CHAPTER 31

Message in a Bottle

EVERYBODY INVOLVED IN THE DELTA PROJECT was sitting around the ten-foot long heart pine table in the dining room where Lisi and her family made important decisions. Lisi and Dr. Yu sat at either end; Joseph, Ada, Carlos, and Chipic on one side; and Rachel, Ben, Amy, and Kate on the other.

"Dr. Yu," Lisi said, "you're in charge here. Before we open the bottle, we'd like to hear news from the Arctic."

"Thank you, Dr. Morse," Dr. Yu said. "I have some news for the group, and some other issues to discuss."

"Let's start with the news," Lisi said.

"Ada, you fill us in."

"Okay, here's the deal," Ada said. "Max has been scanning the polar bear denning areas in a light plane equipped with an infrared camera that picks up heat from animals in their dens. When Max flew over one den that we knew contained a polar bear last year, the camera found something very different this year."

"So what was that?" Joseph asked.

"Well, the heat image recorded was about the size that a human being makes. Chipic searched the area later and found that someone had recently enlarged the old den into an underground room a little larger than a closet. It's supported with timbers that had to have been brought in from outside. Inside the room there was a rifle, a cot, a sleeping bag, blankets, and a supply of food."

"So they're still at it," Joseph said.

"Looks to me like the people who hired Sally have set someone else up to do their dirty work—probably to kill bears as they come out of their dens in the spring," Ada said.

"Wait a minute," Lisi said. "Who are these people?"

"That's what we don't know. The sniper who was arrested for killing Delta's mother is still in custody awaiting trial, probably because of negotiations about a plea bargain," Dr. Yu said.

"So what's a plea bargain?" Carlos asked.

"Well, Sally pleads guilty, and she gets a lighter sentence," Ada said. "She might get off completely if she reveals the names of the people she was working for."

"Okay," Dr. Yu said. "You now know as much as we do about the sniper case. Sally hasn't gone to trial yet, and she may not if she agrees to a plea bargain."

"So what's next?" Joseph asked.

"Well," Dr. Yu said quietly, "the next matter is Delta's habitat."

Suddenly everyone became very serious, especially Chipic and Ben, who had built the outdoor habitat and made sure that Delta had everything she needed to enjoy her indoor space. They were afraid that the habitats didn't meet the requirements for the permit to keep the captive cub for "educational and research purposes."

Everyone looked at Dr. Yu and waited for the verdict. Finally he said, "Concerning the habitats, I have both good news and bad news."

"Give us the good news first," Chipic said.

"The good news is that the habitats go beyond what I'd hoped for. You have more cold water, enrichment objects, and sleeping space than are required by our permit. Delta can swim, play with balls, swing from the tire, climb on rocks, and find places to hide. It's truly a wonderful habitat."

"So what's the bad news?" Joseph asked.

"The bad news is that maintaining the habitat and taking care of Delta is going to cost more money than we have. And to keep the permit, we have to do research about the needs of a captive cub. And we also have to establish an educational program that features Delta and the Arctic. We have to find the funds for this."

"Well, that may be possible," Lisi said. "We'll have to brainstorm about the money later. So, you said you had several issues to bring up."

"Well, one problem we need to talk about is that Delta's not a normal bear. We know that she has a serious deficiency of growth hormone, and that she's much smaller than she should be. In fact she's only gained about three pounds since she was rescued. We have to decide if we're going to try to give her growth hormones and see if she'll grow, or if we're going to let her be small and not interfere, but just let nature take its course. Dr. Carson, what can you tell us about this?" Dr Yu said, glancing over at Amy.

"Dr. Yu, I've researched Delta's condition, and very little has been written about hormone abnormalities in polar bears, or any bears for that matter," Amy said. "I've also talked to veterinarians who specialize in marine mammals. Everybody agrees that we have no idea what to expect if we give Delta synthetic growth hormone. And we don't know what'll happen to Delta in the future if we do nothing. Her own hormones may kick in, and she'll start growing. Or she may stay like she is. Again, we don't know what to expect. We do know that she's doing well now. To use an old-fashioned expression, I think we should let well enough alone."

"That's what I've been thinking," Dr. Yu said. "What do the rest of you think?"

No one said anything. Lisi smiled to herself, thinking that Dr. Yu was managing this gathering as if he were holding a department meeting at the University of Montana.

Finally Kate spoke in a quiet voice. "I think Amy and Dr. Yu are right." And in a matter of a few minutes, everyone at the table was in agreement. Delta would be left to grow or not grow, but no one would try to change her.

"I think she's perfect just as she is," Ada said.

"Let's talk some more about the money problem," Lisi suggested.

"The permit that allows us to keep Delta requires that we

carry out ongoing research and educational projects. It'll be renewed once a year as long as I write a report that includes convincing evidence that the work we're doing is important and that Delta has everything she needs. The problem is that doing this will cost money we don't have," Dr. Yu explained.

"How much money?" Ada asked.

"That depends on how we design our research and educational projects. There are foundations that give money for research and others that support educational programs about polar bears," Dr. Yu said. "Finding the money will take some time. Kate, Lisi, and I will look into places where we can apply for grants."

"Anything else, Dr. Yu?" Lisi asked.

"That's it for now. I think it's time to open the bottle. Chipic, are you ready?"

The bottle with the mysterious paper inside lay in a shoebox where Lisi had put it for safekeeping. Everyone sat quietly at the table while Chipic removed the bottle from the box, placed it on a cookie sheet, and proceeded to moisten a piece of string with kerosene, tie it around the bottom of the bottle, and light the string with a kitchen match. Before anyone knew what was happening, the glass cracked evenly, leaving a round opening big enough for Chipic to reach inside and remove the fragile paper.

"Don't get up," Chipic said just as Joseph and Ada were standing up to see better. Lowering themselves back into their seats, they craned their necks trying to read what was written on the paper Chipic was studying so carefully. Finally, he looked up from the paper with a puzzled expression on his face. "I'm not sure I can read this. It just looks like a jumble of letters. See what you think, Lisi," Chipic said as he passed the paper to her.

"It's a jumble of letters, all right, but the letters themselves are legible. There were no fountain pens in 1863, so they would have been written with a quill or dip pen."

"Lisi, read the letters out to us so we can write them down," Joseph said as he jumped up to get pencils and paper for everyone at the table.

Lisi slowly read out the letters, making sure that she read them correctly:

December 21, 1863

"It's obviously a code," Dr. Yu said.

"Cool," Carlos said. "Can we break the code?"

"Sometimes I use complicated codes in my work, but this one is probably simple," Dr. Yu said. "Whoever left this message must have wanted it to be deciphered."

Soon everyone was trying to make sense of the letters. They tried the backward alphabet code, shifting letter codes, and letter frequency codes. All for nothing.

"I've got it!" shouted Ada, who had been studying the letters, whispering to Joseph, and scribbling feverishly. "I should say 'we've got it.' Joseph and I figured it out together."

"So what have you got?" Chipic asked.

"I've got Julius Caesar," Ada said excitedly.

"What do you mean?" Chipic asked.

"I mean that the message was written using the Julius Caesar code—the one he used to send messages to his troops."

"So how do you know about the Julius Caesar code?" Chipic asked.

"On the days when Joseph and I were in Barrow together, we decided we needed to learn about codes in case we needed one. We researched different codes in the library and settled on the Julius Caesar code. It's easy, but we figured that employees of oil companies wouldn't know about it."

"Ada, tell them what the message is," Joseph said.

Suddenly everyone was silent. They looked at Ada and waited for the message. Then she stood up and read from her notes. "Look where the winter light first falls. Otis Paxton. December 21, 1863."

"Otis Paxton was the man who built this house. He died in 1865 when he was sixty-four years old," Lisi said quietly. "December 1863 was only a few months before General Sherman invaded Georgia. Like a lot of other Georgians, Paxton probably would have hidden—maybe buried—anything valuable. This message that Chipic found in the springhouse may be a clue to the whereabouts of something important."

CHAPTER 32

The Next Morning

The sky was clear, the air unusually dry, and the moon low in the western sky. The stars were so bright that they were the first thing Dr. Yu noticed when he walked out of Lisi's house toward a hill on the eastern side of the pasture. There he stood looking westward until the faintest of lights revealed the pasture, sloping up to the northwest and leveling out to a small plateau. There he could just make out a space enclosed with an iron fence, the far side bordered with a row of red cedars. Inside was the Paxton family cemetery. The early morning light came so gradually that Dr. Yu was not sure when he first made out the human figures scattered around the landscape. But as the diffuse light of the still hidden sun chased away the darkness, he spotted Joseph and Ada signaling their presence on the high side of the pasture, just inside the fence around the cemetery.

On the other side of the pasture were Amy, Rachel and Carlos, and in between were Kate, Ben, and Chipic. They were all quietly watching for a beam of sunlight to strike the earth. Everyone had agreed that the first to see it would shout the words "First light!"

It was Ada who broke the silence. "I see it. First light!" she shouted. As Dr. Yu had told them to do, she and Joseph stayed where they were and pointed to the exact spot where they saw the first rays of the sun spotlighting an old moss-covered marble gravestone. By the time Dr. Yu scrambled down the hill, crossed the pasture, walked up the slope and through the iron gate, a bright clear day had dawned.

Soon all the others gathered around the rectangular stone where the first winter light fell at sunrise, December 21, 2005, the shortest day of the year. Joseph and Chipic carefully cleaned the stone, removing dirt and mold to reveal the words inscribed there:

HERE LIES MY PRECIOUS AURELIA
RETURNED TO THE EARTH
DECEMBER 21, 1863

"Is someone buried here, or is this a clue?" Joseph asked after reading the words aloud.

"I think it's a clue," said Ada, who had wandered around the cemetery reading the inscriptions on the other gravestones. "All the other graves have the dates of birth and death. This one only mentions the day Aurelia was buried."

"Okay, what else did you see?" Chipic asked, seeing that Ada and Joseph had shifted into full detective mode.

"Ask Carlos," Ada said, smiling at her new friend.

"Well, I notice that all the other graves have headstones. This one is just a small flat piece of rock to mark the spot," he said.

"I've noticed something else," Lisi said quietly. "All the other inscriptions include the first and last names of the dead. Aurelia may not be the name of a person."

"What else could it be?" Chipic wondered.

"We may not be able to find out without digging up what's under this stone," Lisi said, not mentioning that the word Aurelia means "golden."

"We can't dig unless we're reasonably sure there are no human remains here," Amy objected. "It's against the law to disturb the dead in cemeteries."

"But how else can we ever know?" Joseph asked.

"I know a dog who may be able to help," Amy said. "His name is Luckie, and he's a yellow lab trained to find human bones. He's part of a team called the Delta Dogs."

"That can't be right," Kate said. "It's too much of a coincidence that we would have a polar bear cub named 'Delta' and that nearby there's a dog team with the same name."

"Actually, it's not a coincidence," Amy explained. "My friend Pam, the trainer, was trying to decide on a name for the team. It's common to use Greek letters. There were already Alpha, Theta, and Omega teams in Georgia, so I suggested the name Delta. I guess it was on my mind since I knew Kate and Joseph were taking care of a cub with that name."

Search dogs were Amy's favorite patients. She examined them twice a year to make sure they were healthy and had the strength to do the strenuous work of a search. Occasionally, she removed thorns from sore paws, cleaned and bandaged scrapes and cuts, and checked out limps. Sometimes Amy went out with the team, and just a week before she watched Luckie at work searching for and finding very old Indian bones for a group of archeologists.

As it turned out, Luckie and his trainer Pam were available, and within a little more than an hour they were on the job. Ada, Carlos, and Joseph watched as Pam presented Luckie with old bones to smell. Next Amy took him to a spot where he couldn't see his trainer, who then hid the bones in the brush at the edge of the pasture. Luckie had an easy time finding them here. During a second trip out of sight, Pam put the bones in a shallow hole and covered them with dirt. Luckie needed a little longer for this search, but in a few minutes he located the buried bones. Both times he sat down patiently by his discovery, the signal to Pam that he had been successful. Both times she rewarded him with his favorite treat.

"He's ready to work," Pam said, as she passed by the kids on the way to the cemetery. "Come sit just a few feet outside the fence. You can watch, but stay still and quiet." Not wanting to disturb the work, everybody else went back into the house.

Once inside the gate, Pam and her dog stood on a grassy spot surrounded by tombstones. The spot where Aurelia was buried was in the far northeast corner of the graveyard.

"Go to work," Pam said in the firm voice she used to give commands. Luckie began scouting, making what is called a "scent inventory." He sniffed here and there, coming back to the same spots again and again. Finally, he sat down by the most recent grave, that of Nathan Paxton, the last of his line, known to locals as "Old Man Paxton."

Without a reward or a rest, Pam gave the command and Luckie sprang into action again, sniffing, circling, and sniffing some more. He focused on one grave in particular, and finally sat down, saying with that action, "I found that odor again." This time Pam rewarded him before sending him back to work.

Luckie was interested in all the old graves—all except the small one with no headstone. When Pam directed his attention to it, urging him to go work that spot, he scouted the area haphazardly and without focus, working as long as she wanted him to. Signaling him that the search was over, Pam suggested that they all go back to the house. Luckie waited on the porch while the people gathered around the table.

CHAPTER 33

A Dilemma

"Pam, tell us what you think, or perhaps I should say what Luckie thinks," Amy said.

"Well, here's what happened. Luckie sniffed around until he picked up the scent. He sat down near the place where it was strongest and waited for me to give him the signal to keep on searching. He continued to locate the scent until I took him over to the small gravestone. He searched carefully, but he never found any scent, so I don't think there are bones there."

"So, what we have is a dilemma," Lisi said. "Should we dig and risk breaking the law, or not dig and never find out what's hidden there?"

"So what will it be?" Dr. Yu asked, looking around at the others.

"It's not for me to decide," Pam said. "But I do know that Luckie's hardly ever wrong."

"There has to be a reason that Otis Paxton wanted someone to look under this stone. I say let's dig," Lisi said.

"I'll do the digging," Chipic said, getting up to go outside.

"I'll get the tools," Ben said. "We'll do it together."

It was already 3:00 PM, and it would be completely dark at 6:00 PM. Chipic and Ben began work immediately. Pam and

Luckie never stayed around for the digging unless they were asked. Amy had not told her about the message in the bottle, the code, or the location of the light first striking the earth.

"Luckie and I better be getting on," Pam announced as she gathered her belongings.

"Wait," Lisi said. "You have to stay long enough to meet Delta."

As the two women were walking back to the cub's indoor habitat, Lisi noticed that the door to Delta's space was open. "Uh-oh, we may have a problem." Sure enough, Delta was not in her den or any of the places she hides in her habitat. "You go back to the others, while I look for Delta. She doesn't know you, and a stranger might spook her," Lisi said to Pam.

After searching everywhere she could think to look, Lisi returned to the dining room and announced that Delta was missing. "She has to be somewhere in the house, unless someone left a door open to the outdoors. We'll have to search everywhere!" Lisi exclaimed.

"Before we start a search, let's get some information from Luckie," Pam suggested. Everyone turned to her, wondering what she had in mind.

"Luckie doesn't just hunt for bones," Pam explained. "I can bring Luckie in and introduce him to Delta's scent, and he'll follow it when I give him the signal."

"How do we know he won't hurt her?" Lisi asked.

"You don't know, but I do. When he follows a scent looking for the source, he'll sit down in the spot where the scent is strongest. He'll stay there until I catch up with him. He won't hurt Delta any more than he would hurt a lost child he'd found,"

Pam said.

"Let's go," Joseph said. "I'll get Luckie."

"Joseph, that won't work. He only obeys me and other trainers I work with," Pam said, as she opened the front door and motioned for Luckie to come in and wait for another command. "Okay if I take him back to Delta's habitat?" she asked Lisi.

"Sure, but don't you want Joseph to go with you so Delta won't be afraid?" Lisi asked.

"Good idea," Pam said. "Stay right behind me, Joseph."

They walked back to the door of the cub's habitat. Following Pam's hand signals, Luckie sat just outside the door, looking at her for a new command.

"There're too many odors inside," Pam said to Joseph. "Bring just one thing at a time over for Luckie to smell." Joseph brought first her blanket, then a stuffed toy, and finally the blue ball. To Luckie, all had a strong scent of Delta.

"Let's shut the door to the habitat. He's ready to work," Pam said, giving the go-to-work hand signal. Ignoring everything else, Luckie began to scout out every room, sniffing in corners, under chairs, and on top of counters and tables. In the kitchen he finally sat down at the edge of the counter. "Does Delta come in here?" Pam asked Joseph.

"Usually we bring her in here for breakfast. This is the place where she eats her salmon mush," Joseph said. They looked in the cabinets, the pantry, and under the kitchen table. Luckie didn't move until Pam signaled for him to have another look around. He gave every corner of the kitchen one more sniff and walked out into the hall where he stopped at the bottom of the stairs.

"Delta has never been upstairs. There's nothing but bedrooms up there," Joseph said just as Luckie began following what to him was a strong odor—first the bottom step and then one after the other until he reached the top and squeezed inside a partly open bedroom door. Pam and Joseph were just a few steps behind.

When they peeked inside, Luckie was in full search mode, sniffing here and there as he did in the cemetery, but he didn't sit. Next he followed the scent into the adjoining bathroom, and finally he sat down by the tub.

"He's found her," Joseph said as he looked into the tub at the sleeping cub.

Pam praised Luckie and gave him a treat. Then she signaled for him to follow her back down the stairs. "We found her!" she announced as she opened the front door to leave. "Call us next time you lose Delta," she said as she waved good-bye.

CHAPTER 34

Ice Storm

Joseph entered the dining room carrying Delta, who was squirming and making her "feed me" sounds. She had never been around so many people at once, but to Joseph's surprise, she was not afraid. Delta had learned to eat mainly solid food a few months before, but sometimes Joseph gave her a bottle when he wanted her to be still and quiet. This was one of those times.

Just as Delta was settling down in Joseph's lap to take her bottle, Ben pounded on the front door. "We've got something! Can't come in until we've cleaned up. Bring us a bucket of water and a brush," he said loud enough for everyone to hear. "We'll also need a chisel, a sharp one, and a hammer."

"Everyone stay put and don't frighten the cub with loud talk," Lisi said as she got up to take Ben what he needed. Back inside she reported that clouds were gathering and the temperature had dropped at least twenty degrees since noon.

It had been about thirty hours since Chipic took the message from the bottle. During that time, no one had mentioned what everyone was thinking, that maybe they would find something really valuable. Now they were about to learn what the coded message, written so long ago, had brought to light.

Ben hefted onto the table a discolored wooden chest, darkened by the heavy coat of pine pitch used to seal it. Its brass fittings were tarnished almost beyond recognition. Stunned by the appearance of the chest, no one said a word. Finally Lisi spoke.

"I'm kind of afraid to open it," she said.

"Remember, Mom, whatever's inside belongs to you," Kate said.

"How's that?" Joseph asked.

"Before I bought this house, I made sure that everything above ground and below ground belonged to me. It's in the contract."

"So this box and its contents are yours, too?" Joseph asked.

"That's right," Lisi said.

Ada, who wanted to prolong the mystery, suggested that they guess what was in the box. After some discussion, everyone agreed to go along with the game.

"Remember, whatever you guess had to be around during the Civil War and must fit in the box," Joseph said, happily joining in the game.

"So we need to know the exact size of the chest," Ada said. Joseph went into the kitchen, came back with a measuring tape, and went to work.

"It's twenty-four inches long, sixteen inches wide, and eight inches deep," he said.

"And it's heavy," Chipic chimed in. "So what do you think is inside? Everyone gets one guess." And so they went around the table as they competed for the most outrageous possibility, ranging from confederate money to dinosaur teeth. No one guessed what everyone was thinking.

All but Lisi and Dr. Yu had suggested what the box might contain. "So Lisi, what do you say?" Chipic asked.

"I say the box contains the past," Lisi said mysteriously.

Everyone looked at Dr. Yu, who remained silent. Finally he spoke. "Maybe the box holds the future."

Again there was silence, followed by a flash of lightning, thunder, and darkness. "Not again," Joseph said, remembering the last time the lights went out just as he and Carlos were examining the contents of the aluminum case Chipic had left for them. He jumped up, went to the kitchen, and soon came back with two kerosene lanterns that he placed on either side of the chest.

"We hardly ever have thunderstorms this time of year, but we sure have our electrical problems," Lisi said, as she stood up and walked outside. "Everybody come; you won't believe this," she called from the porch. There was more lightening, more thunder, more wind, more she-wasn't-sure-what. Snow? Sleet? Hail? At first she thought she was seeing a little bit of everything, but when the wind quieted down for a few moments, she saw that ice was already collecting on the trees.

Everyone went out to watch the storm except Carlos and Joseph, who stayed behind to talk. "This storm reminds me of what happened when we opened the case Chipic left us. Do you think we should tell them about the intruder?" Joseph asked.

"You mean the ghost?" Carlos said.

"Well, whatever it was," Joseph said. "I guess it seemed like a ghost because we never heard a knock. Someone we know would have knocked or called out to see if anybody was at home."

"Remember as soon as we climbed into Delta's den, we hid so no one could see us. With the lights out and no car parked outside, whoever or whatever it was might have figured that nobody was at home," Carlos said.

"I think we should confess," Joseph said, just as everybody trooped back in and took their places at the table.

"Is there anything else that anybody has to say before we open the chest?" Dr. Yu asked.

"Actually, Carlos and I need to tell everybody something strange that happened right after Thanksgiving. We'll tell it together. You start, Carlos," Joseph said.

"Well, the day that Lisi took Chipic and Kate to the Atlanta airport, Joseph and I were here alone with Delta. It was almost dark and just as we opened the case full of stuff that Chipic found when he was building her outdoor habitat, a storm came up and the lights went out," Carlos said and nodded to Joseph to take over.

"Then we heard a noise outside that at first we thought was someone walking up the steps," Joseph said.

"And onto the porch," Carlos interrupted.

"Right. But there was no knock on the door and nobody called out," Joseph said.

"The truth is we were scared, and so we ran into Delta's habitat, shut the door behind us, and hid in the den with her," Carlos added. "And while we were hiding, we heard something outside the door."

"Then we didn't hear anything else, but we did see a pale light moving around the room," Joseph said.

"Who was it?" Chipic asked.

"We never knew. We stayed in Delta's den for a long time, and by the time we came out there was no sign of an intruder," Joseph said.

"So, Joseph, who do you think it could have been?" Ben asked his son.

"I don't know. I can't imagine why anybody would break into a house and leave without taking anything," Joseph answered.

"What makes you think it was a break-in?" Ben asked.

"Well, the door was locked," Joseph said.

"Was there any sign of a break-in?" Ben asked.

"No, there wasn't," Carlos said, "and that's why I thought the intruder was a ghost. In Ecuador where I was born, many people believe that the spirits of the dead linger near where they were buried, especially if they have unfinished business with the living. That's why I thought the ghost of Otis Paxton might have paid us a visit," Carlos said.

"Dad, you always said you don't believe in ghosts, and that people who do are just superstitious," Joseph said.

"That's true, but it sounds to me like you and Carlos are toying with the possibility of ghosts."

"How else can you explain what happened?" Joseph asked.

"Yeah, Mr. Morse," Carlos added, "Do you think we imagined the whole thing?"

"Well, let's see," Ben said. "You said this happened the day Lisi had gone to take Chipic and Kate to the airport. Maybe Lisi got stuck in traffic and called me on her cell phone to tell me she'd be late. It's possible that I would have told Lisi not to worry, that I'd come over here to check on you. Maybe I took the key from its hiding place and opened the door. Maybe, since it was dark, I had a flashlight that I used to look around, and when I didn't find you, I figured you were at Carlos' house."

"Dad, is that what happened?" Joseph asked.

"Well, what do you think is more likely, that I came to check on you, or that Otis Paxton's ghost floated through a locked door?" Ben asked.

Joseph looked at his friend sheepishly, thinking that Ben probably was the intruder, but Ben could see that Carlos was not completely persuaded.

"Carlos, suppose I told you that I did in fact come to Lisi's house that night, and that I left thinking Joseph must have been at your house. Would you believe me?" Ben asked.

"Well, did you?" Carlos asked.

"I did," Ben said.

"Then I believe you," Carlos said. "And so does Joseph, don't you?"

"I do," Joseph said.

Then it was Kate's turn to speak. "Ben, don't forget that when we were kids we believed the house was haunted," she said.

"And sometimes we heard noises in the attic that we decided must be ghosts," Ben said. "Especially on stormy nights."

"Mom told us we were hearing raccoons, but there were times when the noises we heard were hard to explain. Do people in China believe in ghosts?" Kate asked as she turned to Dr. Yu.

"Actually, many people do, probably a lot more than here. For some, ghosts are real; for others, the word just refers to the lessons of the dead. But the more educated people

241

become, the less likely they are to hold on to beliefs in literal ghosts and spirits."

"Here we are," Lisi said, "talking about ghosts when we are about to see what's inside this box. Whatever we find once belonged to a man who died almost a century and a half ago. And I think we can safely say that the contents of this chest haven't been seen by human eyes since they were buried in 1863."

With these words, Lisi leaned back in her chair and became silent, as did everyone at the table. All looked at the dark chest, which in the flame of the kerosene lamps seemed to almost glow. Without saying a word, Joseph and Ada, sitting across from each other, stood up. Joseph reached out and slowly lifted the top, just as Ada came around to stand beside him. Together they were the first people to see the contents of this carefully sealed chest that was buried a few months before General Sherman invaded Georgia. Just inside was a letter enclosed in a sealed bottle like the one found in the springhouse.

CHAPTER 35

A Voice from the Past

To the person who opens this chest,

As I write these words, a tragic war is taking the lives of thousands of young men, both Union and Confederate. My only son left home in 1862 at the age of twenty-three to join the Confederate forces as a member of the medical corps, leaving behind his wife, Pearl, and his infant son. I have been ill since he left, and I fear I may not be alive when he returns to the homestead. To my son, if you are the one to first read this letter, I say that you will know to use the contents of this chest only for good, to relieve the suffering caused by this horrible war and to improve life for all creatures—both human and animals, whether domestic or wild. But someone else—my grandson, his children or theirs, or even someone beyond the family living at a time very different from this age of greed, war, and disease—may be the first to read this letter. And to that person I say, know that you are the caretaker of this treasure and your responsibility is to use it for good.

Otis Paxton

"Lisi, what does this mean?" Joseph asked softly as he finished reading the letter for all to hear.

"It means that we have to look at what's inside this box that has been sealed for nearly a century and a half," Lisi said.

"You look first," Joseph said as he got up to make room for his grandmother. The box was filled with leather pouches. Joseph and Ada stood behind Lisi and watched as she pulled out the first pouch and spilled its contents on the table—twenty-four five-dollar gold coins known as half-eagles, all made in the U.S. mint in Dahlonega, Georgia. Riveted to the sight of the gold glowing in the light of the kerosene lamps, everyone at the table once again sat in silence. Finally Lisi replaced the coins in the pouch, and opened another one containing twelve one-dollar gold coins. Touching the others, she concluded that each pouch contained coins, probably all gold.

"Wow! This is awesome—no, beyond awesome! What do we do now?" Joseph whispered.

"The kids at school won't believe this," Carlos added quietly.

Lisi took a deep breath, and slowly lowered the lid of the treasure chest. "First we need to talk about how important it is that no one except those in this room knows about the gold."

"Does that mean I can't even tell my parents?" Carlos asked.

"Not yet. Normally I would never advise you to keep secrets from your parents. But this gold must remain a secret until we decide how to keep it safe. Can you keep a secret?" Lisi asked.

"Yes, I can," Carlos said emphatically.

"When the weather clears, we'll go to town and store the box and gold in a safety deposit box," Lisi said. "After we get the electricity back on, I'll go on the Internet and research the value of the coins we have. Then for sure we'll have to hire a reliable coin expert to help us. This will take time."

"So where do we hide the gold until we can get to town? How about Delta's den?" Joseph asked.

"That's perfect," Ada said.

CHAPTER 36

A New Day:
A New Year

It was early in the morning, January 1, 2006, the day that Ada and Chipic would fly back to Barrow, and that Kate and Dr. Yu would fly to Montana. Sitting around the breakfast table were the ten people sworn to keep the discovery of the gold a secret.

Kate, Dr. Yu, and Chipic were discussing their plans for the following summer in Barrow. Ada, Joseph, and Carlos were clearing up the breakfast dishes. Ben was explaining to Rachel that he would take Ada, Chipic, Kate, and Dr. Yu to the airport in his soccer van that afternoon. Amy was feeding Delta, and Lisi was bent over a notebook with page after page covered with the names and dates of coins and their value. On a yellow legal pad, she was jotting down numbers, multiplying, and finally making long columns of figures to be added. After the table was cleared and the breakfast dishes washed, Joseph came over to Lisi's place at the head of the table and asked if he could help her with the numbers.

"Please," Lisi said. "It would help a lot if you would get a calculator and check my results. There's got to be something wrong. The sum of these figures is way bigger than I thought it would be."

Joseph took the yellow pad from Lisi and started adding the columns. "Okay, Lisi, I've got a total," he said as he passed the pad back to her.

"That was fast," she said as she looked down at the total. "It's the same as mine." Suddenly, everybody stopped talking, waiting to hear what Lisi would say next. Looking around the table at each person, Lisi stopped and addressed Dr. Yu. "Otis Paxton really did leave us a huge responsibility. If my figures are right, and the gold coin expert who came up from Atlanta is correct, this gold is worth a small fortune."

"You mean like a million dollars?" Ben asked excitedly.

"More than that," Joseph said. "Tell them Lisi."

"I've gone over the figures several times, and Joseph has checked them with the calculator. Based on what collectors are paying for these rare coins today—and if we can find buyers—they would sell for several million. With that kind of money, we could create a nonprofit organization that could make all of our projects possible," Lisi said, her hands shaking and her voice full of emotion.

"So are you going to sell the coins?" Joseph asked.

"Well, first I'll probably sell just one especially valuable coin. There are single coins in the Paxton collection worth tens of thousands of dollars, enough to pay a lawyer to set up the nonprofit organization with enough money left over to keep Project Delta going for a year or more. Then I've decided to give the gold to the organization to be used in ways we decide are best." Lisi said.

"Lisi, how many coins are there?" Joseph asked.

"There's a complete set of all the coins struck in the U.S.

mint in Dahlonega, Georgia. That's every coin struck from 1838 to 1861—fifty-eight different coins. But there are many more. All of these coins are in what's called 'mint condition.' That means they've never been circulated. We know that Otis Paxton came from Saratoga Springs, New York, and got in on the early years of the 1830s gold rush in north Georgia, the first gold rush in America, and he struck pay dirt. We don't know all the details, but we do know that for the lifetime of the Dahlonega Mint, some of the gold Otis Paxton found was made into coins. He probably spent some of it to buy this land and build this house, and then saved the rest."

Dr. Yu stood up and looked at Lisi, then at Joseph, Ada, and Carlos. "With the money from this gold in a nonprofit organization, we can take on whatever projects we choose. For now, we know we'll continue with Project Delta, and do what it takes to give her what she needs. We want people to understand about global warming, and I believe that Delta can help us get the message out. I know Joseph, Ada, and Carlos want to be part of this and help other kids understand that they don't have to be adults to do important work. Now, I'd like to hear what they're feeling about this."

"I'm feeling right now like we can do anything we decide to do," Ada said. "And what we've done so far has been a lot of fun."

"I agree with Ada, and I feel like I'm the luckiest kid alive," Joseph said.

"I'm lucky the same way Delta is," Carlos said quietly. "My mother died in an earthquake in 1995 when I was about a year old, and I ended up in an orphanage in Maca, in the

Morona-Santiago Province of Ecuador. I don't know what happened to my father. My adoptive parents came to Ecuador and brought me back here when I was five years old."

"You never told me you were adopted," Joseph said.

"I was going to tell you, but I was waiting for the right time. Like Delta, I have you for a friend and good people to take care of me."

Once again, Joseph, Ada, Chipic, Kate, and Dr. Yu were gathered together at an airport, this time, the world's busiest airport. Soon Ada and Chipic would be on the first leg of a trip that would take them from Atlanta to Anchorage, then Fairbanks, and finally to the tiny airport in Barrow, Alaska. From there the Arctic Ocean would be frozen over all the way to the North Pole. The mother polar bears would be in their dens nursing tiny newborn cubs.

Kate and Dr. Yu would board a plane that would take them first to Salt Lake City, where they would take a much smaller plane to Missoula, Montana, home of the University of Montana. Kate's Ph.D. work would include a study of Delta, and she would be back in Barrow the next summer helping Dr. Yu.

In August when they parted at what surely must be among the smallest airports in North America, Ada stayed in the Arctic, and Joseph left to go back to Georgia, neither knowing whether they'd ever see each other again. Now Joseph was staying, and Ada was flying home. But this time they had already planned to get together again so they could continue their sleuthing in the Arctic and working with Delta

in north Georgia.

Now instead of an ending, everyone felt they were on the edge of a new beginning. Ada and Joseph knew they would see each other again; Kate and Dr. Yu would travel from Montana to the Arctic, and probably to Georgia as well; and as usual, Chipic would show up wherever he was most needed.

All of their lives and work in the world were tied together in ways that never would have been possible if Delta had not been rescued and the Paxton collection of gold coins had remained buried forever. Dr. Yu was right. The chest did contain the future, not only for Delta, but also for the lives of Ada and Joseph, Kate and Chipic, Dr. Yu and Lisi.

GLOSSARY

Antarctic: The region from the Antarctic Circle at about 66 degrees south latitude extending south to the South Pole. Unlike the Arctic, the Antarctic includes a continent, Antarctica, consisting of a large land mass that is 98% covered by ice. This continent belongs to no country but has been set aside by international agreement for scientific research. Penguins are found in the Antarctic, but not in the Arctic.

Arctic: The region from the Arctic Circle at about 66 degrees north latitude extending north to the North Pole. This includes the Arctic Ocean, much of it covered with ice, as well as parts of eight countries, including Canada, Russia, Greenland, the United States, Iceland, Norway, Sweden, and Finland. Unlike the Antarctic, there is dispute among these countries as to who has the rights to arctic resources, including gas and oil under the Arctic Ocean. Polar bears are found in the Arctic but not in the Antarctic.

Arctic tern: A bird that nests in the Arctic during the summer but then flies south to the Antarctic to spend the summer there during the arctic winter. Altogether arctic terns fly about 24,000 miles per year. They may live for as long as thirty years, but even those who live to an age of twenty years may cover a distance of 500,000 miles in their lifetime. This is the distance to the moon and back.

Artifact: Any object created or modified by a human culture. Examples include tools or sculptures made from stone or bone and clothing made from animal skins. The study of these objects is an important part of archaeology and anthropology.

Baleen: Plates in the mouths of some whales that serve to filter out their food—small drifting organisms called plankton or shrimp-like creatures called krill—from seawater.

Beluga: A species of whale that lives in Arctic waters. Belugas are toothed whales and do not have baleen like the baleen whales. They are 15–18 feet long, white, and are known for the high-pitched squeals and whistling sounds they make.

251

Biologists: Scientists that study living things. Biologists who study plants are known as botanists and those who study animals are known as zoologists. There are many different kinds of zoologists, including wildlife biologists who study wild animals and their habitats, and herpetologists who study reptiles and amphibians.

Bears: There are eight species of bears in the world. Only one of these species, the spectacled bear of the Andes, lives south of the equator. Polar bears live only in the Arctic and are mainly carnivorous, or meat-eating. Giant panda bears, which live in China, are completely vegetarian and only eat bamboo. All other bears are omnivorous, or eat both meat and plants. The other bears that live in North America besides the polar bear include the black bear and the grizzly or brown bear.

Blubber: The thick layer of fat between the skin and muscle layers of whales and other marine mammals. Blubber provides insulation from cold water, is a source of energy, and also aids buoyancy, or the ability to float. Muktuk, the Inupiat or Eskimo name for blubber used as food, is a healthy form of fat, and an important part of the traditional Eskimo diet.

Bog: A type of wetland, also called a muskeg, where water stands and decayed vegetation—mosses, lichens, and other plants—builds up as peat.

Bowhead: A species of baleen whale that can grow up to eighty-eight feet in length, second in size only to the blue whale. This species of whale does not migrate but lives only in Arctic seas and is an important traditional food source for Inupiat or Eskimo people in Alaska.

Buckeye: The seed of a buckeye tree. Some people in the southeastern United States carry a buckeye in their purse or pockets because they believe that it will bring good luck.

Caribou: Deer that live in the Arctic regions of Alaska and Canada, related to reindeer, that live in the Arctic regions of Europe and Greenland. Caribou and reindeer are the only deer in which both males and females grow antlers. Caribou are very important to the native peoples of Alaska and Canada as a source of food and hides.

Contraband: Goods that are against the law to possess and/or transport, such as illegal drugs and hazardous materials. Other examples include fossils and artifacts found in wilderness areas and other publicly owned lands.

Growth Hormone Deficiency: Growth hormone is a chemical produced in the pituitary gland, which is attached to the base of the brain. Growth hormone is carried by the blood to all parts of the body and stimulates growth. A deficiency of this hormone can cause an animal or person to remain small.

DNA: An abbreviation for deoxyribonucleic acid, the chemical found in the nucleus of all cells. DNA contains the genetic instructions or information used to control the growth and development that determines the particular characteristics of each living thing. Except for clones, which have identical DNA, each individual plant or animal has a unique genetic profile—unlike any other organism. This genetic information is passed on from one generation of animals or plants to the next, and so are very similar in the parents and the offspring, making it possible to match a parent to its descendants.

Equinox: The two days each year when day and night are of about equal length. One equinox occurs on March 20 or 21 each year and the other on September 22 or 23. (see Solstice)

Eskimos: The native people living along the Arctic coast in North America, Greenland, and northeastern Siberia. Eskimos living in Alaska are also known as Inupiat and those in Canada as Inuit.

Floe: A floating piece of ice no more than six miles in its largest dimension that has broken off from the ice field of the Arctic Ocean. An iceberg is a floating mass of ice that has broken off or "calved" from a glacier. Floes are frozen saltwater, whereas icebergs are frozen freshwater.

Foundation: An organization—usually established by wealthy individuals or families—for contributing money for scientific research, the arts, education, health care, or other activity to benefit others.

253

Frost heaves: An elevated area of land caused by alternate freezing and thawing of the soil.

Glaciers: A slow-moving river of ice that gradually slides downward due to its own weight. Glaciers form when snow accumulates, usually on mountains, and is gradually compressed to form ice.

Global warming: The gradual warming of the earth, the oceans, and the atmosphere, Scientists believe that global warming is due to human activities, including release of carbon dioxide into the atmosphere, which acts to trap the sun's heat. This warming can result in changes in rainfall patterns, rises in sea level, and a wide range of impacts on plants, wildlife, and humans. The effects of global warming are greatest near the poles, that is, in the Arctic where sea ice is melting rapidly and in the Antarctic where large glaciers are disappearing.

Grappling hook: A metal device, usually having three hooks, attached to a rope. At sea, a grappling hook can be thrown from a boat toward land, ice, or another vessel, and then used to pull alongside.

Grits: Coarsely ground corn commonly boiled and served for breakfast in the southeastern United States.

Grizzly: see Bears

Habitat: In nature, the place that an animal is most likely to be found, or normally lives and calls home. A suitable artificial habitat, such as those in a zoo, will provide similar conditions to those where an animal usually lives.

Herpetologist: see Biologist

Hibernation: A state of inactivity similar to a deep sleep, usually during the winter. There are different kinds of hibernation. A true hibernator has a very slow pulse rate, body temperature drops considerably, and the animal may appear dead and be very hard to rouse. Examples would include ground squirrels, frogs, snakes, and even ladybugs. Bears are not true hibernators. They go into their dens in winter, spend most of their time sleeping, and live mainly on stored body fat, but they can wake up, move, and some black bears even leave their dens, walk around, and look for food.

Infrared camera: A special camera used for night vision by the military, which makes images by measuring the infrared radiation given off by the warm human body rather than measuring visible light. These cameras can also be used for rescue work in dark or smoke-filled areas, and in the Arctic can be used to detect infrared energy waves given off by warm animals hibernating under the snow. The use of an infrared camera may also be referred to as infrared thermal imaging.

Inuit: see Eskimo

Inupiat: see Eskimo

King Eider: A large duck of Arctic coastal waters, one of North America's most spectacular waterfowl species. These ducks may form flocks of as many as ten thousand birds during spring migration and may dive to depths of eighty feet to feed.

Larvae: The immature worm-like forms of insects that go through growth stages before becoming recognizable adults.

Llave: The Spanish word for "key."

Lower forty-eight: The forty-eight contiguous states of the United States, not including Hawaii and Alaska.

Marine mammals: Mammals that live in or around the ocean and depend on the sea for food. The group of 120 species includes whales, seals, sea otters, walruses, and polar bears.

Medic: A member of the medical corps in the military. Medics may function as members of medical evacuation teams or as nurses trained in battlefield medicine.

Mint: a government facility where coins are manufactured for circulation. The main United States Mint is in Philadelphia, but there are branches in Denver, San Francisco, and West Point, New York. Before the Civil War there were also mints in North Carolina, Georgia, and Louisiana.

Muktuk: Whale skin and blubber, a traditional Eskimo food (see Blubber).

Narwhal: A medium sized whale that lives in Arctic waters. The male Narwhal is distinguished by a 7-10 foot long tusk that arises from the upper left jaw. Male Narwhals engage in a social activity called "tusking" in which they rub their tusks together.

Orca: Sometimes called a "killer whale," this animal is actually the largest member of the dolphin family. Resident orcas remain in one area, don't migrate, and feed mainly on fish. Transient orcas move about from one place to another and mainly feed on other marine mammals such as seals, walrus, sea otters, and even large whales.

Paleontologist: A scientist who studies prehistoric life by using fossil evidence.

Permafrost: Soil and rock near the North or South poles or in alpine regions near the tops of tall mountains that is permanently below the freezing temperature of water. On top of most permafrost lies what is called the active layer, which thaws out during the summer and supports plant growth. This may be 2 to 12 feet thick.

Pine pitch: Sticky resin or sap from pine trees. Pitch can be used to seal or caulk the seams of wooden boats so that they won't leak, or to waterproof wooden containers.

Prospecting site: A location where valuable resources—minerals, gas, or oil—are thought to exist.

Scat: Animal droppings. Wildlife biologists often look for scat to identify the animals in a given location and to determine what the animals have been eating.

Scientific objectivity: The effort by scientists to avoid allowing their own prejudices, values, feelings, or assumptions to influence their conclusions about the subject being studied.

Solstice: Either of the two times each year when the sun is most distant from the equator. In the northern hemisphere, the summer solstice, which is the longest day of the year, occurs on or about June 21, and the winter solstice, which is the shortest day of the year, occurs on or about December 21. The solstices and the seasons are caused by the changing tilt of the earth as it rotates around the sun. When there is no tilt of the earth, as occurs on the spring and fall equinoxes, days and nights are equal. The dates of the summer and winter solstice correspond to the dates of maximum tilt of the earth, which is about 23 degrees.

Sorpresa: The Spanish word for "surprise."

Spring house: A small building constructed over a spring, or a place where cold water bubbles up out of the earth. Before electric refrigerators became available, food was stored in spring houses to prevent spoiling.

Tundra: An area where there is little or no tree growth due to low temperatures and a short growing season. Most tundra is found in the Arctic and Antarctic, but tundra also occurs on mountain tops (alpine tundra). There is often permafrost (see Permafrost). In the summer, tundra is generally very wet, and there are many lakes and bogs. Plants of the tundra include grasses, mosses, and lichen as well as small low-growing bushes such as blueberries.

Tusking: see Narwhal

Tussock: A thick cluster of grasses and other small tundra plants growing together in a mound about eighteen inches high and a foot or so across. Walking across the tundra can be very difficult. Hopping from tussock to tussock risks loss of balance, falling, and maybe breaking an ankle, but in between the tussocks there is often mud or even standing water.

Umiak: A traditional Eskimo boat made of animal skins stretched across a driftwood frame and used for whaling and other purposes.

Whiteout: A weather condition in which snow or fog severely limit visibility.

Wildlife rehabilitation center: An establishment that provides medical and other kinds of care to injured or orphaned animals in hopes of restoring health so that the animal can be released back to the wild.

Wildlife refuge: A place offering protection and habitat for wild animals, designated by the U.S. government as part of the National Wildlife Refuge System, or by a conservation organization such as the National Audubon Society.

RESOURCES

FURTHER READING

Banerjee, Subhankar. *Arctic National Wildlife Refuge: A Photographic Journey*. Seattle, WA: Mountaineers Books, 2008. Stunning photographs taken in one of the most pristine and beautiful wilderness areas on earth, which is threatened by those who wish to drill there for oil.

George, Jean Craighead. *Julie of the Wolves*. New York, NY: Harper Collins, 1972. Newberry Medal winning adventure story of a thirteen-year-old Eskimo girl.

Guravich, Dan, and Downs Matthews. *Polar Bear*, San Francisco, CA: Chronicle Books, 1993. A collection of photographs by biologist Dan Guravich, with text by nature writer Downs Matthews, who explains mysteries like how a nine-hundred-pound polar bear can cross a thin sheet of ice that wouldn't support a person.

Kazlowski, Steven. *The Last Polar Bear: Facing the Truth of a Warming World*. Seattle, WA: Mountaineers Books, 2008. Explains with text and photographs why global warming threatens polar bears and what can be done to help them survive.

Kenny, David et al. *Klondike and Snow*, Boulder, Colorado: Roberts Rinehart Publishers, 1995. The Denver Zoo's remarkable story of raising two polar bear cubs, as told by the zoo staff, with many photographs.

Kidder, Lyn. *Tacos on the Tundra*. Anchorage, AK: Bonaparte Books, 1996. The story of Pepe's North of the Border restaurant in Barrow, Alaska.

Mangelsen, Thomas, and Fred Bruemmer. *Polar Dance: Born of the North Wind*. Omaha, NE: Images of Nature, 1997. Beautiful coffee table book with exceptional photographs and text that outlines a typical year in the life of a polar bear.

Milse, Thorsten. *Little Polar Bears*, Munich, Germany: C.J. Bucher Verlag, 2006. A photographer's account of tracking polar bear cubs with a camera in Canada's Wapusk National Park.

Revkin, Andrew. *The North Pole Was Here: Puzzles and Perils at the Top of the World*. New York, NY: New York Times Books, 2006. This book by an excellent writer blends adventure, science, and history in a fascinating firsthand account of a trip to the Arctic.

Rosing, Norbert, and Elizabeth Carney. *Face to Face with Polar Bears*. Des Moines, IA: National Geographic Children's Books, 2007. Factual, informative firsthand account of encounters with polar bears with excellent photographs.

Ryder, Joanne. *A Pair of Polar Bears*. New York, NY: Simon and Schuster Books for Young Readers, 2006. The story of orphan polar bear twins rescued in northern Alaska by wildlife biologists and flown to the San Diego Zoo, where they were raised. Text appropriate for younger children, but photographs interesting to all ages.

Stirling, Ian. *Bears: Majestic Creatures of the Wild*. Emmaus, PA: Rodale Press, 1993. Authoritative book about the eight species of bears in the world, their behavior and biology, and their interactions with humans, written by a variety of bear experts.

Stirling, Ian. *Polar Bears*. Ann Arbor, MI: University of Michigan Press, 1998. Very instructive book, with many photographs of polar bears and chapters with titles like "How Do You Study a Polar

Bear?" and "What Makes a Polar Bear Tick?"

Woods, Shirley. *Tooga: the Story of a Polar Bear.* Allston, MA: Fitzhenry & Whiteside, 2004. A novel about the adventures of a young polar bear growing up on the coast of northern Labrador and learning to hunt and survive on his own.

MYTH BUSTING In reading about polar bears, you may come across statements about how their hair, which is colorless and hollow, conducts sunlight to their black skin, which then absorbs the sun's heat. This widespread myth has recently been "busted." For more on this topic, go to www.gi.alaska.edu/ScienceForum/, and then go to the search window, and type in the words "polar bear hair."

USEFUL WEBSITES

Defenders of Wildlife, www.defenders.org/wildlife
Useful website. This organization sponsors a kid's site at www.kidsplanet.org/

Great Bear Foundation, www.greatbear.org
Located in Montana, the Great Bear Foundation is concerned with protecting and studying all types of bears, not just the polar bear. Good source of detailed bear lore.

Polar Bears International, www.polarbearsinternational.org
Comprehensive and searchable site that includes tools for teachers and students.

National Geographic, www.nationalgeographic.com/kids
Kid-friendly site. National Geographic even publishes a magazine for kids.

National Wildlife Federation, www.nwf.org/
This large organization's website offers a search feature and is very kid friendly. NWF is the publisher of *Ranger Rick* magazine, a nature- and science-oriented magazine for kids.

Natural Resources Defense Council, www.nrdc.org
Take a look also at www.savebiogems.org/polar/, kid oriented and full of information about the Arctic.

North American Bear Association, www.bear.org
Excellent source for videos, photos, and detailed information about the bears of North America. Especially valuable for learning about the lives of black bears. Be sure to see videos of nursing cubs and their vocalizations—the varied sounds they make.

Sea World, www.seaworld.org/animal-info
The famous polar bear cubs Klondike and Snow, now grown to adulthood, live here in Orlando. Website very friendly for both kids and teachers.

Sierra Club, www.sierraclub.org
Oldest grassroots environmental organization in the United States with over one million members. Great site for surfing, as Sierra Club is concerned with many environmental issues. In addition to learning about polar bears and the Arctic, kids can search using the words "kids" or "students" and can also see which issues are important in the state where they live.

Wildlife Conservation Society, www.wcs.org
This organization sponsors a special website for kids at www.kids-gowild.com/ with good information about polar bears and the Arctic.

FILMS

An Inconvenient Truth, by former Vice President Al Gore, is a film based on the well-known book by the same name. This is probably the best available explanation of the complexities of climate change for nonscientists.

Arctic Tale was released in 2007 by Paramount Classics, produced by National Geographic Films, and narrated by Queen Latifah. The film follows a polar bear cub and a walrus pup as they struggle for survival in an ice-bound world that is rapidly melting beneath them.

Klondike and Snow: A Tale of Twin Polar Bears, coproduced in 1996 by the Denver Zoo and two local TV stations, tells the year-long story of how twin polar bear cubs abandoned by their mother were cared for by dedicated zoo staff and eventually grew to become media sensations.

Bears, presented in 2002 as an IMAX film by the National Wildlife Federation, is now available on DVD and contains footage of polar bears on the Arctic tundra, black bears in Montana, and grizzlies in Alaska.

Growing Up Arctic is a two-hour DVD produced in 2008 for the TV channel Animal Planet, and contains four episodes entitled "Growing Up Walrus," "Growing Up Seal," "Growing Up Polar Bear," and "Growing Up Penguin." The "Growing Up Polar Bear" episode tells the story of Inukshuk, whose mother was killed by hunters. A dedicated team of Toronto Zoo curators cares for this charismatic young cub during the first year of his life.

KIDS IN ACTION

www.arborday.org/kids

Website dedicated to inspiring people, including kids, to plant, nurture, and celebrate trees. Kids' page has a special section for older children and youth as well as materials/downloads for teachers.

www.earth911.com/

Useful information about where to recycle different kinds of trash from home or school.

www.pbskids.org/zoom/activities/action/way04.html

This is the website for *ZOOM*, the PBS TV show for kids, and includes things kids can do in their neighborhood to make a difference.

www.ran.org/new/kidscorner/

The Rainforest Action Network's kids' corner suggests things kids can do to help save the rainforests.

ACKNOWLEDGEMENTS

Writing *A Place for Delta* has been a pleasure from the beginning. Although fiction, everything that happens in the book could happen and is consistent with science and history. To make sure that was true required traveling both to the Alaskan Arctic and the Canadian Arctic and interviewing people who know these harsh but beautiful places intimately. When I asked a polar bear specialist if animals suffer from growth hormone deficiency, he told me that of course they could, but that in the wild, animals with such a disability would surely die. Veterinarians have also assured me that what happens could happen. And so I thank the many people who helped me understand topics ranging from Arctic mammals to search-and-rescue dogs in Georgia. Never once did anyone refuse to answer my many questions. All were accommodating.

Since childhood I have spent time hiking and camping in the Appalachian Mountains of north Georgia, and I still do, so I know the area well. But the far north was another matter. In the summer of 2005 I traveled to Barrow, Alaska, where I met the people who helped me understand the flora, the fauna, and the native people of the Arctic. Thanks go to Fran Tate, Joe Schultz, Henry Gueco, Ellen Sovalik, and Charlie Brower who generously shared their time and knowledge and pointed me in the right direction. Among the scientists who taught me about the wildlife and the evidence of climate change are Craig George, wildlife biologist with the department of Wildlife Management of the North Slope Borough; Glenn Sheehan, executive director of the Barrow Arctic Science Consortium; and Geoff Carroll, state biologist of the Alaska Department of Fish and Game Division of Wildlife Conservation. Teresa Heaston, who runs the veterinary clinic in Barrow with only the occasional support of a veterinarian, explained the challenges she faces taking care of animals in a place where rabid foxes invade the town every winter and polar bears regularly pass through.

Scott Schliebe, marine mammal biologist and polar bear specialist with the U.S. Fish and Wildlife Service, granted me a lengthy interview. From Scott I learned about research methods used to study polar bear dens and many details about the nature of polar bear habitats and what threatens them.

I went with a small group to see and learn about polar bears near Churchill, Manitoba. Jim Halfpenny, director of The Naturalist World, was our knowledgeable guide. There I watched more than two dozen bears as they passed the time play fighting, resting, and sleeping while they waited for Hudson Bay to freeze over so they could go out on the ice to hunt. I also appreciate the scientists and the staff at the Churchill Northern Studies Center and Polar Bears International who made my time there an intense learning experience. Special thanks to Kim Daley, a polar bear biologist, who showed me her observation tower.

Much of this book was written during summers I spent in a cabin above Kachemak Bay near Homer, Alaska. Surrounded on three sides by tall hemlock and Sitka spruce, the simple cabin had everything I needed—a bed, a worktable in front of an open window, and a coffeemaker. Almost as important as the coffee pot was the quiet, solitude, and beauty of the place.

When I looked up from my work, I saw the bluer than blue delphinium in a perennial garden to the south, and from there I gazed out across a wide meadow of blooming fireweed to a crescent border of spruce that opens up intermittently to views of the bay and the mountains on the other side of Cook Inlet. I will always value the summers I spent there, and I am grateful to Kim and Gordon Terpening for making the cabin available to me and for introducing me to their community.

Thanks to Kim and Gordon and their son Traveler, I met so many people in Homer that I feel that I belong there. Among those who have welcomed me into their homes and taken an interest in my writing are Ed Bailey and Nina Faust, Roger and Denise Clyne, Asia Freeman, Rika and John Mauw, Eileen Mullen, Mavis Muller, Miranda Weiss, and Bob Shavelson. Sue Post at the Homer Book Store was especially helpful when she sat down with me on several occasions to talk about children's literature. Andy and Sally Wells, owners of the Old Inlet Bookstore, suggested that their then eleven-year-old daughter Oceana would be a good reader of the manuscript. And indeed she was. Jazz Maltz, son of Kevin and Donna of the Sourdough Bakery, read a very early version of the book and offered valuable suggestions.

Other children who have read and contributed to the development of *A Place for Delta* and contributed ideas are Anais Sanchez in Phoenix, Arizona; Catherine Taylor in Acton, Massachusetts; and Sarah Stubbs of Decatur, Georgia. Sarah's grandmother, Mary Emma McConaughey, added her own insightful comments.

For multiple readings of the manuscript and for fine editing I thank Amy Bauman. She believed in the book from the day we sat in a rose garden in Berkeley, California, while she gently but firmly suggested changes that have improved the structure and unity of the book. I'm also indebted to Kate Buechner, who provided substantive editorial guidance as well as excellent proofreading.

Others who have read the manuscript at various stages and made valuable comments and suggestions include Diedre Murphy, a fourth-grade teacher in Quincy, Massachusetts, and Sylvia Villarreal of Houston, Texas. Sylvia has been my cheerleader through this and other projects—and in life. I am also grateful for Robin Strauss's very helpful evaluation of an early version of the book. Ongoing conversations with Jackie Wilkerson, children's librarian, have been very helpful.

There are people whose lives touch so many aspects of mine that it is difficult to be precise about the many ways they enrich my work. I am grateful for all they've meant to me. They are Cecylia Arzewski, Bobbie Wrenn Banks, Roselyn Davis, Sue

Dennard, Dorinda McCauley, Lynne Moody, and Pisha Rearden. In my effort to make sure I got the facts straight, I met and talked to many interesting people whose expertise lies in fields that were unknown to me. Pam Nyberg taught me about the fascinating world of search-and-rescue dogs. Bob Harwell spent considerable time educating me about coin collecting and the value of gold coins.

Creating *A Place for Delta* has been a family affair. My daughter, Laura Hollis Sanchez, not only read the manuscript in various stages but also gave the cub her name. My son, Richard, created the kind of art for the book that would best capture the spirit of the story. His woodcuts and drawings speak for themselves. His sons, Joseph and Max, participated in the process from the beginning—giving me some of my best ideas and warning me to leave out passages that wouldn't interest children. I am deeply grateful that Monica Walker and Alberto Sanchez are part of this family.

Then there's the contribution of my husband, Jerome Walker. Rather than resort to the usual formula and insist that the book could not have been written without him—which may or may not be true—I prefer to think about the good times we've had while the story of Delta unfolded. How many times he read various versions of the manuscript, how much of the editing and proofreading he did, and how often he urged me to sit down and write—all of this will remain our little secret.

It's with profound gratitude that I acknowledge Tess Pendergrast for undertaking at a critical time, the many crucial tasks needed to bring *A Place for Delta* into the world.

Laurie Shock, book producer and designer, is in a category of her own. Her commitment to quality, her attention to the smallest detail, her belief in *A Place for Delta*, and her uncompromising insistence on excellence—all of this will be evident to the reader. I am deeply grateful to Laurie for her professionalism as well as her generosity of spirit.